DEATH'S HEAD, BERLIN

Also by Jack Gerson

THE BACK OF THE TIGER
THE WHITEHALL SANCTION

DEATH'S HEAD, BERLIN

Jack Gerson

ST. MARTIN'S PRESS
NEW YORK

 For information, address St. Martin's Press, 175 Fifth Avenue, New York, N.Y. 10010.

Library of Congress Cataloging-in-Publication Data

Gerson, Jack.
    Death's head Berlin.

    "A Thomas Dunne book."
    1. Berlin (Germany)—History—1918–1945
—Fiction. 2. Germany—History—1933–1945
—Fiction. I. Title.
PR6057.E72D4 1988 823'.914 88-30550
ISBBN 0-312-02569-6

First published in Great Britain by W. H. Allen & Co.

First U.S. Edition

10 9 8 7 6 5 4 3 2 1

For Gerry, with love

PROLOGUE

I first met Lohmann the day after I arrived in Berlin. We were introduced by Hardacre. I was taking over from that tired enthusiast as Berlin correspondent for the New York *Post-Enquirer*. At fifty-nine, Hardacre was going back to New York, as he put it, to vegetate behind a desk until the inevitable retirement to a cottage in New England. And the novel he'd been promising himself he would write since he was nineteen. Of course, for me in my turn, I wouldn't wait so long. That's what I told myself. But I was still pleased . . . no, more, much more to get the Berlin desk.

'Where the action is,' the editor-in-chief Harrison Buckley had said, always the man for a cliché. Of course he was right.

Berlin, August 1934. Where the action was. Where the Weimar Republic had given way to the Third Reich. But people hadn't quite realised it yet. Not the ordinary Berliner, who believed life would go on as before. Except for those big swastika flags. More uniforms in the street. And a different, louder voice on the radio; a harsh strident voice pushing out key words so that the context of the speeches was forgotten, but the words remained. Words like 'Greater Germany', 'Room to Live', 'Strength', 'Renewal', and, with disparagement, 'Jew'.

Apart from the voice, the city was filled with gossip. About the new leaders, about what had happened two months before. The time known as the 'Night of the Long Knives'; when the voice had made peace with the army and the financial power by purging the street element. So it went in the cafes, on the streets, in the beer gardens. Also, regarding the private lives of the leaders. What was he really like behind the moustache and the falling forelock? And had one heard about Goebbels and the latest UFA starlet? Of course Göring was all right, he'd flown with Richthofen. And was now running to fat. Or was it strength? And there was the man with the metal spectacles who looked like a nasty schoolteacher. He had been just that.

Of course there were people who could see what was happening. Or there had been. Those who knew Mister Norris had already changed trains; Herr Issyvoo had gone back to England, Sally Bowles had moved on . . . to Vienna or Paris. The brothers Mann, Thomas and Heinrich, have America and Hollywood to look forward to; as had Brecht, and Billy Wilder, and Marlene. And all those who recognised that something insidious was creeping into the streets of the city, into the country.

Certainly, this is hindsight. It didn't come to me, these first days in Berlin. It didn't come until much later; until too late. On that November night in 1934, there were still ordinary people in Berlin who couldn't know what was beginning to happen. There were still, too, far from ordinary people.

Like Lohmann.

Sitting in a table in the corner of the Cafe Serre, at the window, looking out onto the Prinzenstrasse. Hardacre pointed him out.

'That's Lohmann,' Hardacre said. 'You should meet him.'

I thought, another dignitary, or another of Goebbels' clerks from the Ministry of Propaganda. Although this one looks different. Tallish man, long faced, in a leather raincoat, soft hat on the table beside him, lank dark hair a little too long and falling forward over his forehead. Eyes looking out into the street.

'Find him sitting at that table more often than in his office,' Hardacre went on.

'Who is he?'

'Inspector Lohmann. Criminal Police. The best detective in Berlin. Maybe in Germany.'

I wasn't enamoured of policemen in Germany even in those early days. A growing suspicion of men in uniform was already there. The sense too, that the ones not in uniform might be even more dangerous.

Hardacre seemed to read my mind. 'That one's different,' he said.'So far he's resisted joining the Party. He might have been out, but Arthur Nebe, the big chief, thinks he's too good to lose. Even though he's not a Nazi. He's apolitical. Come on, I'll introduce you.'

Weaving our way through tables, sidling past loud Berliners and quiet Berliners, through argument, discussion and gossip, we came to the table in the corner.

'Inspector Lohmann!'

He stood up and was not quite as tall as I thought. About five-ten or eleven. Almost awkward, in movement possibly shambling. A slight flush on his face.

'Herr Hardacre!' In English, good English with not too heavy an accent.

'As you know, I'm going home soon,' said Hardacre, urbane and confident. 'I'd like to introduce you to my successor. This is David Conway.'

We shook hands. A deliberately firm grip from the German, as if he had to assert himself.

'Very pleased,' he said.

'I've heard a lot about you,' I lied. Although it was to be true later.

Hardacre found it necessary to fill in, for the time being. 'The man who was instrumental in capturing Kurten, the Düsseldorf killer.'

Lohmann shrugged modestly. 'A number of people were involved in taking Peter Kurten. Will you join me, gentlemen?'

Hardacre demurred. We were due back at the office. He was finishing his final dispatch from Germany, and then we were expected at a party in his honour organised by the London *Times* man at the Adlon. Lohmann nodded impassively and we left.

I saw him once or twice over the following weeks. We nodded to each other, professional strangers passing by. Busy, busy, busy. I was getting to know my job, the people, the officials with their swastika armbands and their nervous eyes. At the beginning, in those days there were a great many nervous eyes. One could progress upwards to the heights, or one could make a mistake and end up in a cellar underneath Gestapo headquarters. Such things were becoming commonplace.

Then I heard Lohmann was in trouble. Something to do with a high ranking Nazi official involved in some scandal. The man had attempted to evade arrest and Lohmann had shot him. It was expected that the Inspector would be arrested at any time. Yet it wasn't so, not at once. Lohmann was at his place in the Cafe Serre the next day. And was involved in another investigation. I had some idea of doing a feature about him, not just an interview but perhaps a diary of some days with him on an important case.

It never happened. I went to Austria for some weeks, to Vienna where the Nazis were already stirring, one Fascist group making threatening noises against another Fascist group, the government of Chancellor Dollfuss.

When I returned, Lohmann had gone. Where or why, whether he was alive or dead . . . or in that Gestapo cellar . . . I was not able to find out. No one would speak, either officially or otherwise. He was no longer listed in the establishment files of the Criminal Police. His address, which I had previously obtained, was an apartment building in the west of the city. His name was no longer among the brass plaques listing residents. To my request for him, a caretaker blinked at me uncomprehendingly, shrugged and turned away. It wasn't simply as if he'd gone away, or even died. It was as if he'd never existed.

I went on with my job. I was there until 1938, when I was transferred to the London desk; to the other side of the story. I went with relief.

It was in 1942, eight years after my first meeting with Lohmann, that I finally heard his story. In wartime England, in a Nissen hut outside of Dorking, Surrey.

This is that story. Lohmann's story, as told to me. Perhaps I've embellished it a little, it was always a temptation to do so, but not too much. The main thing is that I believe it. The embellishments can be forgiven. My excuse for them is that I was trying to get into the mind of another man.

So, Lohmann's story . . .

ONE

Lohmann at the corner table. Eyes peering out of the window, through condensation into the street. Yet still, he was listening to the fragments of conversation that came to him from the other tables.

'Of course he's going too far. But he has the right idea about the Jews!' An instant, sweeping condemnation that offended Lohmann's sense of justice. Yet, could be heard too often this day throughout the city.

' . . . he's not only queer, he's positively perverse . . . he only sleeps with men, because women always turn him down . . .'

' . . . I told Franz, there's no point in him joining the air force. If God had meant him to fly, he should try Lufthansa!'

' . . . I know Goebbels very well. And he does have a club foot. Easier to use it as a club than as a foot . . .'

' . . . never again have to carry one's wages home in a wheelbarrow. Hitler'll see to it. The mark will get stronger and stronger . . .'

'It's a new beginning . . .'

'It's the end of the old ways . . .'

'Of course it's true. Why do you think he's against the Jews? Because Hitler is half Jewish.'

Night after night, day after day, the fragments came. Often the same fragment repeated again and again. As if time was telescoped. Heard at lunch, whispered at dinner, muttered throughout the afternoon. When Lohmann was there. He preferred to be there rather than in his office. The unofficial atmosphere was less claustrophobic, the coffee was better. And the fragments of conversation painted their own picture of the city; indicated the changes in thought and circumstance. Only months before, there had been much said about Röhm and the SA, the ubiquitous Brownshirts. The *Sturmabteilung*. Not now. Except in whispers. Röhm was dead, the Brownshirts purged. Those who still survived, the rump of the bully boys of the street, they were still in evidence, but much subdued. And nervous.

Lohmann sipped his coffee and glanced at his watch, a gold hunter. Nine minutes past nine. He was waiting, this night. Waiting to be informed of the results of an operation he had set in motion. Not, he thought, to do with politics. Not directly anyway. He wanted nothing to do with politics. Ostrich-like, he would bury his head, not wishing to be involved. As a servant of the public, it might be said, he knew his place. That place was in the combating of crime. Specifically, for Lohmann, serious crime, major infractions of the law. Those which would occur no matter what government was in power. His vocation. The rest was not his affair.

Not then.

Achille Serre approached his table. The cafe's owner, a small, rotund man, a round ball of a man, Serre was from the disputed Rhineland, half French, half German; and assertive of the German half. But then his livelihood was in Germany. His emotions, he maintained, were German; his politics, non-existent until Hitler had become Chancellor, had suddenly flowered into a full-blown National Socialism. But, even before the flowering, there had been a devout respect for authority; at this moment illustrated by his attitude towards Lohmann.

'The coffee is all right, Inspector?' The tone was unctuous, the attitude deferential. Lohmann nodded.

'Real coffee,' Serre went on. 'Only real coffee at the Cafe Serre.' Again Lohmann nodded, concealing an impatience that had nothing to do with the cafe proprietor.

A burst of laughter came from the bar, echoing across the chatter in the room. Serre looked up, frowning. Two SA men at the bar loudly expressing their amusement at some private joke. Loudly, but not too loudly. Not now. Not after so many recent events.

Serre smiled at Lohmann. 'Not so noisy these days, are they? Not since the Führer took care of Röhm and the other bully boys.'

Lohmann made no reply, but politely raised an eyebrow to illustrate an amiable agreement. At another table, a blonde young woman quoted a price to a middle-aged man, bowler hat on the back of his head. The figure induced a paroxysm of coughing in the man.

Lohmann turned away to continue gazing out of the cafe window. Outside it was raining, rivulets of water streaming down the outer surface of the window. Beyond, the night crowd swarmed under mushrooming umbrellas. A car pulled up at the kerb, a Mercedes-Benz, its hood shining in the rain. A man jumped from the driving seat and crossed the paving stones towards the cafe.

Reiner entered, his eyes moving at once towards the corner table by the window; Lohmann's table. Reiner pushed his way through the crowd at the end of the bar and moved through the forest of tables towards Lohmann. Reiner was in his early thirties, an inch shorter than Lohmann, his crumpled suit, under a long raincoat, a year older than Lohmann's blue serge. Reiner wore a flat cap, damp hair protruding at the back and over the furrowed brow. The brow indicated a degree of consternation.

A woman said loudly, 'Julius is worse than a pimp. He's a romantic. Much more difficult to get rid of . . .', as Reiner moved around her table and reached Lohmann.

The Inspector looked up.

'They lost him!' Reiner said.

Lohmann swore under his breath. 'How could they lose him?'

Reiner, who was Lohmann's sergeant and principal aide, shrugged awkwardly, sliding into the seat beside his chief.

'He came off the Hamburg train, as we expected. Took a taxi to the north of the city. Holtz and Werner followed him. He left the taxi at Waldenstrasse and started to walk. They lost him when he cut up some alley.'

Lohmann, sad eyed, swallowed the dregs of his coffee. 'Take me there,' he said, standing.

They made their way back around the tables and towards the door. This brought them to the side of the bar. As they passed, they drew level with the two SA men. The larger of the two, brown shirt bulging over a large beer belly, was addressing a small dark man with an oriental cast of features.

'You look like a Jew to me! Yes, you do. A dirty little Yid! I don't like drinking near yids. Gives me an acid stomach.'

Serre, behind the bar at that moment, tried to intervene. 'Excuse me, sir, but Herr Kovel is a regular customer.'

Herr Kovel threw Serre a look of gratitude. But it was to no avail. The large Brownshirt was in full spate and not to be cut off.

'*Was* a regular customer! But he's changed his mind. He doesn't want to drink here any more. Do you, Jewboy?'

Lohmann had stopped behind the SA man. The scene offended him. The anti-Semitism produced in him a feeling of disgust. But more than that, the growing feeling of violence about to erupt upset his desires for calmness, for peace in the streets, indeed in all public places. Violence was unlawful and untidy, and he abhorred it.

The violence erupted. The SA man grabbed a bottle by its neck and smashed it against the heavy wood of the bar. He held the jagged, evil edge of glass, in front of Herr Kovel's face.

'If you still want to drink here, Yid, then you'll do it through a face that looks like mincemeat!'

Behind Lohmann, Reiner, the sergeant, braced himself. He was accustomed to his chief's temperament, to the challenges Lohmann threw at a possible ugly fate. Lohmann stepped between the Brownshirt and the small dark man.

'I don't think so,' the police inspector said quietly.

The face of the Brownshirt, large in front of him. The face, ill-shaped as if by improper usage. A thick nose, scarred, not with the delicacy of a duelling scar, but flattened, at some time broken in a street brawl. The eyes, deep-set, surrounded by puffed-up flesh, were small and dim. A misshapen jaw under a loose mouth and wet lips. Damp with anticipation.

From between the wet lips, 'Well, well, a Jew lover!' the jagged fragment of the bottle rose towards Lehmann. 'Mincemeat is mincemeat, whoever's face it's made of . . .'

Lohmann was calm, almost serene. 'Name is Lohmann,' he said quietly. 'Criminal Police. Now use the bottle. Be my guest.'

The Brownshirt hesitated.

Lohmann went on, 'If you want two years . . . yes, at least two years of pain, then use the bottle. But, if you do, I'll break both your arms.'

The Brownshirt stared at the policeman. The hand holding the bottle trembled. The warning from the eye, through the brain, down the cortex causing the trembling.

'But . . . but the man's a Jew!' said the SA man. As if this should explain, permit, excuse any action he chose to take.

'The man's a citizen,' Lohmann replied. 'I'm a policeman. My job is to protect law-abiding citizens.'

It was difficult for the SA man to take in, difficult to absorb the concept that a Jew could be so considered. From the mild prejudice instilled at school or by family, a prejudice against anyone different, to the virulent prejudice of the Party; all that shaping his attitude, impregnating his psyche. Now, this ranking police officer was refusing to acknowledge his basic beliefs. And the police officer had a strength, an authority that the SA man had been conditioned to accept without question.

He lowered the jagged glass.

'Now, you go,' Lohmann went on. 'Out! And you will not come back.'

The second SA man, smaller, less aggressive, and only too aware of the recent culling of the Brownshirts, took his companion's arm.

'Come on. Let's go.'

Still looking at Lohmann, the large Brownshirt said, 'I haven't finished my lager!' Eyeball to eyeball, challenging.

Lohmann lifted the half-full stein of lager on the bar, and, with meticulous precision, poured the liquid down the front of the Brownshirt's trousers and boots.

'You've finished now,' Lohmann said.

The man flushed scarlet. A vein throbbing in the neck stood out like a cord. Fists clenched and unclenched. And clenched again. The narrow eyes narrowed even further; nothing resembling more than an angry Chinaman.

Lohmann, ignoring physical indications, went on, 'Weren't you one of Ernst Röhm's boyfriends? Yes, I must check the *Sicherheitsdienst* files, Sergeant Reiner.'

Reiner nodded, as he was expected to do. The Brownshirt looked from Lohmann to Reiner and back. At the mention of Röhm, the flush had gone from his face. At the mention of the *Sicherheitsdienst* . . . the Security Service of the SS . . . the man's face had gone white, an instant blanching of skin; a deprivation of blood. Then, automatically, he backed away, without speaking although the lips moved, a futile search for words that would not come, that could not be formed into any phrase that would suit the occasion. His companion was already at the door of the cafe. The large man turned abruptly and marched out, followed by the door-holding companion.

Behind the bar, Serre, a cork bobbing on water, head up, head down, acknowledged a debt.

'Thank you, Inspector Lohmann, thank you!'

'Please, yes, thank you, sir.' The small dark Kovel echoed the cafe proprietor.

'No need, Achille,' Lohmann replied. 'I like your coffee and I like drinking it in peace.'

So saying he moved towards the door followed by Reiner. Outside it was raining still, and heavily. Paving stones gleamed in the lights from cafes and shops and a nearby cinema. Umbrellas further reflected the lights. And bowler hats, bobbing in the busy thoroughfare, provided their own shining reflection. A trolley car passed, clanking and *snorting*, a dragon with no Siegfried to slay it, destined for Koepenik. Another trolley car swung left, destination, on its signboard, the Stettin station.

Lohmann settled in the passenger seat of the Mercedes, as Reiner climbed in behind the steering wheel. Rainwater dripped through a tiny hole in the hood of the car onto Lohmann's cheek. He ignored it. Reiner started the ignition and the car moved off into the night streets.

They moved through long avenues of lights, and shadows of buildings. A flag, hanging from some official window, sagging against the stonework, revealed a sodden mass of scarlet in the centre of which was an equally sodden, black swastika. Despite the incessant downpour, the streets seemed crowded. As always. As every night. A mass search for entertainment, for enjoyment, for escape from coming realities, so it seemed to Lohmann. And not in hindsight, but the thought with him, here and now.

Reiner took a cigarette packet from his pocket with one hand, and, the other still on the wheel, lit a cigarette. As an afterthought, he offered the packet to Lohmann, who took another cigarette from it.

'Thought you'd stopped,' Reiner said.

'Yes. Buying them. Haven't stopped smoking,' Lohmann replied, lighting the cigarette, staring straight ahead at the shining cobbles.

Reiner inhaled. And ventured a statement. 'We'll have to move carefully, if we pick up his trail. He's . . . he's an important character.'

Lohmann's eye was caught by a large illuminated sign. AEG LIGHT AND POWER. The word POWER seemed brighter than the others.

'He's a multiple murderer,' Lohmann said, the glare of the sign causing him to blink. 'That's his only importance.'

'We still have to find the bastard. And prove it.'

'We will.' Thus the Inspector, face expressionless. The AEG sign retreated behind them.

The Mercedes took a bend too fast, and Reiner pressed on the brake. The car responded with a screech of protest orchestrated on oil-sodden cables. And now, they were in a side street, ill-lit, narrow, the buildings on either side leaning forward as if the stone was stretching outwards to embrace the opposing façade. The street seemed at first deserted, and then Lohmann caught a movement at the corner of his eye. A tramp shuffling from doorway to doorway, a scavenger of waste waiting the dawn's garbage collectors.

The car moved into a small square, iron railings enclosing a sad oblong of grass, now sodden and patched with mud. Two figures stood at the kerb on the southern side of the square, men in raincoats and soft hats, muffled to the ears in thick scarves. Holtz and Werner, detectives, Criminal Police, Berlin Central, both working under Lohmann. Werner, by Lohmann's choice, Holtz by administrative direction. Which meant Holtz was not only a Kripos detective, but also a *Sicherheitsdienst* spy . . . a Gestapo man. Both men waiting. The Mercedes drew up beside them.

'Sorry, Inspector,' Werner said as Lohmann climbed down from the Mercedes. 'He was too quick for us.'

'Wouldn't be hard,' the Inspector muttered. 'Show me where you lost him.'

Holtz led the way, Lohmann and Werner following and Reiner bringing up the rear, adjusting his cap, that it might keep the rain from dripping down the inside of his collar.

'I don't think he spotted we were following him,' Holtz said over his shoulder to Lohmann. 'We were being very careful of that, as you ordered.'

'I'm sure,' Lohmann replied dryly, long legs striding energetically over the cobbles.

They came quickly to the alley, a narrow gulley between two tall tenements.

'This is where he turned down,' Holtz explained. 'When we got here, there was no sign.'

'He could have gone into one of the houses,' Reiner suggested.

Lohmann nodded to himself. 'Only one place he would have gone in this neighbourhood. Come on.'

He led the way down the alley with the step of a man assured of his destination. Half way down he veered to his left. There was a narrow passage, devoid of street lamps, leading between two of the tenements. It was narrow enough for a man to touch either wall with his arms barely outstretched. It led into wider street running parallel to the alley. On the far side of this street was a large, elegant building, steps leading up to a doorway.

'Holtz! Werner!' Lohmann said decisively. 'Around and cover the rear of that house. Anyone trying to get out, stop them.'

The two detectives looked at each other, as if uncertain

of where they were, and what the other meant. Werner nodded first and led the way towards the side of the house. Holtz followed reluctantly, disappointed at seeming to miss the main action. Reiner stared up at the doorway. Double doors, a brass knocker, and a light visible through the transom above the door.

'What is this place?' he asked.

'The one place in this district our man would head for,' Lohmann replied, moving up the steps to the doorway. Grasping the heavy brass knocker, he thumped it against the door energetically. The sound seemed to echo somewhere within the house. As Reiner stepped up behind him, the door opened.

To say the face that greeted them was raddled, a combination of lines spreading out across skin like a spider's web, and shadowy folds of fat turning in upon themselves, was not an exaggeration. Past middle age, approaching some dark age of both body and soul, she peered at the new arrivals with a myopic intensity.

'This is a private club!' she said, the voice unpleasantly hoarse. 'Go away!'

'Criminal Police!' said Reiner, assuming at once his customary role of advance interrogator and spokesman for his chief. Before the woman could reply Lohmann, with determined purpose but lacking any brutality, pushed her gently aside and stepped into the brightly lit hallway. Reiner followed.

'You have a search warrant?' The woman demanded.

'Didn't you just invite us in?' Lohmann said. Her jaw dropped as she searched for a reply.

'Elsa Kunst, isn't it?' Lohmann went on. 'Tantchen Elsa.' And then an aside to Reiner. 'She has a police record going back to when the Kaiser was a boy.'

Elsa Kunst flushed scarlet with assumed indignation. 'You fucking bastard, you've no right in here!'

Lohmann turned away from her and surveyed the hallway. 'Elsa, you know I can go anywhere,' he said, not unpleasantly, staring at a small statuette, a not very good miniature reproduction of Michelangelo's *Boy David*. The police inspector shuddered slightly.

'I daresay it sets the tone,' he said, turning a full three

hundred and sixty degrees to take in everything. Pseudo-Grecian pillars led towards a set of double doors. An imitation marble fireplace had seen no flames. A mural on the left wall depicted a Greek or Roman bath, young men with, and without, togas. No sign of the female of the species, Lohmann thought. Except of course Elsa Kunst, if she could so be described. At the side of the pillars, completely out of period, was a maplewood desk, as if for new arrivals to register their names. But there was no registration book. Lohmann could only presume that volume existed only in Frau Kunst's head.

He stepped towards the double doors and threw them open. Reiner was at his heel, and behind, almost stumbling, Elsa Kunst moved reluctantly forward, hands wringing.

It was a luxurious lounge into which the two policemen stepped. The Graeco-Roman motif was there in the mock-marble items in the room . . . yet another fireplace . . . and pillars everywhere. But the furniture was Louis Quinze, or a passable imitation, and the room was illuminated by a large chandelier. A staircase swept upwards on one side of the room. Chaise-longues abounded, by the staircase, on either side of the fireplace, in this corner and in that. On three of them sat three youths, one to each piece of furniture; each with room for a companion. And as Lohmann stepped into the room a large man, dressed in black trousers, a striped shirt, waistcoat and bow tie, moved in front of him. The man had large hands even for his size, and a well-defined broken nose. Both hands and nose, with small eyes above, expressed a threatening attitude.

'It's all right, Gregor!' Elsa Kunst called out just as Reiner drew a Mauser pistol from under his coat.

It was always Reiner who took the elementary precautions when his chief was threatened. Lohmann never acknowledged this fact but seemed to accept it, as a matter of course.

Now the large man, Gregor, backed away, seemingly disappointed at Elsa Kunst's warning. He moved back across to a pillar near the foot of the staircase and leaned on it, scowling at the room. Ignoring him, Lohmann turned his attention to the nearest of the three youths.

'I know you! The Pretty Boy, they called you. Used to work the Unter den Linden, didn't you?'

The youth looked up. His cheeks were carefully rouged and powdered, his lips shining with lipstick.

Lohmann went on. 'Fritzie! That's what they call you. Four convictions for soliciting. Or is it five? What brings you to this particular sewer?'

'So?' the youth said arrogantly. 'Why shouldn't I be here? It's warmer than the streets, and I have to eat, don't I?'

Shaking his head sadly, Lohmann turned to the next youth, a gangling figure spread over his chaise-longue, dressed inappropriately in Lederhosen, the face also smeared with make-up.

'I know you too. Age?'

'Seventeen.'

Reiner was at Lohmann's side now. 'I know him, too. Seventeen, going on a hundred and five.'

Elsa Kunst suddenly took a step forward, hand-wringing continuing, but the need to ease the situation obvious upon her.

'Gentlemen, if you are so interested . . . I mean, one understands even the police have to relax . . .'

Reiner cut her off. 'Shut your filthy mouth!'

The woman rocked back on her heels, as if she had been struck. Ignoring her, Lohmann turned to the third youth. Here, the face, unsullied by make-up, presented a mild touch of acne. The youth was wearing a none-too-clean open-necked shirt, a pair of trousers woven from some thick, cheap cloth, and a jacket of similar material, ill-fitting and stained.

'You! I don't know you,' said Lohmann. 'You're new. When did you get to Berlin?'

The youth's face was scarlet, his lips trembled fearfully. 'Y . . . yesterday, sir,' he stammered. 'From Westphalia. M . . . m . . . my f . . . father has a farm in Westphalia.'

'What happened? Have a row with the old man? Took off to see the bright lights. Fame and fortune in the big city. And who do you meet but Tantchen Elsa. Everybody's favourite aunt. You fell into bad company, boy.' The Inspector stared down at the youth in silence for a moment. Then he went on. 'Got any money, boy?'

'No, sir.'

'Name?'

'Karl, sir.'

Lohmann reached into his trouser pocket, then hesitated and, seeming to change his mind, turned to Elsa Kunst.

'Give him the price of a train ticket back to Westphalia.'

Elsa's face twitched in some attempt at protest. 'But, Inspector . . .'

'And the price of a decent meal,' Lohmann pressed on. 'Do it. Now!'

The woman fumbled in a bulky reticule that hung from her wrist. The spider-web face seemed to crack even more, deeper chasms of flesh appearing. She produced a bundle of notes, and carefully selected three. Impatiently, Reiner stepped forward, took the bundle from a reluctant hand, doubled the amount she had selected, added a couple of extra notes and, handing the remainder of the bundle back to the woman, turned and pressed the notes into Karl's hands.

'Now get out!' Lohmann said harshly. 'Back to Westphalia. If I see you again in Berlin, I'll slap you behind bars quicker than a flea'll bite you!'

The boy stared at the money, half rose from the chaise-longue, looked from Lohmann to Reiner and back. Then, crouched, he ran from the room to the hallway. A moment later they heard the front door open and, a second later, slam shut.

Lohmann turned to the first youth, Fritzie. 'You! A man came in here about half an hour ago. Freiherr von Glauber. Which room? Show me.'

Fritzie looked questioningly at Elsa Kunst.

'Don't look at her, look at the Inspector,' Reiner shouted and the youth turned, shaking, back to Lohmann.

'I'm not sure . . .' he started to speak but was cut off by a scream from the floor above. It was a horrendous sound, a shriek of pure physical agony trailing off into a whisper. And then dying away.

Lohmann leaned forward, grabbing Fritzie by the scruff of the neck and propelling him towards the staircase.

'Up!' he shouted. 'And show me!'

Fritzie stumbled but, under the grasp of the Inspector, regained his balance. Reiner followed them up the stairs. At the top they were faced with a long, ill-lit corridor. There were four doors on either side. Fritzie pointed to the third on the right. Lohmann released him and he sagged against the wall. Reiner, Mauser pistol in hand, ran to the door, stopped and looked to Lohmann close behind him. The inspector nodded and the sergeant took a pace backwards, and kicked out at the lock of the door. There was a tearing, snapping sound of wood breaking and the door swung open. Reiner went in and his chief followed.

The room was brightly lit, illumination coming both from a centre bank of lights on the ceiling, and a large lamp beside the bed. All these were reflected by mirrors on the wall, and a large mirror on the ceiling over the bed. The bed itself dominated the room, a large, double bed with an ornate gold headboard. It was not the bed that drew their eyes, but what was on the bed. Lying on top of rumpled sheets was the body of a youth of about sixteen. The body, naked, was lying face downwards. Across the exposed back and buttocks were a series of slashes, criss-crossing the flesh, soaking skin and sheets with the violent scarlet of newly shed blood. Still uncongealed, small trickles and streams of this blood flowed in distinct if tiny rivulets across the body and on to the bedding. And, just under the headboard, the youth's head, twisted in a peculiar and unreal position, was drenched with blood at the neck. The throat had been slashed across the Adam's apple to some considerable depth.

The two police officers stood, Lohmann in the doorway, Reiner in the centre of the room, both momentarily immobile, as they took in the horror of the sight on the bed. It was Lohmann who turned first to face the man standing by the side of the bed.

Von Glauber, middle-aged, a full head of sleek black hair, so black as to be certainly dyed, stood clad only in a pair of striped morning trousers which he was hurriedly pulling on over ample hips. The belly, streaked, as was the chest, with the blood of the youth on the bed, protruded over the trousers, the navel a gross eye suffused also with blood. The man's face, heavy jowls trembling, bore an expression both surprised and terrified. The mouth, margined by thick lips, twisted, moved awkwardly, as if the effort of speaking was too much for it. Yet the words finally came.

'A . . . an accident, I assure you . . . a dreadful accident.'

Reiner, eyes still riveted to the horror on the bed, swore softly but violently under his breath. But even the oath was stifled by a rush of phlegm to the back of his throat. He gagged. Lohmann, ignoring everything else now, had his eyes on von Glauber. In the intense light, the man's figure seemed to shimmer in front of his eyes, almost a mirage. Lohman had waited a long time to come face to face with this mirage. When he spoke, his voice was hoarse with disgust.

'Makes the fifth accident, Freiherr. Now, you will not move. Otherwise it will give me some pleasure to shoot you.' Lohmann produced his own Mauser pistol.

Von Glauber babbled. No other word for it. His trousers now securely buckled, he swayed against the side of the bed, his mouth still working violently.

'Told you . . . accident . . . yes, an accident. Please understand . . . no harm intended.' Swallowing hard over and over again, Adam's apple bobbing up and down. Searching for an answer to the unanswerable. Then, grasping at a straw, asserting himself. 'You must know. I am an important man. I hold high position in the Party. Personal friend of General Göring . . . also Alfred Rosenberg . . . .'

'You *held* high position in the Party,' Lohmann replied, stressing the past tense.

Still swaying, von Glauber tried to steady himself by placing his left hand on the bedside table. Behind him, the only window in the room reflected Lohmann's image back at himself. The tall, thin figure holding the pistol, this caught his eye. In that second he had taken his eyes off von Glauber. And the man saw this and took his one fleeting opportunity. The left hand circled the heavy lamp on the bedside table, grasped it, and threw it at Lohmann. It struck the police inspector on the chest and he stumbled backwards. The bulb in the lamp exploded with a loud bang. At the same time, von Glauber spun around and threw himself through the window. The glass fragmented with a crash as his body disappeared into darkness. Reiner, still unsettled by the sight on the bed, fired once, a reflex action taken without aiming. The bullet went into the wall at the side of the window.

Lohmann, unhurt but momentarily surprised, moved first, running to the broken window. Staring out, he found himself faced not with a yawning drop but with the metal of a rusting fire-escape. His first thought had been that the murderer had deliberately attempted suicide. Now he stared down at an escape route he had not reckoned on; and he could hear the sound of clanging, rattling metal, as Von Glauber, apparently unhurt by his leap through glass, was climbing down towards the ground. Brushing aside shards of glass still in the window frame, the Inspector climbed onto the escape and started downwards.

Below him, he caught a flash of movement in the darkness. He fired one shot, hearing it clash on metal, seeing a spark strike off, somewhere below. As he continued a headlong descent his ankle scraped against flaking iron and a second later he felt the cutting edge of pain. To be ignored. One thought only. Stop the fugitive. He had been on the man's trail too long to permit even the thought that he might, for a short time, escape. Certainly, if he did so, an alert police force in the city would surely find him. Unless, and there was the fear, he might reach one of the influential friends who could hide him.

The sound of a thud came from somewhere below. Von Glauber was off the fire-escape and on the ground. Freed of a lower weight, the metal swayed even more, bucked and jumped, as Lohmann struggled downwards.

Holtz or Werner must be down there somewhere, Lohmann determined, gripping the rusting sides of the escape. The metal ladder led onto a lane at the rear of the building. They should certainly be able to stop the fleeing man.

He reached the end of the escape, and jumped the remaining five feet to cobblestones. As he did so, as if in answer to his thoughts about Holtz and Werner, he heard a shout from the end of the lane, followed by a scream of agony. He raced along the lane. Werner was lying, curled up on the edge of a puddle. Cupped hands nursed his crotch. Face contorted in pain, he managed to nod in the direction of the street beyond the lane. Von Glauber had obviously disabled the detective with one unexpected kick. Yet where was Holtz? He should have been there to back up Werner. One man can be disabled but, with two, the other can easily use the time to draw his weapon and shoot the antagonist.

Lohmann ran on into the street.

Von Glauber had turned to the right and, in doing so, had made his mistake. The street came to a dead end, a high stone wall barring further progress. But the man was able to make use of any opportunity that presented itself. The opportunity came in the form of the Westphalian farm boy Karl who, clutching his railfare home, had taken a wrong turning and found himself in the dead-end street. Then he had found himself staring at a half-naked man, body mottled with another's blood, hand clutching a thin shard of glass; ready to use the shard as a weapon.

Lohmann stopped fifteen years from the two figures. The fugitive had grasped the farm boy by the neck, twisted him around to face Lohmann; and was holding the dagger-like splinter of glass at the boy's neck. Lohmann stopped, gun in hand, and stared at the two figures huddled under the shadow of the end wall. He heard running feet and half turned to see Holtz hurrying towards him.

'Where the fuck have you been?' he demanded of the detective.

'I . . . I was just down the road . . .' No explanation, the man flustered and embarrassed.

Lohmann turned towards von Glauber and the youth. Von Glauber's hand, clutching the shard, moved closer to the youth's throat.

'One step and I kill him!'

'So, kill him. And then I shoot you,' said Lohmann.

'You . . . you don't care if I . . . if I kill him?' Von

Glauber was gasping for breath, sucking air into his lungs with a desperation compounded not only of exertion but also of fear.

'Did you care, when you killed that boy back there? Or the others in Hamburg and Bonn?'

Von Glauber blinked, trying to work out some reply.

'After all, they were only rent boys,' Lohmann went on, a feeling within him of disgust at the play-acting he was forcing himself to indulge in. At the same time, he was studying the figures in front of him.

Karl's body was completely shielding that of the fugitive. His head was bent to one side, straining away from the cutting edge of glass close to his neck. Von Glauber's nose, eyes and forehead were clear of the boy's head. Yet, if the boy moved, he could still cover the man's head. Time to take a chance? Or time to wait? Lohmann's decision. The Mauser's grip, sticky in his hand. Holtz at his side, staring. Unable to do anything but stare. Not one to take a decision. Not when there was no compulsion to do so. Not when there was a possibility of making the wrong move. That was Holtz.

Then there was a movement on the top of the wall. A cat had leaped out of darkness on to the wall, and was balanced on a loose brick. The brick rocked and dust fell to the ground. Von Grauber had been at that moment distracted by this, as had Lohmann. But it was the police officer who, acknowledging the cause, turned back to the situation. And saw von Glauber's head was completely clear of the youth's head and body.

With both hands he brought the Mauser pistol up to eye level, aimed and fired.

A small round spot appeared on von Glauber's right temple. His fingers, gripping the shard of glass, trembled violently and then the glass slipped from between them and fell. It caught for a second on the boy's jacket before falling onto the cobbles where it shattered. Karl, feeling the grip around his shoulders relaxed, leaped aside, turning away from his erstwhile captor. Von Glauber, a surprised expression crossing his face, was against the stonework, now sliding slowly to the ground. As he slid, his head twisted around and showed an exit hole as large as a fist, blood and other material matting the black hair.

Lohmann turned away, to face Holtz. 'You!' he said, not bothering to conceal his irritation with the man. 'Get that boy out of this. Then phone for the meat wagon and get everything cleared up!'

'At once, Inspector!'

'And by the way, where were you when this character attacked Werner?'

Holtz stiffened, almost came to attention. When he spoke it was with a self-conscious arrogance.

'I was required to telephone the *Sicherheitsdienst*. An earlier order. There's a phone in the cafe off the square . . .'

Lohmann raised an eyebrow with some deliberation. 'You'll have to make up your mind, Holtz. Whether you are a police detective or a member of the Security Service.'

'With respect, Inspector Lohmann, they will soon be one and the same.'

Heavy irony in the reply. 'Until they are, Holtz, you will do exactly as I tell you. And you will not desert a fellow detective when he is relying on you to back him up. Now get back to your phone and get the wagon here.'

Holtz moved off, his face flushed.

Ten minutes later, Lohmann stood in the hallway of Elsa Kunst's establishment, addressing himself to Reiner.

'How is Werner?'

'Apart from sore balls where von Glauber kicked him, he'll survive,' the sergeant replied. 'What about the woman and her people?'

'Take them in. Charge them. Accessories to murder. Incitement to illegal sexual acts. Procuring. And running a disorderly house. That should guarantee Elsa Kunst and her friends quite a long vacation. Holtz is phoning to bring in the wagon and the murder squad. You take charge. I'm going home to get some sleep.'

As he said it, Lohmann realised he was, at that moment, physically exhausted. Not by the brief pursuit of a killer, that required little effort. Something else. Something he would not dwell upon. The killing of von Glauber. Christ, not that the man did not deserve to die. Five perverted killings, reason enough. But the act of extermination of another human being, the killing itself; that could disturb Lohmann. If he allowed it to do so. He must *not* permit himself that masochistic luxury. Von Glauber was the fourth man Lohmann had been forced to kill. The others, a bank robber on the run, two murderers who had attempted to kill him; and now von Glauber. Despite the necessity, the justification, there was a part of him revolted against the act. A part that nauseated him; that, when he was alone in the darker reaches of his existence, he felt loath to acknowledge. And yet, he would repeat to himself, none of the killing could have been avoided. Still, the remembrance of each act had to be avoided.

Holtz appeared in the doorway of the house.

'Inspector, you have to report to Chief Inspector Murnau at headquarters.' The pronouncement uttered with some degree of enjoyment at Lohmann's possible discomfiture.

'In the morning, Holtz.'

'With respect, sir, at once. There seems to be some concern at the death of the Freiherr von Glauber.'

Holtz turned away, a smug expression on his face.

'Oh, go and do something, Holtz!' Reiner said. 'Go and tidy up the Freiherr's body.'

Holtz disappeared down the steps into the darkness.

'He's joined the SS,' Reiner went on. 'Little bastard wants to hide inside a big, black uniform.'

'Poor sod,' Lohmann responded with irony. 'All those conflicting loyalties. He'd be much happier in the traffic division.'

'You could still go home, sir. We could say Holtz didn't deliver the message?'

The Inspector yawned. 'No. It appears I have shot an important Party official. Be interesting to see how they deal with it, don't you think?'

One half hour later. Lohmann striding into the main office of the Criminal Police. At least, he is on familiar territory. His own office in a tiny cubicle against the wall to the right. He moves towards it, acknowledging the nods, and in some cases the embarrassed looks, of his fellow officers. In his own office, he sits behind the small desk and waits.

The summons came within three minutes, delivered by a uniformed policeman.

The Chief Inspector's office was larger and better furnished than Lohmann's cubicle. The prerogative of rank. A large oak desk, deeper leather seats (two only), a small drinks cabinet, the interior of which was illuminated when its doors were opened . . . in dubious bourgeois taste . . . and, on the wall behind the desk, a portrait of Field Marshal Hindenberg (soon to be replaced by another less distinguished if equally notorious portrait). On a side table, laid out in all its glory, the new uniform of an SS officer, the Death's Head badge gleaming in the cap.

The uniform embarrassed Chief Inspector Murnau. He was normally a plump, pleasant man, son of a policeman under the Kaiser, grandson of a policeman under the Kaiser's father. A Prussian who did not look like a Prussian; a man determined to do his best under whatever circumstances arose. A man without jealousy, proud of the fact that his force contained a detective officer as good as Lohmann.

Greeting the Inspector, he saw Lohmann glance at the uniform with ill-concealed amusement.

'Damn it, Lohmann, I have to join,' Murnau explained. 'As you will if you wish to have a career here.'

'You mean, if I still *have* a career here?'

'Ah, yes. The Freiherr von Glauber. Did you . . . did you have to . . . shoot him?'

'Yes.'

Murnau shook his head wearily. 'Of course, you were right. But will they see it that way?'

'What other way can they see it? The man butchered five kids.'

'These people have a different perspective.'

'Whatever that may mean?'

Murnau glared at him. 'I don't know what it means. I'm not sure what our job means any more. But . . . one of them will no doubt explain it to you. And I hope, in God's name, you survive the explanation. There are two SS men waiting outside. Their orders are to take you to Colonel Heydrich. You may have heard of Reinhard Heydrich. One of the coming men in Germany today.'

TWO

It was after midnight, yet, despite the lateness of the hour, the building on Prinz Albrechtstrasse was ablaze with light. The necessity, Lohmann determined, to show that the security services of the new Reich were ever alert. For this was the headquarters at once of the Gestapo and the Security Service of the SS. Here, the former schoolteacher with the steel-rimmed spectacles, Heinrich Himmler, was busy establishing his empire. Here, too, were his principal aides, Reinhard Heydrich, Sepp Dietrich and the young Walter Schellenberg. And, lower down the scale, burrowing his way through official documentation, the clerk, Adolf Eichmann.

Lohmann had been escorted from Police Headquarters by two black-uniformed figures, taciturn monosyllabic SS men. The black uniforms were impressive although, as in Murnau's office, the Death's Head insignia on the caps were disconcerting. Why, Lohmann wondered, should any organisation take as its symbol a sign of death? Whose death? Shouldn't the building then bear the telegraphic address, 'Death's Head, Berlin'?

The interior of the building was a hive of activity. The black uniform predominated, although there were civilians, a few, it seemed, moving with eyes averted. The uniform seemed a guarantee of superiority. There were also a number of grey uniforms, the officers of the *Sicherheitsdienst*, the Death's Head still in evidence. In the entrance hall, a roped-off area comprised several rows of wooden benches. Here were seated other civilians, not employees, but those who had seemingly been invited to report to officials. They sat, infinitely patient, nervous, hand-twisting, handkerchief-ringing; some even with a nervous defiance. Waiting.

Lohmann was led past them to a desk behind which sat a black-uniformed male receptionist. A few words from his escort and they were waved through. A wide staircase led upwards. The higher the rank, the higher the floor. They stopped on the fifth floor and went along a corridor. At the end of this corridor, Lohmann was shown into another office, an ante-room. Here a female secretary in black skirt, white shirt, swastika armband, blonde hair in a severe bun, looked up.

'Inspector Lohmann, for Colonel Heydrich,' said the smaller SS man.

The woman did not even glance up from the document she was studying.

'Thank you. The Colonel has no further need of you.'

The two men clicked their heels, presumably, Lohmann thought, in deference to the office of the Colonel rather than to the secretary, and departed. Still the woman did not look up, but lifted what Lohmann presumed was an internal telephone receiver.

'Inspector Lohmann is here, Colonel!'

Lohmann could not hear the reply, but the woman now looked up.

'Go in. The Colonel is ready for you.'

Heydrich's office was large, three walls panelled, the third taken up by a vast, glass-fronted series of book-shelves. The desk was in proportion to the room; huge and yet immaculate. A family photograph on one side, blotter and pen and ink stand in the centre and, on the other side, a neat pile of papers. Behind the desk, the framed photograph of Hitler, this one personally signed. And on one side of the photograph, an SS regimental banner.

The man behind the desk was dressed in an impeccable grey uniform. The SD emblem was low on the left sleeve; the lapels framed the laurel insignia. And there was a row of medal ribbons. The face was thin, the eyes narrow, almost slanting under a broad forehead, the blond hair short and slicked down around a left-sided parting. Yet the nose was the dominant feature, long, narrow with large nostrils. As Lohmann entered, he looked up, appraising the police officer from head to foot.

'Inspector Lohmann! Please sit.' The voice was low, deliberately cultivated to eradicate any trace of regional accent.

Lohmann sat in an upright chair facing the desk. He said nothing, aware of the eyes still appraising him. Then the eyes were turned down to a solitary sheet of paper on the blotting pad.

'You have an excellent record, Lohmann.'

'I do my job,' Lohmann replied, aware that he sounded surly. That was not politic, yet he could not help himself. He had been ordered to this office; had come unwillingly and was prepared for the torrent of indignation that must surely fall upon anyone who had shot an important party member. It did not matter, he was convinced, that the dead man was a murderer.

Heydrich began to read from the sheet of paper. 'Instrumental in the arrest of Peter Kurten. Also Karl Tetzner, Klaus Vogel, Eichner, the Leipzig bank robber. Also Beekmann, the child murderer. You haven't got Erwin Müller yet, but a case is being assembled. . . .'

It was irresistible. Lohmann cut in. 'And, as of tonight, Freiherr von Glauber, murderer of young men.'

Heydrich looked up. 'Ah, yes. Von Glauber. He was a Party member of some standing.'

'He was also a murderer and a pervert. He killed at least five youths . . .'

'And you shot him in the line of duty, of course?'

'Of course.'

Heydrich ran his fingers down the length of his nose. 'Von Glauber was also a member of the officer class.'

'I didn't have time to ask him for references.'

Heydrich suddenly laughed. It was a high-pitched laugh, and unmatched by the eyes which remained expressionless.

'Of course not,' the Colonel went on. 'No time for references. Not that his reference would have impressed me. I have no love for the officer class, Lohmann. And I was, myself, a naval officer.'

'I believe I knew that,' said Lohmann, restraining himself from mentioning he was aware that Heydrich had been the subject of a naval court-martial.

'I think you did the Party a favour tonight,' Heydrich said, to Lohmann's ill-concealed surprise.

'I'm . . . I'm pleased . . .' he stammered.

Heydrich looked again at the piece of paper on his desk. 'You are not a Party member, Herr Lohmann?'

Lohmann cleared his throat, giving himself a moment to absorb the surprise. 'I've always believed the law should be above political parties and their considerations. Impartial, if you like.'

The Colonel's expression changed. No sign of a smile now. A wintry look. 'You are wrong! The Party will be the law!'

He paused as if to underline the statement. Then he seemed to relax. 'However, I appreciate your position. I'm told you are the best detective in Berlin. If not in Germany.'

Lohmann shrugged. 'I told you, I do my job.'

Heydrich now rose from behind the desk. He was taller; taller than the police inspector, a tall, lean man. Imposing in his height and uniform. He pressed a button on his desk. Fingers drummed on the polished wood for a moment.

The door opened behind Lohmann. The man who came in wore the uniform of an SS captain. He was about the same height as Lohmann but with broad shoulders. Also thick black eyebrows under the peak of the black cap.

'My personal aide,' Heydrich explained. 'Captain Zoller. This is Inspector Lohmann. You two have to meet. You may see a great deal of each other.'

Zoller stared at Lohmann and then inclined his head in a curt acknowledgement.

'Captain Zoller,' Lohmann responded.

Heydrich took his cap from a drawer in the desk. 'The car is ready?'

'Waiting, Colonel.'

Lohmann found himself following the two uniforms. He was retracing his steps along the corridor, but this time they passed the staircase and proceeded to another door, an elevator entrance at the end of the corridor. The elevator took them down to a basement garage. A new Mercedes-Benz, the insignia both of the SS and a staff officer on the front. Zoller climbed in beside the uniformed driver and Heydrich beckoned the Inspector into the rear. Lohmann settled into soft leather, Heydrich beside him. The car started and moved up a ramp and into the night city.

Only then did Lohmann ask the question. 'Where are we going?'

Heydrich lit a cigarette before replying, as an afterthought proffered the gold case to Lohmann. 'They're Turkish,' the Colonel explained. Lohmann took one and Heydrich lit their cigarettes with a gold lighter. The back of the car filled with the sweet scent of Turkish tobacco.

'There was another murder committed in Berlin tonight. Or should I say, last night. Apart from the von Glauber affair,' Heydrich said, exhaling through his nostrils.

'Surely,' Lohmann replied. 'Statistically more than one. But I haven't seen the night's incident report.'

'It will not be on that report. It has been referred to higher authority.'

'To you, Colonel?'

'To me. And higher. Much higher.'

He's enjoying himself, Lohmann thought. Strong, silent, taciturn. Always, when the authority is new, it has to be savoured. Let the inferiors wait until you condescend to explain. Part of the childish game of utilising power. Lohmann had long outgrown it. But not Heydrich.

Outside, it was still raining and the lights of the city were blurred, the interiors of the windows misted. The streets were empty of people, the hour and the downpour driving even the night scarecrows to cover. The Mercedes swung around a corner and the glimpse of a building brought recognition to the detective. They were in the Wilhelmstrasse. After a moment the car turned again, under an archway and into a courtyard, pulling up in front of a row of steps. The steps led to large double doors. On either side of the doors, in the shelter of another arched entrance, stood two, black-uniformed sentries.

Zoller jumped from the seat beside the driver and

opened the rear door of the car. Lohmann followed Heydrich into the building.

Now he knew where he was. The Reichschancellery of Germany. The old Reichschancellery. There was talk of plans to build an even newer edifice to house the offices of the Head of State. But not yet.

Again Lohmann found himself crossing a large hallway. But this time, apart from a manservant in striped trousers and tailcoat, there was no one else in sight. A chandelier above his head was unlit, the only illumination coming from a small lamp on a table at the foot of the sweeping staircase which itself led up to semi-darkness.

'We are expected,' Heydrich had said quietly to the manservant as they entered the hall. The man gave no reply but led them upwards. At the top of the staircase, dimly discernible, a portrait of Field Marshal Hindenberg. Below the portrait, a smallish figure, rotund, running to fat. Short hair and a brown uniformed jacket devoid of insignia.

'Bormann,' Heydrich said, barely acknowledging a lesser authority.

'He's waiting,' the man said, and led the way along the corridor, also lit only by a solitary lamp.

Through a high, arched doorway they went into a large office in which were three empty desks. Secretaries, Lohmann thought, long since departed to their homes and beds. Where he devoutly wished he was at this moment. Yet the wish did not overcome the growing curiosity he felt for the meeting he knew was about to take place. Higher authority Heydrich had said. The highest would have been more appropriate.

Facing the further door, Heydrich hesitated and turning, said to Zoller, 'You will wait here.' Zoller's heels clicked automatically. He froze.

The man called Bormann knocked at the door, and waited. After a moment the knock was acknowledged.

'Come!'

Bormann opened the door and indicated that Heydrich and Lohmann should enter. He himself did not do so, but drew the door closed behind them.

The marble floor stretched some twenty yards to the

desk. The walls on either side were draped with swastikas. Between and beneath the swastikas were other portraits. Lohmann made out the exiled Kaiser, his father, and another large portrait of Frederick the Great. The others he did not recognise. But then, after a moment, his eyes were on the figure behind the desk.

The face was pale, the cheeks fleshy, the eyes a watery blue. The dark hair was neatly parted, the familiar forelock surely deliberate as it fell over the forehead. A uniform jacket similar to the one worn by the secretary, Bormann, bore however one decoration, the ribbon of the Iron Cross. As the man looked up at the new arrivals, the impression, despite the surroundings, was one of insignificance. Adolf Hitler resembled nothing more than an undistinguished commercial traveller.

Heydrich broke the silence by coming rigidly to attention in front of the desk, clicking his heels and raising his arm in the Party salute.

'Heil Hitler!'

How disconcerting, it occurred to Lohmann, to be perpetually hailed with one's own name. A return to the customs of the Roman Empire must surely be embarrassing to a modern Caesar. Yet Caesar showed no sign of embarrassment. He merely acknowledged the salute with a slight raising of his own right hand. The watery blue eyes were however directed not at Heydrich but at Lohmann who offered no greeting but stood, self-consciously, hat in hand.

Heydrich, seeing the direction of the eyes, cleared his throat and went on, 'Führer, may I present Inspector Lohmann of the Criminal Police?'

Hitler nodded, still staring at Lohmann, almost peering as if a sufferer from myopia. Lohmann could only return the nod, with a muttered, 'Herr Reichschancellor!'

There was no way, Lohmann determined, he would address this man as 'Führer'. Hitler was due his official title, yes, he was Reichschancellor; as to 'Führer', 'Leader', he may be that to members of the Party. But he, Lohmann, was not a Party member.

'They tell me you're the best detective in Berlin,' Hitler said, echoing the phrase used earlier by Heydrich. The voice was strong but harsh to the point of hoarseness. As if it had been over used, as if he had been shouting loudly and was now suffering for so doing.

'Tonight, they keep telling me that,' Lohmann replied with a small smile, his attempt to lighten the tone of the conversation. Hitler was unsmiling. It occurred to Lohmann there was no way of lightening a conversation with this man.

Hitler glanced briefly at Heydrich. 'They tell me you are not in Colonel Heydrich's Security Service?'

'No, sir. I am in Kripos. Criminal Police. Since I became a detective officer.'

'And, you are not a Party member?'

'I keep out of politics.'

There was a pause. Hitler continued to stare at Lohmann and, as he did so, he rose to his feet. Lohmann noticed for the first time he was wearing immaculately creased black trousers. The impression was of Spartan smartness.

Hitler finally broke the silence, repeating Lohmann's own words quietly, and with deliberation. 'You . . . keep . . . out . . . of . . . politics. So!'

He paced around the desk until he was standing, leaning against it, arms folded, eyes still on Lohmann. The steady, piercing gaze was not comfortable. The man seemed to be trying to stare inside the police inspector; to examine mind and soul. Lohmann felt the hair on the back of his neck tingling, and his face was surely flushing.

'You may be right to keep out of politics, Inspector!' Hitler suddenly burst out, the voice rising in pitch, an intimate exhibition of studied platform technique. 'There are no longer politics in Germany, as there were. No longer divisive, doctrinal whining by the little men! There are only the politics of the National Socialist Party. As determined by me.' He took a breath now, with deliberation. Then his voice dropped. 'You know why you are here?'

'Regarding a murder last night?' Lohmann replied tentatively and cursed himself inwardly for sounding so tentative. Especially in front of this man.

'Three murders!' Hitler went on. 'Over the past two weeks. Members of the Party. Old comrades.'

'I have heard nothing, Reichschancellor.'

'Heydrich has all the details. But I repeat, these were old comrades. His eyes now drifted from Lohmann, staring into space, remembering. 'Franz Rudig. As a youth, he marched with us in Munich. A young naval officer, he was then. Now he is . . . was a captain in the Documentation Branch of the civil authority. Konrad Preuss, Accountant, Party Records Section. Before coming to Berlin, he was one of the first party members in Saxony. And last night, Karl Bruckner, formerly in the Prussian Police. Before that, also in the navy. He was now in the Party's legal department.'

Again Hitler became silent, beads of perspiration on his brow. He produced a large white handkerchief and proceeded to mop his face. This was done while staring at the floor. Handkerchief returned to his trouser pocket, he continued.

'These three men were all strangled . . .'

Heydrich coughed and Hitler stared at him. 'You have something to say?'

'Not simply strangled, Führer. Garrotted!'

Lohmann was surprised. 'Garrotted?'

The blue eyes swivelled around to him again. 'Inspector?'

'It is an unusual method of murder,' Lohmann explained.

To his surprise Hitler seemed to flinch. A slight shudder. Perhaps a pang of fear.

'Yes. So. They were garrotted. Unusual.' Another pause. 'These men, you understand, were not as yet high ranking Party officials. But they were good men, working for the party. And, as I said, although not old in years, they were comrades of long standing. Someone has perpetrated this criminal act of murder on three old comrades. Colonel Heydrich has all the details, photographs, reports of the investigations so far . . .'

'Surely the SD has come up with something?' Lohmann said.

A glare at Heydrich. 'Neither the SD nor the Gestapo has succeeded in discovering anything. Which is why you are here.'

Lohmann acknowledged this by wiping his hand against his damp forehead. 'Can you be sure the three killings were carried out by the same person?'

Heydrich answered. 'The *modus operandi*. The Medical Examiner assures us each killing was by exactly the same method. A rope and a strong piece of wood. Similar to the technique of the Spanish executioners.'

Hitler broke in with a degree of irritation. 'Details later. I simply want the murderer found. With the Nuremberg Congress to take place shortly, I can devote little time to this matter. That is why you are here. I might suggest that with such an exotic method of killing, you may find you are dealing with an exotic, possibly oriental mind. In other words, a Jew. I want the man found. Preferably alive. If not possible, then otherwise. I gather you yourself have no scruples in such matters.'

'I beg your pardon, sir . . .?'

'The Freiherr von Glauber!'

Lohmann drew in his breath. He did not, he had to admit to himself, care to be classed as an unconcerned killer. He had justification. Perhaps Hitler had not been informed of the circumstances.

'Von Glauber,' he said, with precision, '. . . had just killed one youth and was about to kill another. I had no alternative.'

'Yes, yes, Lohmann,' Hitler replied, irritation now mixed with impatience. 'Doubtless you had cause. And the man was no loss.'

The instigator of killings, *en masse*, less than three months before must of course easily excuse the killer of the previous evening. In the name of some kind of justice. Or was it that Lohmann could now consider himself at one with the assassins of the "Night of the Long Knives". Was a von Glauber so different from Röhm and his slaughtered Brownshirts? No, Lohmann insisted to himself, there had to be a difference. Otherwise there was no morality left in the world. The thought brought another question to mind.

'Is it possible these men were killed . . . perhaps accidently, by . . . by those who carried out the recent executions of a number of SA men?'

Hitler took the question with surprising serenity. Turning again to Heydrich, he spat out the question.

'Well, Heydrich?'

'Not possible,' the SD man replied. 'As you know, sir, the execution of traitors was brought to a halt . . . anyway these three men were good Party members.'

Lohmann was unable to resist the thrust at the SD leader. He'd heard stories of that night. Innocents slain because they happened to have the same names as a number of SA men. Even a friend of Hitler's, so the stories went, Father Bernhardt Stumpf, had been killed during the purges, the rumour being that an error had been made. Much to Hitler's fury. Even Himmler, the Führer's faithful acolyte, had been called to this office and humiliatingly berated by the Führer himself.

'Again I say I would prefer the assassin delivered alive,' said Hitler.

'Of course,' Lohmann said. 'To stand trial. Under due process of the law.'

The watery eyes were again on Lohmann. 'Yes, under the law. Lohmann, I am that law henceforth. I am the only law in Germany today. Understand that.'

'Yes, sir.' Meaning damn you, sir, but I could never admit to that. Fortunately unspoken.

'You will be given every facility,' Hitler continued. 'Apart from the services of your own Criminal Police, you can call upon the SD and the Gestapo. And the Party you have not yet seen fit to join, Inspector. Of course you will join. In time. We plan to amalgamate the police under the SD. And no one who is not a Party member can expect to continue. You understand?'

Of course he understood. He had no choice but to understand. No choice, no alternative, yet. Meanwhile three men had been murdered, and if the Gestapo and the SS were blameless, then there was a murderer on the loose. Lohmann's job to apprehend the man. That went on, despite the Party, and the *nouveau* politicos, despite Enabling Acts that would place this white-faced man in front of him with absolute power in Germany until he died, or chose to retire.

Hitler half turned and took a second sheet of paper from

the top of his desk. On it was emblazoned the seal of the Reichschancellor's office. Below the seal, scrawled across the paper, handwriting thin and spidery, a single paragraph.

The Bearer is on the business of your Führer and the Reichschancellor of Germany. He is to be granted without question, every aid and facility. He is permitted to travel anywhere; to detain anyone in the pursuance of his mission.

Signed

Adolf Hitler
Reichschancellor

Lohmann took the paper from Hitler's hand, folded it and placed it in his wallet. And thought, God, the power of that single sheet of paper, in Germany today, was immense.

Hitler was nearly finished with them. He returned behind his desk, sat down and waved a dismissive hand. This was followed by an afterthought.

'You will furnish daily progress reports to Colonel Heydrich who will pass them on to me. When the task is successfully completed, you may bring the final report to me personally.'

A further wave of the hand. Heydrich clicked his heels and turned. The heel-clicking seemed inappropriate to Lohmann's civilian status and he contented himself with a final nod of acknowledgement before following the SD Chief from the room. He had a final absurd thought that, as in the presence of some oriental potentate, they should have perhaps withdrawn walking backwards. Not that Hitler would have noticed. He was peering at yet another sheet of paper, while his right hand groped in a desk drawer for the pair of spectacles he was at pains to conceal were necessary to him.

Only when they were out of the Reichschancellery and back in the Mercedes did Heydrich speak.

'Find this man and you can choose your own job in the police.'

'Also be invited to join the Party?'

'Of course.'

'I'm not sure that I'd like the other guests.'

The aroma of Turkish cigarettes filled the car. But this time Heydrich had not bothered to offer Lohmann one.

'You can choose your own company today, Lohmann. That letter he gave you, it makes you the second most important man in Germany. For the time being. Until your investigation is complete. But only until then.'

'After which, next to the murderer, I may be the second most wanted man in Germany.'

Heydrich smiled. 'It is the nature of things.'

Lohmann peered through the car window. 'Where now?'

'To the scene of the third crime. Karl Bruckner's apartment. You will find nothing has been touched since the body was found. By his housekeeper. Only four hours ago.'

'I want my own people.'

'I anticipated that. Sergeant Reiner should be there by now. I will send for your own murder squad at once. Although the SD have some very efficient officers.

'I'm sure. But they're not my people. Colonel.'

Heydrich inhaled deeply. He showed no sign of irritation but stared straight ahead, a slight smile on his lips.

'As you wish. Of course you will furnish me with the reports required by the Führer.'

'I will furnish you with the reports required by the Reichschancellor.'

The Mercedes cornered, coming into a quiet street, tree-lined. Behind the trees, shadowy apartment buildings. Not the tenements of the working class, but comfortable bourgeois residences.

'However,' said Heydrich, 'since you are not using my people, I have one request. One of my men, as an observer. To study your methods. We are not too proud to learn from the master.'

'Please be my guest.'

Heydrich leaned forward, the high pitched voice sharpening in tone. 'Zoller!'

The captain twisted around, like an automaton. 'Colonel!'

One of the robots in Capek's RUR, Lohmann thought.

'You will work with Inspector Lohmann, from now until relieved.'

'Yes, Colonel.'

The car came to a halt under a tall, goose-necked street lamp. Lohmann recognised the street; the Ferdinand-strasse in Lichterfelde-Ost, a prosperous residential district.

'I thought the captain was your personal bodyguard,' said Lohmann, still staring out of the window.

'He's always expressed a desire to better himself. Perhaps some of that desire will adhere to you, Inspector.'

'Perhaps. Also, perhaps you will have a spy in my camp, Colonel.'

'Naturally.' Heydrich smiled again in aloof acknowledgement of Lohmann's perspicacity. 'I shall leave you and Zoller now. I'll await your reports with interest. You will catch this man, won't you? The Führer expects it.'

Zoller opened the car door and Lohmann stepped onto the kerb.

'I will try to live up to the Reichschancellor's expectations.'

'Good. Bruckner's apartment is on the first floor.'

A deeply carpeted but impersonal foyer led to elevator doors and, beside the doors, a staircase. Ignoring the elevator, Lohmann slowly mounted the stairs followed by Captain Zoller. Lohmann, deep in thought. Not about the murder he was about to face, not yet. His thoughts were of the people for whom he was working. People he had avoided in the past years. Ignored. At times, he had acted as if they didn't exist; certainly would not endure. Yet they did exist and were enduring. They were on every street corner. They were the government of his country. He was working for them. Still, he told himself, he need not be concerned. Even Karl Bruckner, an insignificant Party official, deserved to have his murderer found and brought to trial before the law. If there was to be a trial. If there was still Lohmann's kind of law.

Reiner was waiting for him at the top of the staircase.

'Chief! They tell me you've been with Heydrich?' A glance at the black-clad figure of Zoller.

'This is Captain Zoller, Colonel Heydrich's . . . representative. Sergeant Reiner.'

The two men eyed each other warily and exchanged curt nods.

'Go in, Zoller,' Lohmann said affably. 'Make yourself at home beside the corpse.'

Zoller went into the apartment.

'Why are icicles forming at the base of my spine?' Reiner asked.

'Rigor mortis is setting in. Throughout the country. Tell me about this.'

As Reiner spoke they moved into the hall of the apartment. A mirror and an old fashioned hat stand, devoid of hats but holding underneath a number of walking sticks, were the only furnishings.

'Karl Bruckner. Aged thirty-five. Formerly in the Prussian Police. A protégé of Göring. Now in the Party secretariat. Also as a young naval officer was a member of the Stahlhelm.'

Lohmann remembered the Stahlhelm. A para-military group of Fascist-minded officers in the early twenties. Their weight thrown around against Socialist and Communist opposition.

'Unmarried,' Reiner went on. 'Lives here with an elderly housekeeper. A precise kind of man. Very regular in his habits. Off to work in the Party offices regularly every day. Home at precisely the same hour . . .'

'Unmarried?'

'Nothing queer there. According to the housekeeper, quite a ladies' man. When he entertained a lady, she shut her door and read romantic novels. Very appropriate. The ladies are confirmed by the neighbours. With some envy on the part of the male neighbours.'

'You've already questioned them?'

'Some of them. While I was waiting for you. Didn't do too much around the body. The place is full of black uniforms. Very depressing.'

Lohmann smiled. He sympathised. All those Death's Heads. 'Our people are on their way,' he reassured the sergeant. 'Anything else?'

'You'll see for yourself. He was sitting in an armchair.

Somebody came behind him, whipped a rope around his neck and twisted a piece of wood attached to the rope. He was strangled.'

'Garrotted. The Spanish used to execute people that way.'

'And I thought the Spanish were a romantic crowd. Goes to show.'

'There have been two other killings by a similar method in the last two weeks,' Lohmann informed the sergeant.

'You mean there's a mad Spaniard in the city!' Reiner frowned. 'We should have seen reports on these.'

'They were kept from us. Until tonight. Now we are ordered to find the assassin.'

'Why should they keep it from us?'

'Higher authority. The highest. I saw him tonight.'

Reiner's eyes widened. 'You don't just mean Heydrich? Or Nebe?' naming the Chief of the Berlin Police. 'You do mean . . .'

'I mean the Reichschancellor.'

'Jesus Christ! Hitler!'

'They are not one and the same. Despite rumours to the contrary. About Bruckner's body? You say he was sitting in an armchair?'

'You'll see for yourself.'

Lohmann was working now. 'He was relaxed. Awake. In an armchair?'

'That's how it looks.'

'No sign of a break-in?'

Reiner shook his head. 'I checked. No break-in. The housekeeper went out an hour before. To the cinema. When she came back she found him. I gather you could hear the scream two streets away.'

'Then he must have let the murderer in himself.'

The sergeant's brow wrinkled in thought. 'Hadn't got that far yet. But it looks like it. Somebody he knew . . .'

'Certainly somebody he had no reason to fear. He lets the man . . . or woman . . . in. And is relaxed enough to sit at ease in a chair.'

'Yes. It could have been like that.'

'Let's have a look.'

They went into the living room. A large room with two

large windows looking out onto the Ferdinandstrasse. On the walls some framed reproductions. *The Battle of Austerlitz, Frederick of Prussia on Horseback.* Others in a similar vein. Deep padded armchairs. On one of them, facing a marble fireplace, Bruckner, head at an awkward angle. The face was an unpleasant sight. Almost black, tongue protruding, eyes bulging. Very dead. A bookcase containing *Mein Kampf,* a book by Rosenberg on racial purity, and a number of detective novels, Edgar Wallace predominating. And, standing around the room, presumably awaiting orders, Heydrich's black-clad SD men. Zoller was staring at the body. His face was tinged with green.

'Surely you're used to dead bodies,' Lohmann said to the SS man. 'In your job, it must be commonplace.'

'I've seen dead men before,' Zoller replied, a look of disgust on his face. 'But I don't like to see them lying around.'

'Very untidy,' Reiner chimed in, sardonically. 'I'm sure the SS is much tidier with its corpses.'

'You should know,' Lohmann turned to Reiner, 'the three victims were all party officials. And old comrades of the Füh . . . the Reichschancellor.'

'Chilling, isn't it?' Reiner shuddered. 'We're at the North Pole. And it's cold outside.'

'We can do without the weather forecast. I'd like to see the housekeeper.'

Frau Essen, Lohmann reckoned, was in her sixties. A World War widow. Sitting in her own room, the smallest of the three bedrooms in the apartment, she was surrounded by souvenirs of a life that had been altered radically by a shell somewhere near Cambrai. The mantlepiece was covered in small framed photographs; a soldier on leave with his wife, a fading youthful Frau Essen probably when she was still Fräulein Schmitt. Her late husband's Iron Cross (Second Class), in its original case. Fragments of a life. Iron-grey hair to match the medal. Reiner knocked and entered the room followed by Lohmann. She presented a tear-streaked face to them. Reiner introduced Lohmann, and asked her if she'd mind repeating all that had passed that evening.

She replied, her voice trembling, 'I was at the cinema.

I had made Herr Bruckner his evening meal and . . . well, he knew it was my evening off . . . he said he hoped I'd enjoy the cinema . . .'

'Was he expecting any visitors?' Reiner prompted her.

'No, I . . . I don't believe so. He said he was having an evening in. Reading. He was a great reader. . . Anyway, I went off. Came back about ten-thirty to find him . . . him . . . like . . . that . . .' The tears flooded down the cheeks again, coursing through a light surface of powder. 'It . . . it was horrible . . .'

'You were fond of Herr Bruckner?' Reiner asked.

'I've known him since he was a boy. I was a maid in Saxony to his mother. Then I married and lost touch. Some . . . some years ago, I answered this advertisement for a housekeeper. And it was Herr Bruckner. Such a coincidence. But the moment he saw me, the job was mine. You see, he knew me, knew I'd lost my husband in the war . . . he was a good employer.'

'He had never married?'

'Always said he was looking for the right girl.'

'He . . . looked quite extensively, didn't he?'

Her back stiffening, Frau Essen bridled. In defence of her employer. 'Why shouldn't he? He was single. Without obligation. Yes, he had his women. A number and varied. His business, not mine.'

Lohmann, who had hitherto left the questioning to Reiner, now asked his first question. 'Was he friendly . . . or even acquainted with a Captain Rudig. Or a Herr Karl Preuss?'

'He had many friends . . .'

'That is not an answer. Rudig or Preuss?'

'Possibly. The names mean nothing. But then I never bothered about names. He had many friends.'

'And enemies?'

She was silent for a moment. She seemed to gulp before replying. And then she replied hesitantly. 'No . . . no enemies. He was a good man.'

The hesitancy had registered with Lohmann. There was, in that pause, a hint of fear.

'I'm asking the question again, Frau Essen.'

She waved her right hand in front of her face, a gesture

of trying to brush the question away. The fear became more obvious.

'I'm not . . . not a young woman, Inspector. And I am not entirely alone. I . . . I have responsibilities. I have two cats. My own cats. To look after. When one has no children, the cats become like children . . .'

'Never mind the cats, Frau Essen . . .'

'But I have to . . . I have to mind them. How would they survive without me?'

'What are you trying to tell me?'

'I . . . I . . . would not . . . would not wish to get into trouble. Not with powerful people . . .'

'Bruckner had made an enemy of someone powerful?'

'I have not said that!'

Lohmann took a deep breath. Pressure had to be applied. 'Frau Essen, I'm going to tell you something. I was told tonight that I am just now the second most powerful man in Germany. I have in my pocket a letter that says so. It is signed by Adolf Hitler. Now I require you to tell me about this powerful enemy of Herr Bruckner's. Otherwise you will be in greater trouble. With the most powerful person in the country. Now, tell me . . .'

The woman trembled. Her hands shook. Her face, drawn, still streaked with tears, became a shade whiter. Her hands, on her lap, twisted nervously. 'It was . . . an argument. Over a woman. An actress . . . or rather a singer. Her name is . . . Lys Lysander. I had heard of her. He brought her here several times. Late at night. And during the day. She stayed overnight at least once. And then, there was this argument with this important man . . .'

'His name?'

'Please. You will not say I told you. Goebbels. Herr Doctor Josef Goebbels.'

Behind Lohmann, Reiner gave a deep whistle. Goebbels. Reichsminister in charge of propaganda. With a known penchant for attractive women. In the cinema and in the arts. And more than that, Reiner had heard, an evil little bastard.

From outside came the wail of a police siren. Lohmann's murder squad had arrived. Back in the living room, the

Inspector gave instructions to Zoller. 'Thank your SD men for a good job and try and explain tactfully that they are no longer needed and can at once get the hell out of here. Excluding yourself, of course.'

Zoller carried out the order with quiet alacrity. As Lohmann's detectives filed in, the SD men left. Lohmann was relieved to see Holtz was not among his men. Obviously off duty. He was grateful. One representative from the building in Prinz Albrechtstrasse was enough.

His men set about their work. Flashbulbs lit up the room, and the musty aroma of fingerprint powder assailed the Inspector's nostrils. At this stage he always began to feel superfluous. This was the part of the investigation he could leave to his squad. He decided to do so. Dawn would soon break. Home, he determined, was his next move. Taking Reiner by the arm, he drew the sergeant into the hallway.

'I'm going home for a couple of hours.' He informed Reiner. 'When you're finished here, do the same. But I want medical, fingerprint and interview reports on my desk by mid-day. Have two men go round everybody in this building.' He yawned. 'I think I'm getting too old for all this.'

'By the time it's over, I'll be at least as old as you, sir,' Reiner replied.

'The only way to become a father-figure in the department,' Lohmann responded. 'Oh, two other things. Get the complete files on the murders of Rudig and Preuss. The SD will have them. Make sure they don't short-change us. *Complete* files. Zoller should be of help. Second thing . . . what was it? Yes, Zoller. Try and keep him away from me as much as you can. We are landed with him. But let's not overdo it. Have him compile files on the lives of the three victims.'

'What about the Goebbels angle?'

'Nothing. I'll have to handle that one. Like walking on the edge of an abyss.'

'I've heard him called a lot of things. But an abyss . . . I like it.'

Lohmann moved down the stairway, the sergeant following.

'That was quite a story,' Reiner went on. 'About this Hitler letter. Frau Essen swallowed it whole . . .'

'She was right to. I'll show you the letter, some time.'

In the street, it was still raining. Lohmann commandeered one of the smaller police cars.

'I'll drive myself,' he informed the police driver. 'Get a lift back to the station in one of the other cars.'

He had originally intended to go directly to his apartment off Frederichstrasse but, as he drove off, he changed his mind. There was one more place he had to visit.

THREE

It was on the north bank of the Spree. An area of derelict tenements, waste ground and rubble. In his mind, Lohmann called it the Wasteland, his wasteland, a refuge, a haven for down-and-outs, tramps, the human refuse of the city; more, the rejects and failures of society. Some would call themselves the walking dead; no emotion left, no contact; loners without ambition, hope or desire.

The numbers who existed in and around the Wasteland had increased during the Weimar Republic. The waxing and waning of the mark had caused catastrophe, bankruptcy, suicide. Men who had lost everything found they no longer wanted anything but the kind of oblivion that could be found in the Wasteland. Around those who existed here at night there had grown up colonies of scavengers, of small-time criminals, touts and informers. Somehow a knowledge of everything that happened in Berlin filtered down to the Wasteland. Someone always knew something. Some, and not only the professional informers, lived on scraps of information sold to the law, or to the Party; to anyone who had enough interest, and a little money to pay.

Car parked in a quiet street nearby, Lohmann walked to the derelict ground. Almost anyone, walking here at night, was risking at least robbery, possibly a beating. Murder, too, although that would be accidental and irrelevant. Those who attacked strangers did so to acquire whatever possessions might be there, not necessarily to kill. There were those too, like Lohmann, who were known and feared. If recognised, they would not be assaulted; this partly because the law was hated and feared, partly because there was the knowledge that such persons would be armed.

Lohmann walked steadily across the open space. A hoarse outbreak of laughter on his right. Laugher without humour. A shape moved on the ground in front of him. Rags, some form of life within. A woman's voice in the darkness made a suggestion, obscenely phrased. More laughter at the obscenity. Then a man Lohmann knew, name of Osvald, embracing his own knees, staring up at the policeman. Osvald, dressed in a once-expensive suit now dirty, crumpled and torn, bowler hat on balding head, the last symbol, held on to, of a long-gone respectability.

'I shall be back,' Osvald said, partly to Lohmann, partly to the darkness and himself. It was said he once owned a bank. Or had once robbed a bank. Or robbed his own bank. Here, it had no meaning.

Lohmann moved on. Searching. Not quite sure for whom he was searching. A voice, a fragment of knowledge, a tout, a police informer. Underfoot, dirt, earth, on a warm night sometimes flesh. Those who slept under the stars. On a damp night like this, only the strays, the masochists, the more hopeless of those without hope.

Then, in front of him, looming up above his head, a great shadow, shapeless, amorphic. Then defined into a mass of coloured balloons, not that the colours were visible, at the end of strings. The Blind Man, holding the strings with one hand, a white cane with the other, moved in front of Lohmann.

'You're up early this morning, Inspector.'

No one knew how he could recognise those in front of him, but he always seemed to do so. Or was it true that, as he had once insisted, he could smell a policeman yards away; identify that policeman within two yards. Any doubts about his blindness being genuine had been settled years ago at a police medical examination when he was arrested for some petty misdemeanour.

'As a bat,' the medical officer had assured the police. 'No sight whatsoever. The optic nerves have long been destroyed as have both retinas. How? God knows.

Perhaps in the war.' This had suited the Blind Man at the time. He had talked loudly about his war wound. It was possible. On another occasion, he had insisted he was born blind. Yet again, there was talk of a youth attempting to blow a safe with gelignite, and instead blowing out his eyes.

'Yes, early this morning,' the Blind Man repeated.

'No. Up late this evening,' Lohmann said. The Blind Man chuckled.

'I hear you wiped away von Glauber. Congratulations.'

'Thanks. How's Müller?'

'Buy a balloon?' the Blind Man asked.

'Which ones are the balloons, which ones are the contraceptives?'

Another laugh from the Blind Man. 'You don't need those, Inspector Lohmann. Your wife's dead and your lady takes her own precautions.'

'Shut up!' Lohmann said. There were areas he did not permit others to mention. 'I asked you how Müller was.'

Erwin Müller. Described in one newspaper at the tsar of Berlin's underworld. The financier of most big robberies in the city. Involved in money lending, protection, gambling and vice, Müller had flourished in the easy days of Weimar. Now, it was getting difficult.

The Blind Man seemed to read his thoughts. 'It's difficult for him today, Inspector. How can you aspire to being a big time crook, when the bigger crooks have taken over the whole country? Of course I'll be glad if you don't quote me on that.'

It was known that the Blind Man ran occasional errands for Müller: was well paid to do so. The ears, if not the eyes of the underworld. Yet despite rumours that the Blind Man was never without money, he was a *habitué* of the Wasteland. 'My kind of people,' he had once said 'And even blinder than I am.'

'What's the big whisper around the town?' Lohmann asked.

'Oh, your elimination of von Glauber, certainly.'

'Apart from that?'

'Silence.'

'You haven't become deaf as well?'

'I sometimes wish it were so. Life would be easier without sight or sound.'

Lohmann dug the heel of his right shoe into the soil. Either the Blind Man was holding back out of self-interest, or the great silence had descended.

'I'm waiting, Blind Man.'

Still silence. An uneasy silence though. 'What are you looking for?'

'A killer. Three victims. Like Glauber.'

'No! Not like von Glauber. Glauber killed kids for fun,' the Blind Man insisted. 'Your present preoccupation is not with kids.'

'I never said it was. Rudig. Preuss. And last night a man called Bruckner.'

'Should I know them?'

'Party officials. Not top rank. But the top rank wants to know. Anything you hear, I want to hear.'

'Of course. I'm a good citizen. Oh, I did hear you've become a big man. The High and the Mighty has placed you on his right hand.'

'Don't believe everything you hear. Tell Müller too. Anything he hears . . .'

A dubious expression came over the Blind Man's face. 'You know Müller. Taciturn. Not giving to talking. About anything or anybody. But I will mention your request.'

The cane moved forward, and with it, the Blind Man. Passing Lohmann and into the darkness. Lohmann stood for a moment contemplating the disappearing figure. Then turning, he moved again forward towards the outline of a derelict tenement. Somewhere to his right, there was a low moaning sound. He ignored it. When in the Wasteland, ignore everything you cannot see. And do not approach the source of such sounds. Like the Sirens, there were those who lured wanderers to a kind of destruction.

At the entrance to the tenement, there was a movement in front of him, a shadow, followed by a second shadow, flitting across the doorway. Lohmann stopped, feeling under his coat for the comforting butt of his Mauser. He took a deep breath and waited. The shadow again, moving closer.

'I wouldn't try it, Hermann,' Lohmann spoke crisply,

with authority. 'Before you could do anything, you'd have a bullet in your right lung. I got you in the left last time. This would even it up. Wouldn't make for the best of health, though.'

A deep breath, in front of him, only a few feet away. The shadow moved again, this time in front of the inspector. Lohmann reached into his jacket pocket and produced a small pocket torch. The pencil-thin beam illuminated the face of a large man with a broken nose and closely cropped hair. Eyes blinked into the beam.

'Ach, Jesus Christ, I didn't know it was you, Herr Lohmann.' The voice was thick, guttural, and strangely embarrassed.

'And if it hadn't been me, Hermann?'

Large feet shuffled in the mud. 'We was just discouraging sightseers.'

'Tell Rudi to come into the light too.'

Hermann nodded and called out. A moment later he was joined by a short, thick-set figure, the egg shaped head incongruously topped by a battered, mud stained bowler hat.

'Evening, Inspector Lohmann.'

'Morning Rudi. I hear Inspector Manfred is looking for two characters who attacked a well-known businessman in the Kurfürstendamm last week. Took him up an alley and stripped him, not only of his wallet, but all his clothes.'

'Nothing to do with us, Inspector,' Rudi said plaintively. 'We weren't near the Kurfürstendamm last Tuesday.'

'It's so,' Hermann added. 'What would we be doing there? Especially when we hadn't a pfennig between us. Costs money to breathe in the Kurfürstendamm.'

'I think you went there to take a deep breath, Hermann,' Lohmann said. 'From Herr Sachs's wallet. He lost a bowler hat too.'

Rudi's hand went to his hat, stopped, and was slowly lowered. 'What would I do with a bowler hat? I already got one.'

'And how did you know it was on Tuesday that Sachs was robbed?'

'You said . . .'

'I said last week. Still, it's not my case. Of course I could have a word with Manfred . . .'

Hermann rubbed a large grubby hand across an already grubby face. 'Look, Herr Lohmann, we got to eat. Our appetite is as big as that Sachs character's. Bigger, maybe. So he loses a wallet and a suit of clothes. He's got others. From the look of him, plenty. So we roll a rich man. But we give it to the poor. Us.'

'Like Robin Hood.'

'Sure. Who?'

'Three men have been murdered in the last two weeks. Rudig, Preuss and last night a man called Bruckner . . .'

'We don't go in for that kind of thing. You can lose your head trying that . . .'

Lohmann smiled to himself in the darkness. Someday they would go too far, and lose their heads. But not now. This was not their area of operations. But they heard things.

'What's the word on these killings?' he said.

The two men looked at each other. Was it his imagination, Lohmann wondered, was there a trace of nervousness in the look?

'Didn't see anything in the newspapers . . .' Rudi murmured.

'There was nothing in the newspapers. But you have heard something.'

The smaller man shrugged. 'Nothing about last night. About the other two . . .' he hesitated.

'Go on.'

'We . . . we thought . . . thought it was a hangover from . . . from the Röhm business.'

Lohmann shook his head. 'Not good enough. It wasn't to do with the Long Knives.'

'So you say,' said Rudi.

'I say it.'

'They were good Party members?'

'So give me the word.'

Hermann breathed deeply now. 'The word is . . . stay away. Not our affair. Not anybody's affair.'

'That's all?'

'They've opened a new place. Not exactly a prison,'

Hermann said. 'Place called Dachau. Anyone puts their nose into those killings, that's where they'll end up.'

'I'm putting my nose in,' said Lohmann.

'Maybe you'll get away with it, sir. But we wouldn't. Too much noise, there. Too many black uniforms and Death's Head badges.'

'So the SD were investigating. They're entitled.'

Hermann laughed aloud now, a braying sound. 'Sure they are. And they find out what they want to find out. You believe it, Herr Lohmann.'

'I can always talk to Inspector Manfred . . .'

Rudi's face twisted awkwardly in the torch beam. 'Aw, Christ, Inspector, what do we do? Jump from hot fat into burning coals? The word is out: don't talk about anything.'

'You'll listen hard, Rudi. And you, Hermann. Anything you hear, you need talk only to me. Right.'

The two men shuffled awkwardly. 'Right, Inspector.' A reluctant duet.

'And any further incidents like that on the Kurfürstendamm and I will speak to Manfred.'

Hermann became plaintive again. 'We have to eat.'

'Then earn some money. I pay for information.' Lohmann gave a curt nod and, turning on his heel, retraced his steps across the Wasteland. Between the Blind Man, and Rudi and Hermann, the word would be out. Lohmann was in the market for information; and would pay for it. The only thing that troubled him was their attitude. There was fear there. That was unusual. So-called honour among thieves was non-existent. They rarely had scruples about informing on each other. Particularly when the crime was murder. A murder investigation was too liable to hamper their own activities, too much pressure was brought by the police authority in too many areas. Better to sell a stranger than lose the proceeds of their own operations. The customary attitude. But this time there was another element. Fear. Not simply the normal fear of authority; not even the fear induced by the black uniform of the SS of the SD. Or even the Gestapo. This time it was stronger and deeper. The fear of execution. Or worse. Because worse did exist in the New Germany.

'Herr . . . Herr Lohmann . . .!' A voice in the darkness,

from his right. A tentative, trembling voice, not uncultivated, but with the accents of an educated man. Lohmann relit his torch and swivelled it to the right. It lit up a pale, thin face, cheeks dark, hollowed, unshaven. Familiar and yet not familiar.

'I'm Lohmann.'

The man was sitting on the ground, back against the wall. He wore a tattered raincoat over a crumpled mud-streaked suit, a suit that had once been expensive.

'You do not recognise me, sir?'

Lohmann moved a few paces closer. 'I'm sorry . . .'

'Polinski! Reuben Polinski.'

At once the face came into perspective, and was recognised. Polinski, who had owned a bookshop near the Alexanderplatz. Specialist in books on the law. This was the man. In the twenties, the young policeman had browsed through the law books, buying when he could afford to, reading while standing at the shelves when he couldn't. Educating himself in his profession. The law and the history of the law. Young advocates were common in Polinski's bookshop, university students studying law and philosophy were *habitués*. Yet a policeman was a rarity. Reuben Polinski had been at first amused, then intrigued by the young man.

'You wish to learn the law? But you are not a law student?'

'I'm a police officer. I believe those who administer the law should know what they are doing, and why.' He must have sounded gauche, almost naive, in those days.

'Of course, of course,' the bookseller agreed. 'There would be less injustice if the police knew the letter of the law. And such time-saving in the courts.' Of course these were the Weimar days, when there were men trying to achieve a kind of justice.

So Lohmann had been permitted to browse at will; more, to ask questions of the man who not only sold books, but made it his business to read, know and understand what he was selling.

'Of course the Code Napoleon provides the basis for most law in Western Europe.' Polinski enjoyed his own lectures as much as they had benefited Lohmann. 'The

English of course, their law has different origins. Not to be maligned. Based on common law, built over hundreds of years of precedent.'

Eventually Lohmann was promoted and, knowledge of the law expanded if not completed, had abandoned the visits to the bookshop near the Alexanderplatz. Now, here, in the Wasteland, the thin, ageing face of the bookseller peered up at him.

'Herr Polinski!' Lohmann said.

'You know me now?'

'Of course. But what are you doing here?'

'Surviving.'

The one word seemed to chill the already damp air. It was said flatly, factually, without emotion, which served only to emphasise the hopelessness of its meaning.

'But . . . the bookshop . . .?'

The old man shrugged. 'First they burned half of the books. Dr Goebbel's contribution to *Kultur*. Then, of course, they wanted the shop. So they took it.'

'But you owned the shop. They couldn't just . . .'

'Yes, they could. You forget, I'm a Jew. They drove my customers away. A sign on the window . . ."Juden" . . . enough these days. No customers, no shop.'

'But you . . . you're a German citizen!'

'And my father before me. Before that, who knows? Polish, I think. But I thought I had proved I was a good German. I fought in France as a good German soldier. It doesn't matter. They don't wish to know.'

'You should have come to me,' Lohmann said, angrily.

'Why should I have come to you? You were only a customer.'

'I was a friend.'

'Can one be sure of that today?' Polinski shook his head. 'You go to one old friend, and you find he is a Nazi now. Your friendship is an embarrassment. You go to another, he is not a Nazi, but you put him in jeopardy. Friends do not thank you for this.'

'For God's sake, why? What's the point in this stupid anti-Semitism?'

'Read *Mein Kampf*. Hitler tells you. If you wish to gain power in a stricken country, choose a minority, and blame the ills of the country on that minority. Hitler chose the Jews.'

'But now he's in power. There's no need . . .'

'Ah, Herr Lohmann, in some ways you are a clever man. A clever detective. In other things, you are a child. These people come to believe their own fantasies. Say the lie often enough, loud enough, and it becomes, to them, the truth. See, it has brought me here. At least I am grateful my wife is dead. And we had no children. So there is only myself. Therefore, it is not so bad.'

'You can't stay here!'

'I have been here for some months now. I shall stay.'

'But . . . how do you live?'

'I scavenge.'

'You will come home with me.'

'No!' A pause. Then, softer. 'But thank you for the thought.'

'I could get you out of the country.'

'It is my country. I don't wish to leave it. And I am a little old for starting over again. I am seventy-eight. And here, for a time, I am safe. Out there in the streets, I am Jew. To be beaten up, spat upon, to be an amusement for the Brownshirts. No, I stay here. Soon, it will be finished. My only regret is . . . no one to sing Kaddish for me.'

'For God's sake, you have to come with me . . .!' Lohmann felt cold and the chill increased his determination to take the old man from this place.

'Still, the answer is no.'

The two men stared at each other; the police officer, tall, standing stiffly looking down at the crouched figure; the old man sitting against rubble, head looking upwards, eyes shining. Above them, a grey dawn streaked the sky. An impasse. The old man would not move. The younger man would be ashamed to turn away.

'You're stubborn,' said Lohmann.

'My age permits it,' said Polinski. 'Please go now. It was pleasing to see you again.'

Lohmann felt in his pocket. A small bundle of notes, a few marks he had on him. His fingers curled around the notes, and taking them from his pocket he bent down and placed them in Polinski's hand. The old man looked down at them. And shrugged.

'I am not above taking a small loan. It will be repaid . . .'

'Forget it!'

'Oh, yes, to refuse would be not kind to you. If I believe in God . . . something I'm not sure of . . . even wanting the Kaddish to be sung when I am dead. . . . I would be taking your kind action from you. God, if he exists, will repay. Thank you, Herr Lohmann.'

'Look, that's all I have on me. But I can get more money to you later today. You'll be here?'

'I'm helping you to do a good work, Lohmann. Do not ask me to help you overdo it. With this, I may get out of Berlin. In the countryside, I'm safe too. And it is pleasanter there than here. Thank you, Herr Lohmann, goodbye. Shalom.'

Lohmann backed away reluctantly. 'But . . . but where will you go? Where in the country . . .'

'South-east. Who knows? I may even reach Jerusalem.'

There was a sound of scraping in the dirt. Polinski moved out of the circle of light thrown by Lohmann's torch. Lohmann moved the torch to the right. The rubble of bricks. To the left, a flat patch of soil. And around, in the darkness. Nothing. The old man had disappeared. Lohmann stepped forward again, and the beam of the torch circled again. Nothing.

Back in the police car, Lohmann sat for some moments. His hands trembled. Not with fear but with a strong, undefined emotion. He told himself he should have forced Polinski to come with him. Dragged the old man to the car. It should have been simple, there would have been no physical strength there to resist him. Yet there would have been another kind of strength, an unbending determination to go his own way. To die, certainly, but to die with an inner dignity. Not relying on the kindness of acquaintances. A dignity that relied only upon self.

The trembling stopped. The thoughts resolved into other thoughts. What was happening to this country? What was happening to normal human emotions? Old men were kicked to death in the street and the law did nothing. The law Lohmann had all his life believed in turned in upon itself, a reflection giving only the reverse image of what should be. Old men dying and the faces of their compatriots gaping, lips twisting to laughter. A hegemony dominated, laughing at those they had cast aside, thrown to the perimeter of their society. All the time, the danger increasing, the futility multiplying. Around and around in the head, what was, and what will be. Unable to contain it in his head, Lohmann saw himself reflected in the car mirror, a sidelook distraction to be studied only to ease away other thought. A kind of relief. A safety valve to be used before depression turned uglier. Looking at himself in the mirror, looking at anything to prevent the thoughts from becoming more painful.

He made himself think, the Wasteland always made him feel like this. A black, black cloud of depression, hiding the sky, obscuring the top of the inside of his skull. Yet he was to admit to himself now, at once, it wasn't the Wasteland. It originated with Polinski, with the old Jew, what had happened to him, what might henceforth happen to him. Damn the old man for this! Then he would be one of the others; one of those who were fit to join the Party, get in on the game, wear the Death's Head with pride. Thus it might begin. So easy a beginning. Rather go back into the depression.

He started the car. Something to do. Away from thinking. He slipped the gear lever into first and steered off into the road. Away from the Wasteland. Away from his own thoughts.

He drove home.

FOUR

Home was in a quiet, tree-lined street south of the river. Not unlike the Ferdinandstrasse. A ground-floor apartment in a greystone building. A porter was in attendance during the day but at night the residents let themselves into the building with their own keys. Lohmann's apartment was large; three bedrooms, kitchen, bathroom, living-room, and a small den which was his own refuge, study, office, call it what you will. The three bedrooms were necessary. The largest was Lohmann's, had been his and his wife's until her death five years before. The other two bedrooms, of equal size, were his daughter's and his housekeeper's. The housekeeper, Frau Anselm, was a pleasant middle-aged woman, a widow with a grown-up daughter who was married and lived in Cologne. The experience of bringing up one daughter had enabled her to take over the supervision of another's with efficient practicality and a deal of tenderness. All this Lohmann appreciated. He was fortunate. With a profession like his it was necessary to have someone like Frau Anselm. With a headstrong fourteen-year old like Anna Lohmann it was doubly necessary.

Lohmann let himself into the silent apartment and, in the kitchen, made himself a cup of strong coffee. As if its strength would eradicate from his mind the traces of the Wasteland. He was careful to make little noise. Not that he was afraid of waking Frau Anselm. The woman slept the sleep of innocence, or perhaps ignorance, certainly as regards his profession and its extreme ramifications. To Frau Anselm, Lohmann was a pillar of the law, an upholder of the values of her bourgeois society. In this, she loudly and verbally showed her pride. No, he was not afraid of waking Frau Anselm.

His fourteen-year old daughter, that was different. Anna was burgeoning into womanhood, exhibiting some sensitivity, an awakening intelligence, not yet strong enough to allow her to be free of external influences and pressures. And she slept lightly. So lightly that, as Lohmann was sitting at the kitchen table sipping hot coffee, the kitchen door opened and Anna, dressing-gown over nightdress, came in. She was blonde, like her mother, a round, pretty face, still slightly plump with baby-fat, and had keen blue eyes. These days, when Lohmann really looked at her, he was still surprised at the woman emerging from the child.

'G'morning, father.' Eyes still sleep-filled but curious.

'What are you doing up at this time?'

'Hungry. I can make breakfast for both of us.'

'Be supper for me,' Lohmann replied. 'But I'm not hungry. Too tired. Have to get a couple of hours sleep. Coffee'll do me.'

She poured herself a glass of milk and sat facing him.

'Tell me about your night,' she said, adding with an unhealthy, childish relish, 'More murders?'

'You have a gruesome turn of mind, Anna.'

'Can't help it. It's your job. Anyway, children should be interested in their father's work.'

Lohmann smiled and dripped coffee onto his chin. 'Only if the father has an ordinary job. Which I have not. I have a distinctly unhealthy job. And you have a distinctly unhealthy mind.'

Anna grinned. 'I know. It's great! Tell me about it. Please.'

Lohmann stared at the surface of the table. Smooth white wood. He'd have to tell her something. She was persistent. An inherited trait.

'I suppose you might be interested in this. I was called to the Reichschancellery this evening. By invitation.'

A spark of interest.

'Who was it? The Chief of Police? Old Nebe?'

'I went by invitation. From the top.'

'The top . . . did you meet Hitler? Oh, did you . . .?'

He didn't like the enthusiasm. As if it was for a film star. For that man, it was unhealthy.

'I met him.'

'That's wonderful! Wait until I tell the others at school.'

'No!' Spoken sharply. 'You will not do that.' Not to be talked of, not to be boasted about.

'Ach, father . . .!'

'You can tell nobody. That's definite. An order.'

'You mean . . . a state secret?'

It was enough for the time being. 'Yes. A state secret.' And there was truth there.

It did not deter Anna. 'Tell me about him. Was he marvellous?'

'No.'

'Oh, please tell me, father. . . .'

'He's a very ordinary, rather unpleasant little man. And he shouts.'

'He's got to shout. To be heard.'

'I don't like the things I hear from him. He looks and behaves like a mean little commercial traveller. And I don't like this unhealthy fascination with him in you.'

Defiantly she threw her blonde head back. 'But he's . . . he's the spirit of the new Germany.'

They were teaching her well at school, he was sad to hear. Efficient indoctrination, one thing they were good at with the children. And not only with the children.

'I preferred the old Germany,' Lohmann said. 'God, I suppose they feed you this crap at school.'

He was taken by surprise then by the anger in his daughter's face. Angry and near to tears. 'It's not true! It's not . . . not crap. It's our . . . our country. And you, of all people, should be proud . . .'

'. . . of books being burned? Of political opponents being murdered?' His anger matched and over-rode hers. 'Of good, decent, German citizens being beaten in the streets . . .'

'But they're Jews!' Anna said, and then, at once, fell silent. In her eyes was a dawning realisation of what she had said.

Lohmann stared at her across the table, a cold, direct look. 'They're German citizens,' he said evenly. 'They happen to be Jewish. Like your friend, Sophie Maslansky. You liked Sophie, didn't you?'

The anger had gone. She was a small girl now, unsure of herself, ashamed of what she had said. There was still a basic decency left despite the indoctrination.

'They took Sophie away from school.'

'They had to take her away from school. They were forced to . . .'

'You . . . you shouldn't say things like that.' The tears streaked her face now. 'We're supposed to report people who say things like that.'

'What do you mean, report people?'

Still tearful, she struggled to repeat something she'd obviously learned by rote. 'A good National Socialist is expected to report either to his teacher or his Hitler Youth Section Leader anything he hears derogatory to the Third Reich. This is a patriotic duty. Even parents should be reported in order that corrective measures can be taken to ensure their proper instruction . . .'

'Is that what they're teaching you now? How to inform on your family and friends. . . .'

A small flash of defiance. 'You use informers . . .'

'Yes. And pretty nasty characters they are. We have to use them to catch bigger crooks. But we don't like it, and we don't like them.'

'But . . . but this is different.' She was tearful again. 'This is for the good of the country. And you . . . you shouldn't say things like that . . . you should be reported . . .'

She rose, suddenly, unable to suppress a flood of tears, knocked the half full glass of milk over the table, and ran from the kitchen. A moment later he heard her bedroom door slam shut. Lohmann rose wearily, and taking a cloth from the sink began to mop up the spilt milk. Trying not to dwell on what she had said. Aware of the efficiency of their indoctrination. Yet assured she was basically a decent child with decent values.

Ten minutes later he went to bed. Ignoring the neatly pressed pyjamas, he stripped to his underwear and lay under one sheet and one blanket. Determined to wake in two hours.

He slept for three hours and would have gone on sleeping but for Frau Anselm bringing in a large mug of coffee. Gulping it, he showered, dressed and, still chewing a ham sandwich, drove to police headquarters. Reiner was waiting for him.

'Reports on the three victims on your desk,' the sergeant said. 'So far, no connection between them. Except that they were all party members. Didn't seem to know each other. But they obviously could have. We're still checking. Rudig was a widower. Wife died of influenza after the war. Preuss has a wife. And you know about Bruckner. And you look God-awful!'

Lohmann sat beside his desk. He was beginning to waken up. Probably be all right until this afternoon, he told himself, then he'd feel like death. He massaged the bridge of his nose.

'Reiner, did you know school children are being asked to report anybody they hear speaking against the government?'

'That's nice,' Reiner replied sarcastically. 'They'll never have time to do any school work.' A pause. 'Anna being difficult?'

Lohmann nodded.

'I wouldn't worry,' the sergeant went on. 'Still missing her mother. She's vulnerable. And they're clever. But she's intelligent. She'll learn.'

'I suppose so.'

'Still, I'm glad Hilde and I haven't any kids.'

Lohmann glared at the sergeant. 'Forget it! You say Preuss has a wife?'

'The SD interviewed her. Formidable.'

'Good. Let's get out of here. Get some air and interview the formidable lady.'

A police driver was at the wheel of the car this time. The previous night's rain seemed to have gone for the time being, leaving only puddled streets under a weak and watery sun. The trees in the Unter den Linden seemed thin, skeletal in the daylight. And, in that same light, Berlin seemed more its old self to Lohmann. People scurrying from shop to shop, office to office. Busy, even smiling. The city gearing up for the day. Only the occasional swastika banner as an ugly scar on the façade of the occasional building. They drove south to a pleasant suburb, bungalow nudging bungalow, cottage to cottage. Wide streets, and few high-rise buildings.

'Frau Preuss found her husband's body.' Reiner was reading from one of the files he had brought with him. 'In his study. Frau Preuss more indignant than sorry on finding her husband dead.'

'Indignant?'

'As if . . . how dare anyone murder her husband and disturb her routine. A kind of twentieth century Brunhilde, this one.'

She lived up to this description. A woman in her late forties, looking as if she should be in her late fifties. An ample bosom under a thick sweater, polo-necked, more like a man's garment than a woman's. Greeting them in the hall of the bungalow, a square hall with dark brown walls, as depressing as the glare on the woman's face. The only brightness in the room was her blonde hair, plaited and tied around her head.

'I told the SD everything,' she insisted, ushering them into a sitting-room that was even dimmer and more unpleasant than the hall.

'We're not the SD, Frau Preuss,' Reiner insisted, as Lohmann took in the room. Dark brown furniture matched the dark brown walls. A little light filtered around the division in the heavy curtains, also brown, and barely open.

'We're very sorry about Herr Preuss's death,' Reiner went on. It was their old trick. Let the inferior officer ask the initial questions. Leave Lohmann free to come in with the bigger questions. A kind of technique.

Her response was direct and antagonistic. 'Are you sorry? How can you be? You never knew my husband, did you?'

'Eh, no . . .'

'Then don't make meaningless noises. I knew him. For twenty years, I knew him. From Saxony to here. Oh yes, I knew Preuss. And I didn't like him.'

Lohmann spoke now. 'Why was that?'

'I'll show you.'

She ushered them into a side room, obviously Preuss's study. Again the walls were dark brown and depressing. The walls of the room seemed to bend in on them creating a stifling, claustrophobic atmosphere. Around the room, on the walls, were display cases; case upon case upon case. On every piece of furniture in the room, from desk to table to chairs, were stacked more display cases, albums, some bound in morocco, others with thick cardboard covers. On the desk too, were large sheets of paper and, adhering to these, brightly coloured oblongs and squares and triangles. Stamps, foreign stamps. Reiner looked at the nearest display case on the wall. Butterflies. Each neatly pinned to backing paper and below, in small, crabbed handwriting, the Latin appellation for the specimen.

'You see,' said Frau Preuss, lips pursed. 'He was a collector. He collected everything. Stamps, butterflies, cigarette cards. In the drawers you will find his collection of coins.'

'Quite a collection,' said Reiner.

'Obscene!' said the woman. 'Petty. Collecting small . . . small things.' She shuddered. 'I hate small things. They befit a small man.'

Lohmann wandered across the room staring, with a degree of wonder at case after case, artefact upon artefact.

'It swallowed him up,' the woman went on. 'Devoured him. Of course he had the mind of a peasant. One who has acquired middle-class wealth and squanders it like this. A Saxon peasant. From a town nobody had ever heard of. Halle an der Saale.' She drew herself erect. 'I'm a Berliner myself. But Preuss, he was only fit to be a clerk. Even his job was that of a clerk. Listing the names and records of Party members. Collecting them together. And then, coming home to continue collecting. Barely acknowledged my existence.'

'You married him,' Lohmann said quietly.

'A man without charm, without humour. Yes, I married him.'

'Why?'

'God knows. I was visiting Halle an der Saale when I met him. The Depression was on. There wasn't much choice. And he looked all right then. A naval officer. Him and his friends. One of the others might have been better. Tall man . . . his father kept doing a comic Jewish act. Like a cabaret. I might have married the son, only they said the father was really Jewish. Tried to cover it by pretending he was only acting. Well, I couldn't marry a Jew, could I?'

'Why not?'

Frau Preuss glared at him, a look both indignant and puzzled. 'You can't be serious?'

'No, I suppose not.' Lohmann stared at a case of crucified butterflies. 'Why marry at all?'

'My father had recently died. My mother was long dead. I had come to this country village to . . . to live with an ageing aunt. It was either marry or become an unpaid nurse for God knows how many years. Marriage seemed like the way out. See, I'm honest about that, Inspector. I simply picked the wrong man.'

Then, at once, she smiled. A pleased, almost contented smile. 'Never mind. I can do what I've always wanted to do. I was going to do it last week, after his body was found. But there was no one to tell. And I wanted to enjoy the telling of it. See, his collection. Everything tiny, neatly indexed. Years of work. Tomorrow, I will make a big bonfire and burn the lot. Everything. Every stamp, cigarette card, every little corpse of every little butterfly.'

Reiner looked at Lohmann and, away from the woman's gaze, made a face. As if he was about to vomit.

'Some of these things might be of value,' said Lohmann.

'I shan't care. I hate them. I shall watch them burn.' A pause. A reflective look in her eye. 'I hated him, you see. I think I could have strangled him myself.'

'Did you?' Lohmann blew a film of dust from one of the albums on the desk.

Lips pouting, she smiled at him. 'You're out of luck, Inspector. I should strangle him and end up with a paltry few marks as a pension. No, I did not kill him. I was at a meeting. National Socialist Woman's League. Frau Goltz and Frau Kammer accompanied me home. They were invited in for a coffee. Frau Kammer went into the sitting room and found the body. She screamed. A silly woman.

The SD came. They ascertained that my husband was seen after I left for my meeting. Alive. He bought drawing-pins from the shop at the corner. For his specimens. Returned to the house. Someone then presumably broke in and killed him.'

'Why?' Reiner asked.

Frau Preuss looked around, suddenly off guard. 'I . . . I'm sure I don't know.'

'You say somebody broke in?'

'Yes.'

'There was no sign of a break-in. Not according to the SD report,' said Reiner.

'So they don't know how the killer got in?' The woman turned away. Losing interest rapidly.

'Of course your husband could have let him in.'

Now thick eyebrows raised. 'Why should he let in some thug?'

'Because he did not presume the man was a thug. He was either a friend or acquaintance.'

'My husband had few friends. If any. Acquaintances of course, he would have from his work. But I never knew any of them. Apart from my own woman friends, he had no visitors. His entire time was devoted to his collection.'

'Very well. But there was no break-in. So your husband let into this house either an acquaintance or someone from whom he would think he had nothing to fear.'

'This, of course, might be so,' Frau Preuss replied. 'But you are the detective. Not I. It is your task to find the thug who killed my husband, isn't it?'

A slight smile on his face, Lohmann bowed slightly from the waist. 'Of course, Frau Preuss. Thank you for giving us your time. And I'm sure you'll be available if we need to talk to you again.'

'I'm at your service, of course.'

Outside, they settled back in the rear of the car. Lohmann was silent for a moment.

'That woman,' said Reiner. 'Enough to put you off women for life. No wonder Preuss preferred his collections. What now?'

'Have you a cigarette?'

Reiner provided the cigarette. Lohmann lit it and inhaled deeply.

'Have we learnt anything?' Reiner asked, lighting his own cigarette.

'Like Bruckner, Preuss either knew his murderer, or trusted him enough to let him in. That's important.'

'Noted.'

'I think we'll find Rudig's house was not broken into.'

'Like the other two, he admitted his own killer. Right?'

'You'll make a detective yet, Reiner. I think we should visit Rudig's home now.'

'I don't think we'll get much there.'

'Why not?'

Reiner shrugged. 'According to the SD report, he lived alone. Two rooms. And bathroom. Schliemannstrasse. Small apartments. No wife. No housekeeper. And no visitors. According to the porter. All in the SD report.'

'At least one visitor. The one who killed him.'

Reiner was right. There was little to be found at Rudig's apartment. Two rooms, a suite of ageing leather chairs, a table, a gas cooker and a wash basin in an alcove, and a bookcase. None of the books were new. Old, popular editions of old, popular novels. Some of them possibly from the man's childhood. Or his taste was childish. The westerns of Joe May . . . the saga of old Shatterhand . . . *Emil and the Detectives* . . . and a number of German translations of the works of Edgar Wallace.

The bedroom revealed little more. Two civilian suits, not expensive, two sports jackets and two pairs of flannel trousers; all in the wardrobe. Next to an old naval uniform, a captain's uniform. A drawer revealed a Party membership card, a certificate of Rudig's achieving the rank of captain. A discharge book dated 1930, from the navy.

From the porter in the block of floats they obtained a few further scraps of information.

'The Captain, he kept to himself, yes . . . seemed he didn't like people very much . . . no visitors, leastways none I saw. But that don't mean much. May have had visitors. Women? No, not interested. Not men either. Or boys. Least I saw none of it.'

'You found the body, Herr . . . Herr . . .?'

'Bok! Rudi Bok.'

'You found the body?' Reiner persisted.

'Yes. In the morning. His front door was ajar. Hadn't been shut properly . . .'

'Had it been broken open?'

'No, sir. The lock wasn't broken.'

'So it would appear, Herr Bok, that no one broke into the apartment? That whoever killed him was admitted. . . .'

'Could be. I wouldn't know.' A large, unintelligent smile. 'Wouldn't that be your job, sir?'

Lohmann smiled. 'Rudig had been in the navy?' he asked the porter.

'That was his problem, sir. See, they kicked him out. Oh, not for doing anything wrong. When they was having to cut down. They cut him down. Told me that's why he joined the Freikorps. And then the Party. Said they cared about the navy. Said the only time he was happy was when he'd been at sea. Funny, that.'

'Why funny?'

'Him liking the navy. After all, he was a country boy. Always said so. Country boy who went away to sea. And liked it.'

'Do you know where in the country he came from?'

'I don't know. Schleswig-Holstein, Brunswick, somewhere like that.'

'Or Prussia? Or Saxony?'

'Could have been . . .'

'And he now works as a civil servant?'

'That's it.'

Lohmann paused. They were now in the porter's office, a small cell in the basement of the building. A desk, three blank concrete walls and a door. On the back of the door, a cut-out magazine photograph of Marlene Dietrich in *The Blue Angel*.

'He's a Party member?'

'Has to be. Works for . . . worked for General Göring, I believe. Well, not the General personally, but one of his offices.'

Lohmann went to the door, briefly contemplated Fräulein Dietrich, and went out, followed by Reiner.

'Put Honigman and Werner on to looking into Rudig.

Where he came from, what he did for General Göring. Anything they can find.'

'Will do.'

'And Reiner, I want everybody's pet little informer in the city contacted. I want to hear every whisper. If anybody coughs I want to know. And not just fact. I want to hear what they're thinking about these killings. Also I'll grant immunity to anybody who helps . . .'

Reiner looked puzzled. 'Can you do that?'

'The letter from Hitler says I can. We'll see if it works. Now let's get back to the station. You have work to do.'

'How about you, Inspector?'

'You are an undisciplined bastard, sergeant. Why do I keep you with me?'

'Because I'm good.'

'I don't know whether that's a statement or a question.' Lohmann leaned forward. 'Back to headquarters,' he told the driver. The car moved off.

'While I'm getting everything organised, what are you planning, chief?' Reiner asked.

'I shall be moving, hopefully, in more elevated circles. Is Göring in Berlin?'

'He hasn't actually informed me . . .'

'First thing you do. Find out.'

Half an hour later, Lohmann was in his office, feet on the desk, drinking a cup of strong coffee. The SD reports of the three murders were spread out in front of him. He was reading them for the third time.

Reiner came in.

'Göring's in Berlin. At the Air Ministry. Big reception. Foreign diplomats. Pre-Nuremberg Rally thing.'

Lohmann's feet came off the desk. 'Good. I've never been inside the Air Ministry. Life is full of new experiences.'

'Not today, Inspector,' Reiner responded, amused. 'This is the big diplomatic reception bit. No one admitted without Göring's personal invitation.'

'I'll get in.'

'Fifty marks says you don't.'

'I don't take money from my juniors. You forget, I have an invitation from higher authority . . .'

'But will it work?'

'It had better.'

'You be back?'

'Maybe.' Lohmann donned his coat. 'If not, meet me at the Romanische Cafe at eight.'

'The Romanische?' Reiner wasn't pleased. 'Pseudo-artists and would-be poets. Hot air and unemployment.'

Lohmann was at the door now, struggling to disentangle one sleeve of his coat. 'And gossip, Reiner, don't forget the gossip.'

He went out. In the corridor he came face to face with Captain Zoller. The SS man had abandoned his black SS uniform and was in the grey of the SD.

'SS yesterday, SD today, Captain Zoller. What of tomorrow? A captain of Uhlans?' Lohmann said pleasantly.

Zoller brandished a file of papers. 'As you suggested, I've been going through everything I could find on the victims. There's a deal more here than in those original files.'

'Good, good, glad you've been gainfully employed. Leave them on my desk . . .'

'Colonel Heydrich said I was to be an observer of your investigation. Not a researcher . . .'

'Of course he did. But I thought you'd want to do something useful. However, you can accompany me now. The uniform will be of help. Come along.'

Zoller had to trot to keep up with Lohmann's long strides along the corridor, down the staircase, and into the yard. A car was waiting.

'You may drive, Captain,' Lohmann informed the SD man. 'We won't need a driver tonight.'

He settled into the passenger seat beside Zoller.

'Where are we going?' Zoller asked.

'The Air Ministry.'

Zoller hesitated. 'There's a reception there tonight.'

'You're very well informed.'

'We have to know what's going on.'

'Really? Have you a cigarette?'

The Captain provided a cigarette. Lohmann lit it and inhaled.

'Thank you. You spy on each other, then?'

Zoller glared at him. Lohmann ignored the glare.

'You can start the engine now,' Lohmann said.

Zoller sat, unmoving. 'We don't spy on each other,' he said. 'We . . . we like to know what is happening.'

'Ah! Of course. Wouldn't do if Göring did something Reichsführer Himmler didn't know about.' Lohmann exhaled.

'We knew about it. A reception for foreign diplomats. Preliminary to the Nuremberg Rally.'

'So I understand. But it wouldn't do for Göring to be meeting all these foreigners without Himmler knowing what is being said.'

Zoller scowled. 'The Führer himself wishes to know . . .'

Lohmann stretched in the passenger seat. 'Surely Göring will tell him all that passes. Come now, Zoller, Herr Himmler really does want to know what Göring's up to. Any indiscretion can then be reported to the Reichschancellor. After all, Goebbels will have somebody there too. And Admiral Canaris. Are you going to drive, or would you rather I got a police driver?''

'That's the secret, isn't it?' Lohmann went on. 'The left hand must know what the right hand is doing. The wrist has to study the palm. The thumb must observe the small finger. Is that the secret of good government?'

The Captain seized on this. 'Yes, yes, I think that is the principle.'

Outside of the car the streets were darkening. No rain yet, but above the city the clouds were threatening.

'Or perhaps it's simply the secret of National Socialist government. Never trust any hand lest it be raised against you.' Lohmann thought to himself, I sound almost biblical tonight. 'There's one point that worries me though. Who decides?'

Zoller's eyes, fixed on the road, still managed to look puzzled. 'Who . . . who decides what?'

'Who decides what is good for the State and what is . . . dangerous?'

Silence for a moment beyond the noise of the engine and extraneous sounds from the street. Zoller was searching, without success, for some kind of answer. Lohmann decided to help him.

'Or is that beyond your brief as a captain? You leave that to your superiors?'

To this Zoller was able to reply. 'I do.'

'You simply obey orders?'

'Of course. The SS oath . . .'

'Never mind the SS oath. Words, Captain Zoller, words. We're talking about actions. You simply do what you are told.'

'I obey orders, as you said.'

'No initiative? No thought?'

'I don't question the Party, Inspector Lohmann,' Zoller said, vehemently now. 'Nor should you. I gather you are not yet a member?'

'A good detective has to question everything, Zoller. Remember that. Report it to Colonel Heydrich. Show him you're learning something.' Lohmann paused thoughtfully. 'I even question why this investigation was taken from the SD and given to me.'

'The Führer's orders, I was informed.'

'Ah, yes. Very flattering. Because Herr Hitler was informed that I was the best detective in Berlin. Now I wonder who told him that? Colonel Heydrich?'

'No!' Zoller uttered the one word quickly and then stopped. Fearful of saying too much, Lohmann could speculate.

'Of course the Colonel would not want the investigation taken away from the SD. Am I right?'

'Possibly, Inspector.' The Captain was being careful now.

'So who recommended me to the Reichschancellor?' Still Lohmann would not refer to the man as the Führer. 'Come, you must have some idea, Zoller?'

'Herr Nebe, the Chief of Police. Or Count von Helldorf. They say he is to be Berlin Police Commissioner.'

'Yes, yes, I know both Nebe and von Helldorf. I suppose that's possible.'

Lohmann drew again on his cigarette. He had been

enjoying himself. Party-baiting, Reiner would have called it. Trouble was, they all took themselves so damned seriously. He frowned. Perhaps they were right to do so. He, Lohmann, should take them more seriously. In less than a year they had changed the face of the country. And he didn't like the look of the new face.

Ahead of them, gates loomed up, and beyond the gates a blaze of light.

'The Air Ministry, I think,' said Lohmann. 'Please to follow me, Captain. And leave the talking to me.'

The air force sentries came to attention more at the sight of Zoller's uniform than at Lohmann. At the door of the building an officer, winged badge on his tunic, came to attention.

'Your invitations?' A look of undisguised appraisal at Lohmann's trench-coat and soft hat.

The Inspector produced his police warrant-card. 'I wish to speak with General Göring.'

'You have no invitations to the reception?'

'No.'

The officer stared at Lohmann for a moment and then laughed. 'This is a diplomatic reception! Hosted by General Göring. You don't seriously think you can walk in here at this time?'

'But I do,' Lohmann insisted. 'You will please inform the General I am here.'

The officer took a deep breath. 'You will please get the hell out of here. Come back tomorrow and make an appointment. If I'm right, the General might see you within a month or so.'

Lohmann smiled pleasantly. 'And if I'm right, and if I don't see the General now, you will be lucky if you are not cleaning latrines at the rank of private soldier tomorrow morning. You will please read this.'

From his pocket he produced the Hitler letter and presented it to the officer. The man's face was now scarlet with anger.

'I don't care what piece of official toilet paper you give me . . .'

'You'd better care. Read the letter!'

'Damn you, sir . . .!'

'Start with the signature.'

The officer glanced down at the signature. His face now changed colour, a greyish hue taking the place of the scarlet. He read the letter.

'You'd better . . . better wait inside.' He handed the letter back to Lohmann, and turning, ushered them through the door.

The hallway of the Air Ministry was crowded with uniformed figures. Mostly these were the blue uniforms of the air force, Among them were a smattering of civilians in dark jackets and striped trousers, the uniform of the *Corps Diplomatique*. There were also other uniforms, unfamiliar, without the swastika armbands, those of the forces of other nations. A hubbub of noise, conversation, laughter, small-talk, filled the hall. Discreetly, the officer led Lohmann and Zoller around the perimeter of the crowd as if afraid the inspector's informality of dress might be noticed and cause some untoward incident. At the side of the hall he opened a door and led them into a small, elegantly furnished anteroom.

'You will please to wait here,' said the officer, and withdrew. They were left staring at a painting of a large dirigible, the proposed Graf Zeppelin.

They waited in silence.

After some moments, another officer came into the room. He stared at them haughtily, clicked his heels and introduced himself.

'Ernst Udet. Aide to General Göring.'

'Lohmann, Inspector, Criminal Police.'

'You wish to see the General?'

'Yes.'

'You appreciate this is hardly the time . . .'

'I am authorised. You wish to see the letter of authorisation?'

Udet shook his head. 'I have just heard of it. You will wait?'

'We will wait.'

Udet withdrew, shutting the door behind him. Lohmann turned to contemplate another painting, that of Fokkers in action over the Western Front, 1917. Zoller paced up and down. He was smiling to himself.

'Something amusing, Captain Zoller?' Lohmann asked.

'One in the eye for fat Hermann. Colonel Heydrich will be pleased.'

Lohmann kept his face straight despite feeling amused. The internal, petty rivalries of the Party could be considered humorous if the outcome of that rivalry was not, as often, so deadly.

'Captain Zoller,' he said. 'You are speaking of a senior German officer, and indeed, your deputy Führer.'

Zoller's face at once became serious. Of course I meant no disrespect . . .'

'I'm glad to hear it.' Face still straight, Lohmann turned to study again the Fokkers over the Western Front.

Some moments later the door opened and a bulky figure stepped into the room.

The man, despite his weight, looked younger than his forty-one years; not more than his early thirties. The jowls were heavy, the eyes deep set, the figure large and seemingly larger from the weight of the uniform which was immaculate, ornate and be-medalled. A pure white jacket was worn over air force blue trousers. The chin had once been strong but now was puffed out, the flesh divided by a prominent dimple. The general appearance was a cross between a high ranking officer and an over-dressed mountebank. He looked first at Lohmann, a piercing look from slightly reddened blue eyes.

'You are Lohmann?' The voice was stern, the expression slightly irritated.

'General,' Lohmann replied with a nod of his head.

The eyes swivelled around to Zoller.

'Must we have one of Himmler's minions here?'

Zoller flushed, opened and shut his mouth, a fish out of water.

'Not necessarily,' said Lohmann. 'If you'd prefer we talked alone, General . . .?'

'I would!'

'Captain Zoller, you will wait outside,' Lohmann said pleasantly. Again the mouth opened and shut, and then with a smart clicking of heels Zoller went out, shutting the door behind him.

His departure seemed to permit the General to relax.

'Himmler's running dogs. Always waiting for the seeming indiscretion,' he said. 'And reporting it, of course. Not that it can touch me. But the sensation is unpleasant.'

Lohmann said nothing. Waiting.

Göring turned again to him. 'I know why you are here, Inspector. I spoke with the Führer this morning. It is to do with the murder of Captain Rudig.'

'And others. Two others.'

'The Führer is concerned. These were old Party members. Not important men in themselves. But loyal people. I don't see how I can help you. And it is hardly convenient in the middle of a reception.'

'The . . . Reichschancellor believes it important that the killer be found quickly.'

'I appreciate that. But how does it concern me?'

'Captain Rudig worked for you.'

Göring nodded. 'In the Prussian office. But his position was minor. Plenty of officials could have told you more about him than I am able to do. I don't see why you have to come here . . .'

'Because,' Lohmann cut in. 'There could be a plot to assassinate Party members. Starting with the smaller people, it might go unnoticed. As some minor crimes. But it is my belief that Herr Hitler feels this may be . . . shall we say . . . the tip of the iceberg. Preparatory to the killing of more senior officials.'

Had Hitler said that? Lohmann couldn't now be sure. He had perhaps implied it. Anyway, it was useful in impressing the higher ranks of the Party. He had, he knew at once, impressed Göring.

'You think this is so? the General asked.

'I think it is a possibility. Because of that, I felt it necessary to seek both your experience, Herr General, and your knowledge of the one victim who worked under you.'

'Yes. I see. Of course I knew Rudig only slightly. But I did know him. Because he was not an air force man. I employed a great deal of old comrades . . . those who had joined the Party. Rudig was formerly in the navy. However, he was a good man. Good Saxon stock. A dedicated Party man. A position was found for him. Dealt with records and so on.' He broke off for a moment, as if considering all Lohmann had said. And then started again.

'But if there was an assassination plot, who would be behind such a plot?'

'My job to find out. After the recent . . . eh . . . arrest and conviction of the Brownshirts . . .'

Göring laughed loudly, crudely. 'No, no, there are damn few of those types left. We cleaned out that dirty little nest.'

'Party rivalry?' Lohmann suggested nervously.

Göring looked up, his face darkening. 'The Party is united under the Führer. There is no such thing . . .'

'And yet . . .'

'What?'

'There are those who might be jealous of the General's proximity to the . . .' Lohmann now had to force himself to say the word. '. . . to the Führer.'

'Oh, there's that all right,' Göring said pompously. 'There's always jealousy. But, to the extent of murdering small people . . .'

'As a preliminary? To more important people.'

A look of concern crossed the large face. 'You think that, Inspector?'

'I am examining every possibility.'

'Yes, of course. And there are those . . . those who resent not having their fingers in every pie. So to speak.' Tentative now, the words. 'Himmler, y'know, always resentful of my forming the original Gestapo organisation. Out of the old Prussian police. Couldn't wait to take over. Not that it bothers me, of course. My first and only love . . . the air force. The new air force we are building.'

He fell silent, contemplating the Graf Zeppelin, still to be. He then glanced at Lohmann and back to the picture. 'We're building it, you know. Greatest airship in the world.'

'Splendid,' Lohmann said automatically. He had no interest in airships.

Göring suddenly turned on his heel with surprising speed for such a large man. 'The Jews! Could it be a Jewish conspiracy?'

'Of course it's possible,' Lohmann replied. 'And that aspect will be looked into.'

'Hitler was right, y'know,' Göring went on. 'Behind everything, the Jews.'

'Of course I always thought anti-Semitism was a tactic. Nothing more,' Lohmann said, conscious that he was in a dangerous area.

To his relief, Göring smiled. 'You've read *Mein Kampf*. Of course there was always the tactical element. Blame a minority for all our ills. I have nothing against the Jews themselves. But I think the Führer has come to believe what were merely tactics. I have no such feelings. But the recent actions against Jews . . . I suppose that could trigger off a reaction. Rudig was, after all, concerned with weeding out Jews from government positions in the Prussian civil service. And other areas of Party activity.'

'I wasn't aware of that,' Lohmann said, genuinely surprised.

'Oh yes, part of his duties. Make lists, clean out the stables, so to speak. I suppose a conspiracy could have arisen from that fact.'

'Interesting. And very helpful, General.'

'Beyond that, I had little dealing with the man. So there you have it. I can tell you nothing else. Of course I had no social connections with him.'

'And the others? Preuss and Bruckner?'

Göring became irritated. 'These are little people. I have no time for such people. Only if their deaths are the beginnings of attempts on other more important people would I be concerned. Particularly the safety of the Führer. And, though I have no personal fear, I am important enough to the Party and the country to have no desire to be a victim of some Jewish lunatic.'

'We'll make sure such a thing doesn't happen, Herr General.'

'See that you do!' The massive figure stumped to the door. 'I may now rejoin my guests?'

Lohmann gave a small, formal bow.

At the door, Göring hesitated. 'It will be the Jews. You'll see I'm right. I'm no anti-Semite like Streicher but, damn them, they're a pestilential brood! Just wait until after

Nuremberg and they'll sing another song. After the new decrees . . . the enemy, Lohmann, always remember, the enemy are the Jewish international financiers, and the Bolsheviks. . . .'

'In the case of these three murders . . .'

'Even in this case, Lohmann.' Göring insisted, holding the door handle in a large sweating hand. 'Catch the killers, you will find out. Catch them, and we will execute them. Quickly.'

'Isn't there a contradiction, General Göring. Jewish international finance and the Bolsheviks? In league with one another?' Lohmann found himself trying not to smile at the contradiction.

Göring opened the door before replying. The white jacket seemed to flare in the lights from the chandeliers in the hallway.

'There is no contradiction, Lohmann. Hitler says it.'

He went out, closing the door behind him. He went out leaving Lohmann staring at the polished wood of the door. Pondering on contradictions. The man had gone who had 'nothing against the Jews'. Except that he believed they were 'a pestilential brood'. And he believed the enemy was an alliance between Jewish international financiers and the Bolsheviks. Hitler had said it, the Führer had spoken. And Lohmann knew there were names for this kind of thought. Words like schizophrenia and paranoia.

He went out of the Air Ministry into the sanity of the streets.

FIVE

Lohmann went back to police headquarters. Zoller questioned him about the meeting with Göring throughout the drive.

'Göring was helpful,' Lohmann informed the SD man, and said nothing more. There was nothing more to say. On arriving at his office Lohmann asked the SD man to get him a coffee and a piece of apple strudel.

'When you've done that, Captain, I suggest you go home and sleep.'

'You are going home, Inspector?'

'Eventually. Tomorrow, talk to every one of Rudig's associates at his work. See if you can find anything that might be connected with the murder.'

Zoller stood erect in front of Lohmann's desk. 'I am delegated to accompany you . . .'

Lohmann interrupted him angrily. 'You are part of this investigation, Zoller. You will do as I tell you!'

The man was good at taking orders. Face flushed, he clicked his heels and went out, returning some ten minutes later with a mug of coffee and a slice of strudel. Another click of heels and Zoller was gone. Lohmann breathed a sigh of relief. The man's presence was like a cloud hanging over him. Mental skies cleared with his departure.

Holtz came into the office.

'Beg to report, Inspector . . . .'

'Fine. But first, where is Reiner?'

'Gone home, sir. For a bath and a shave. Said he was meeting you later. You'd know where.'

'Also fine. Now, your report . . .'

Holtz cleared his throat loudly. 'Regarding instructions to contact known informers, I visited among others a man called Werfel, a bookseller in the Münzstrasse . . .'

'I know him,' Lohmann interjected. 'Esoteric literature. That's what he calls it.'

'Witchcraft, astrology, that kind of thing, Inspector . . .'

'With an equally esoteric stock of pornography. Anyway, go on, Holtz.'

'The man has proved useful in the past with information. This time, however, I was most fortunate. He actually knew Karl Bruckner, the third victim.'

Holtz had Lohmann's attention now. It was chances like this that often led to the solving of murders.

'Go on.'

'Bruckner had come into Werfel's shop twice.'

'Recently?'

'About two months ago. First of all, he said he was looking for an astrologist.'

'An astrologist?'

'That's what Werfel said. At first I thought he was merely taking advantage of me, this Werfel. You know how it is. These informers hope to get money so they say anything. But no, Bruckner had left his name and address. And he was looking for a particular astrologist. A man called Doctor Gisevius.'

'Werfel knew of this man, Gisevius?'

'He had heard of him. You know these crackpots. They all know each other. It seems this Gisevius had done quite well a couple of years ago. And then, according to Werfel, was caught in some confidence trick. Werfel wasn't sure exactly what it was, but the man had dropped out of circulation. Anyway, Bruckner asked if Werfel could locate the man. He left him a few marks, said there would be more if he could find Gisevius's address.'

'Did Werfel find the man?'

'No. When Bruckner returned he had to admit the man seemed to have disappeared. But he did find a book by Gisevius.'

'A book?'

'On astrology. Seemingly Bruckner bought the book. I think Werfel charged him somewhat more than its value.

Bruckner said he thought he could get Gisevius's address from the publisher. That was the last Werfel saw of Bruckner.'

Lohmann leaned back in his chair. 'Good. May be something to this. You'll follow it up, Holtz.'

'Yes, sir.'

'First, check Bruckner's apartment. See if you can find Herr Doctor Gisevius's book on astrology. Then check the Berlin State Library. Find the publisher. If the publisher is still in business you may just get Gisevius's address from him.'

'I should then interview Gisevius?'

'No. You should then report to me with the address. Don't go near Gisevius. We don't want to frighten him away. If the publisher has no address, then you'll simply have to look for the man. But I'm sure you'll find him. Understood?'

'Understood, sir.'

'Right. That's your sole job just now. And good work, Holtz.'

'Thank you, Inspector.' Holtz went to the office door.

'One thing more, Detective Holtz . . .'

'Sir?'

'I would be pleased if you didn't report this to the SS. I shall inform them in my own good time. And, if there's nothing to this Gisevius business, you'll only be wasting their time.'

Holtz hesitated uncertainly. His brow furrowed. Divided loyalties. A picture of the small man in the middle.

He said with false assurance. 'Of course, Inspector.' He went quickly.

Lohmann leant back, aware of a pain at the base of his spine. It always came after a long day on his feet. Weariness taking its toll. He sat up erect again, and lifted the top sheet of the report on his desk.

Chief Inspector Murnau came in.

'Took a message for you. Colonel Heydrich. Wants to see you. As soon as you came in.'

Forcefully. 'Fuck Heydrich!'

'Understandable. But hardly advisable.'

'I know. He's a promising man.'

'The word is it'll be *General* Heydrich soon.'
'I shouldn't be surprised.'
Murnau cleared his throat. 'Lohmann, I want to keep you here.'
Without looking up, Lohmann said, 'I hope you will.'
'Then, for God's sake, join the Party. As a Party member, and working for Heydrich, you could rise . . .'
'Like scum on water?'
'I didn't hear that.'
'There's going to be a lot of things said in Germany that it will be best not to hear.'
Murnau looked down at his polished shoes. 'Look,' he said with an embarrassed air, 'I didn't join the Party because I believe in . . . in their political philosophy. I'm not even sure what that philosophy is. I was ordered to join. And I believe in taking orders. Also I believe that . . . that Hitler might just manage to make this country great again.'
Lohmann rose from his seat. A twinge of pain hit the base of his spine.
'I'd better get along to Prinze Albrechtstrasse. I have to meet Reiner later,' he said.
'You're not to go to SD headquarters. Heydrich will see you at his home.'

The apartment was large and impeccably decorated. There was about it, however, a Spartan simplicity. The bookshelves, filled with morocco bound volumes, were practical and unadorned, as were the furnishings. The room Lohmann was shown into was high-ceilinged, one picture on the far wall of Adolf Hitler barely discernible in the light of a solitary table lamp.
Lohmann had been waiting for ten minutes. He had studied the portrait of Hitler in minute detail. He had peered at the volumes in the bookcase, noting the works of Nietzsche, Spengler and, surprisingly, *A History of the Jewish People*. He had paced the carpet heavily, glanced at his watch frequently and felt impatience rising within him.
Finally the door of the room opened and Heydrich came in. His uniform was as always immaculate. He was smoking a cigarette from a long holder. His blond hair,

cut short, was oiled down flat on his scalp. Above the long, thin nose, the blue eyes searched the dimly lit room for the visitor.

'Ah, Lohmann, sorry to keep you waiting. My wife and I are having a small dinner party.' The voice was even more pronouncedly nasal than before.

Lohmann said nothing, but waited.

'I believe you went to see Göring?' Heydrich said, delicately tapping the ash from his cigarette into a gunmetal ashtray.

'I see Zoller has wasted no time in informing you,' Lohmann replied.

'Göring was . . . helpful?'

'Possibly. I learned a number of things . . . and we discussed Jewish international finance and the Bolsheviks. They seemed unlikely bedfellows.'

Heydrich laughed, a high pitched, nasal laugh, lacking humour. A reflex reaction. 'These are, of course, the common enemies. As our Führer says. However unlikely it may seem.'

'Hardly a good reason to persecute good German citizens, because they happen to be Jewish.'

Heydrich reddened. 'I wasn't aware that good German citizens could be Jewish. They are another race. An inferior one.'

'Streicher and Rosenberg have propounded that dubious theory, I believe.'

The colonel turned and paced slowly away from Lohmann. 'If you have hopes of joining the Party, Lohmann, I should not question assured racial theories. But this is not all that you discussed with Göring?'

'Of course I made enquiries about Rudig. The General knew of him.'

'Nothing else?'

'Nothing of apparent value.'

Heydrich continued to pace. 'You know, Lohmann, in life, a man is faced with a number of choices. Some of them are trivial, others of paramount importance. It is like that in the Party. There are . . . factions. Each of us attaches himself to one faction. The choice is important. The stronger faction will dominate. It's the way of nature and the way of the Party. You, Lohmann, have to be sure you join the right, the strong, faction.'

'Naive of me to think you were all one Party under the Reichschancellor,' said Lohmann.

'Yes, it is. Of course we all serve the Führer. But some are more loyal than others. Stronger than others. You see why you have to choose carefully.'

Lohmann felt a shiver on his back. Choose carefully? Otherwise, what? Join the Party? Otherwise, how long would he still work for the police? These were questions, he knew, faced by many officials in Berlin, in Germany today. Which was to be more important, their livelihood or their beliefs?

He took a deep breath. 'I've already chosen my faction, Colonel Heydrich. It is . . . myself. And my job. Which is to apprehend murderers.'

Heydrich stared at him for a moment. Then a smile appeared on his lips. 'A man without ambition. Rare in Germany today. You know, I preferred that the SD handle this investigation. I still do.'

'But the Reichschancellor over-ruled you.'

'As you say. Of course I will understand if you fail to apprehend this particular killer. Random killing by a deranged personality . . . the most difficult killer to find . . .'

'If it is that . . . yes . . .'

'The Führer may not understand that kind of failure.'

It was Lohmann's turn to smile. 'I've no doubt you will explain the difficulties of such a case.'

Heydrich looked serious. 'Believe me, I will. A good investigating detective is hard to find. And will be useful to the country. Yes, I may be able to persuade the Führer that one failure should not ruin a career.'

'I should be grateful. If I fail . . .'

'Naturally. Good night, Lohmann. I shall read your reports with interest. They'll be forwarded to me at Nuremberg. The Rally, you understand. This will be the largest to date. Pity you won't be there. It will be quite inspiring.'

'I'll contain my disappointment,' said Lohmann. 'Good night, Colonel Heydrich.'

It was a warm, dry night despite clouds gathering over the suburbs of the city. The Romanische Cafe, for the first time in days with its tables on the pavement, was an oasis of bright lights. Voices argued loudly about painting and literature, less loudly about politics. There was an awareness of the presence of brown-shirted and black-tunicked uniforms.

Reiner was sitting at a table outside the main entrance to the cafe when Lohmann drove up.

'Can I get you something, chief?' he asked as Lohmann settled beside him.

'A lager.' Lohmann looked around at the other tables. Reiner beckoned a waiter over and ordered two lagers.

'Anything happened?' he asked when the waiter had departed.

'Holtz has come up with a possible lead. He's following it up.'

'About time Holtz did something. What about Göring?'

Lohmann lit a cigarette, inhaled, and coughed loudly. When the coughing had subsided, he went on, 'Between Göring and Heydrich, I learn something new every time. Not necessarily about the investigation. But about the Party.'

Reiner grinned. 'Anything I should know?'

'Factions, Reiner. Factions and other factions. Doubtless, factions within factions. Only one thing stops them massacring each other. Hitler. And their own self-interest. Pity about Hitler. Without him it would all fall apart. Something devoutly to be wished.'

Reiner, genuinely nervous, looked around.

'There are some things best not said, chief.'

'You forget, I'm the second most powerful man in Germany.'

'But, for how long?'

'You have little faith, Reiner. That's what I like about you.'

The waiter reappeared with the two lagers. Reiner paid for them, as Lohmann studied the other occupants of the tables. He felt weary now, and the weariness seemed momentarily to distort his vision. Was he indeed surrounded by plump little men in Homburgs and bowler hats; woman with fat, rouged cheeks, large hats and scarlet lips shaped as the petals of flowers which had never grown in any garden? Was the laughter really forced and frantic? Or was his vision in some way distorted? Human beings seemed to have become caricatures of themselves. Georg Grosz paintings come alive. Among the women, there were fewer he could recognise as prostitutes. One or two certainly, there, and there. Less than last year. More, he felt sure, than there would be next year. The puritanism of evil, he thought, and felt pleased with himself at the phrase.

'May I join you for a moment?' the voice said.

Lohmann and Reiner looked up. Lohmann's picture of those around him, made flesh in front of him. Brown bowler, starched collar, striped shirt, jewelled tie pin gleaming, the round face grinned down at them.

'Hartmann!' the round face said, with a small, formal bow. 'You may remember me, Inspector Lohmann.'

It took Lohmann a moment before he identified the face. 'Yes, Hartmann. 1929. You went into Augsberg Prison. False pretences, wasn't it?'

'I was merely trying to make a living,' said Hartmann, sitting on the edge of the seat beside Reiner. 'A misunderstanding. However, I hold no enmity against you, Inspector.'

'Generous of you,' Lohmann replied acidly.

'I'm a generous man. Anyway, what is crime? A few years ago one stole . . . or borrowed . . . a million marks. The next day it's worth toilet paper.'

Lohmann sipped his lager. 'We can do something for you?'

'I can do a small thing for you, Inspector. The Blind Man is looking for you.'

'I saw him in the small hours of this morning.'

Hartmann shrugged. 'He's looking for you now. Perhaps he can be of some service.'

'I'll keep it in mind. Anything you can do for me, Hartmann?'

The bowler hat was raised and plump fingers scratched thinning hair over a shining scalp. 'What are you interested in?'

'The murders of three men. Rudig, Preuss and Bruckner?'

Hartmann shuddered visibly. 'There's a cloud over that business.'

'Why?'

'Isn't the SD investigating? Nobody wants to be mixed up with those people. Criminals, they are. And, if you say it takes one to know one, I can only agree.'

'A lot of fear around?'

'Yes.'

'But not the Blind Man?' asked Reiner.

Hartmann shook his head. 'I don't know anything about the Blind Man. Except that he wants to see Lohmann.'

Lohmann finished his beer. 'If you've nothing to tell me, Hartmann, go away. The Blind Man'll find me.'

Rising, Hartmann leaned forward towards the Inspector. 'People are getting out, Lohmann. Not just the bright people and the Jews. Others. They're afraid. Our people, Lohmann. Yours and mine. They take the law away, none of us have a chance.'

'They haven't taken it away yet. Goodbye, Hartmann.'

The brown bowler was raised with excessive politeness. The smile was still set on the plump face. He waddled into the crowd, merging, disappearing into blackness.

'Huh! Hartmann!' said Reiner.

'Hartmann,' Lohmann echoed. 'A man with little past and less future.'

'Another lager, chief?'

'No. Time we went to work. Bruckner's friend. Fräulein Lys Lysander . . .'

'Starting at the Club Hawai. Off the Kurfürstendamm.'

'Good,' Lohmann rose to his feet. 'You drive, sergeant.'

Reiner parked the car on the Kurfürstendamm close to the entrance of a narrow alley. Nearby, a large man in a heavy coat with a brown fur collar climbed from a Rolls-Royce and helped out a beautifully gowned woman wearing a mink stole. They moved slowly into the alley, the woman's laughter echoing back as the large man muttered in her ear. Four young men in dinner jackets appeared on the street and went down the alley.

Lohmann and Reiner followed. The alley was ill-lit but,

some fifty yards down, flashing lights denoted the Club Hawai.

'New?' Lohmann asked.

'Three months open,' Reiner replied. 'Very chic, very popular. They say someone in the Party's invested in it.'

'Not a very salubrious location.' As if to give point to Lohmann's words, there was the sound from a building on their right of a lavatory flushing. On the left there was a pile of bricks, timber and a broken cement bag, left-over materials from the Club Hawai.

'Expensive place,' said Reiner.

Lohmann sighed. 'You mean, not for the likes of us. But then, we're on duty.'

The club's entrance was a thick wooden doorway surrounded by electric light bulbs in various colours. Beside the door was a small, framed poster. 'Club Hawai presents Lys Lysander and the Girls.' In the centre of the door was a spyhole.

'I presume we knock,' said Lohmann.

Reiner knocked.

An eye came to the spyhole.

'You are members?' The voice came through a small speaker at the side of the door.

'Police officers,' said Reiner, producing his warrant card and holding it in front of the spyhole. The door opened.

Behind the door was a large man with the body of a wrestler. The body was somehow squeezed into a ill-shapen dinner jacket. The head was bullet-shaped and closely cropped. In contrast there was an aroma of strong perfume from the man and, around his right wrist, two large gold bracelets.

'Willi Kopfer,' said Reiner.

'Should I know him?' Lohmann responded.

'Ach, now, Herr Reiner . . . .!' Willie Kopfer said.

'Used to wrestle a bit. Wasn't bad.'

'I was good,' said Willi Kopfer. 'I was near championship form. Until you put me in the Tegel Prison.'

'I didn't put you there,' Reiner smiled. 'You put your hand in a gentleman's pocket, around his wallet, and that put you there. I told you, a wrestler's hand would never make a successful dip.'

'Anyway, I'm straight now, Herr Reiner.'
Lohmann said, 'Who's managing this place?'
'Herr Leni. Paul Leni.'
'I know him. Tell him Inspector Lohmann and Sergeant Reiner are here.'
Willi Kopfer disappeared, leaving them staring at a small counter behind which was a smiling hatcheck girl. They divested themselves of coats and hats as Paul Leni appeared. Lohmann knew him of old. A small, balding man in his fifties. He had managed nightclubs and cafes in and around Berlin since before the war. He had no criminal record that Lohmann knew of, although the Vice Squad had a file on him. Rumour said he had been bankrupted twice running his own clubs and, eventually, had settled for a salaried job running other people's enterprises.
'Herr Inspector Lohmann, how good to see you,' he effused with excessive and calculated insincerity.
'And you, Paul,' Lohmann responded in kind. 'This is Sergeant Reiner.'
'Both always welcome. Any time, any time.' Then the face darkened nervously. 'No trouble, I hope? Please. We have very important guests here tonight.'
'No trouble for the club, Paul. I hear you have a new singer?'
'Fräulein Lysander. She will be on shortly. Come in. You would like a table? Or be my guest at the bar?'
'The bar, I think.'
Leni ushered them into the main club room. To Lohmann it was typical of so many he had known throughout his years in Berlin. A bar at the rear, one step higher than the rest of the room. The room itself was low-ceilinged, tables arranged around a small oblong dance floor. Beyond the dance floor, a miniscule stage, at the rear of which was a piano and four music stands. A five-piece group, playing jazz. At each side of the room were cubicles, leather-lined alcoves for the more discreet private parties. These cubicles could be curtained off so that the occupants could be invisible to the rear and sides, while still permitting a view of the stage. As a concession to the name of the club the side walls were decorated with a

number of papier-mâché palm trees. And the numerous waitresses were dressed in brassieres and grass skirts.

At the bar, Leni beckoned over one of two bartenders. 'You will drink on the house, Inspector?'

'A schnapps for me and a beer for my sergeant,' Lohmann replied, looking around. A haze of smoke hung over the room and, from the bar, the jazz was muted by the babble of voices and the frequent bursts of raucous laughter. Lohmann thought, like a thousand *boites* in a thousand cities throughout the world. There was a sadness in the way the wealthy took their entertainment in this Godforsaken century. Even the thought was not original.

The drinks were placed in front of them.

'I want a word with Fräulein Lysander,' said Lohmann.

Leni shrugged. 'Ach, she is so popular. I don't think she will be able to see you . . .'

'Police business. Alone. After her appearance. Arrange it.'

A look of alarm came over the nightclub manager's face. 'It is difficult tonight, Inspector. She has most influential friends here.'

His glance strayed to a booth at the right, close to the stage.

'You will have to inform Reichsminister Goebbels that he will have to wait. Police business takes precedence . . .'

'But, Inspector . . .'

'Do it! Now!'

Leni, nodding, turned and moved away. His face was ashen and Reiner could almost swear he trembled as he went off. Reiner gulped a mouthful of beer.

'Aren't you taking a chance with the little doctor, chief?' he said.

Lohmann smiled. ' "Second most important man in the country." Remember?'

'I remember, but does Goebbels know it?'

A loud fanfare of music came from the stage. The house lights dimmed and a spotlight flashed onto the centre of the tiny platform. Then into the spotlight danced a small, compact figure in dinner jacket, black tie, wing collar. And started to sing.

'Ferdy Mann,' whispered Reiner. 'Master of Ceremonies. There's a rumour he's Jewish.'

The MC was in full voice now, singing a plaintive, if humorous, ballad. Behind him four scantily dressed girls, none of them seeming to be older than seventeen, performed a kind of dance. The import of the ballad was a welcome to the customers to the depths of the Club Hawai, a place of romance and sadness. The music finally died and Ferdy Mann bowed to a smattering of applause.

'They sound as if they know he's Jewish,' Reiner added.

The MC stepped forward, a fixed grin on his face. The voice, high pitched though it was, carried across the club.

'Meine Herren und Damen! Welcome to the Club Hawai. From here, there's no place to go but upwards towards the gutter! But never mind, the food's good. We serve great Bavarian Hams. There's a party of them sitting at the table over there. We used to serve gefilte fish and matzos too. But they've gone on holiday. To a new holiday resort called Dachau.'

A ripple of nervous laughter ran through the room. And died away at once.

Undeterred, Ferdy Mann went on. 'Ernst Röhm and his men are still served here. Anybody can order roast leg of Brownshirt. Not that we're all meat eaters. We also serve big cheeses. There's at least one small one in the corner booth . . .'

He was staring at the booth nearest the stage.

'Not exactly brilliant material,' Lohmann murmured.

'Or popular,' Reiner added.

Taking a bow towards the corner booth, Mann seemed unconcerned by the lack of laughter. 'They say one of the big cheeses has a club foot. His lady friends tell me they can always hear him coming. Even with both feet off the ground.'

One short, brief laugh was instantly cut off. Leni arrived back at the bar, his face even whiter than when he had left.

'I told the fool not to use that material,' he said, mopping his brow with a large white handkerchief.

Reiner said, 'He's certainly living dangerously.'

The club manager nodded. 'The fool. It's his last night here. Probably his last night anywhere.'

But Lohmann was staring towards the corner booth. An arm rested on the rail of the booth, an arm in a grey tunic. Two large men in dark, ill-fitting suits, emerged and headed for a small door to the right of the stage. Ferdy Mann, taking a barely solicited bow, was introducing the next act.

'The lady whom all Berlin has taken to its heart. Fräulein Lys Lysander!'

She was of medium height, full-breasted, with long dark hair. Her eyes were large, and even from a distance Lohmann imagined them to be of a penetrating blue. She was dressed in a low-cut clinging gown of silver.

Leni's attention was however not on the stage. He was staring at the two men approaching the small door.

'Those are the Reichsminister's men. God, there will be trouble backstage. Please, Herr Lohmann, can you help?'

Lohmann frowned, reluctant to take his eyes from the stage. Lys Lysander was commencing her song, a soft haunting ballad. The voice was clear, if not strong, the notes impeccable. She was good, he thought, and in time, with experience, would be very good.

'Please, Lohmann . . . !' Leni repeated himself.

'Yes, all right. You've told Fräulein Lysander we wish to see her?'

'In her dressing room, after her numbers.'

'Lead the way. Come on, Reiner.'

They followed Leni down the right side of the club, passing by the corner booth. Again Lohmann glimpsed an arm resting on a brass rail. Only when they had passed the booth and reached the stage door was he able to turn briefly and stare into the dark eyes of the small man with the large head, sitting with yet a third aide, this time in uniform. Goebbels had his eyes riveted on the singer. One hand cupped the chin under a petulant mouth. This was the man; Reichsminister, Minister of Propaganda, devout husband, soon to be a father, and notorious womaniser.

Lohmann moved through the door, followed by Reiner. They climbed five steps into a shabby corridor, stage entrance left, and beyond, a row of doors. The tinselled glamour of the club no longer applied here. The floor was wooden planking, uncarpeted but for a film of dust. From the dressing room doors, flaking paint peeled. And, from the first of these, closed though it was, came the sound of a scream followed by a number of thuds, and yet another scream. Leni stood at one side, white face covered in sweat, looking to the two police officers. Lohmann nodded to Reiner. The sergeant positioned himself in front of the door and kicked it open.

Ferdy Mann was on the floor. His face was already bruised, his lower lip torn and bleeding. His two assailants stood over him, taking turns at kicking him; in the stomach, then below in the crutch. Ferdy Mann screamed again, a high pitched, agonising sound, a human animal in pain. Lohmann stepped into the room in front of Reiner, grabbed the nearer of the two men by the shoulder, turned him around and, with the side of his hand, chopped him across the throat. The force of the blow was considerable, but calculated. The man went backwards across the tiny dressing room and collapsed, choking, under the dressing table.

The second man turned to face Reiner. He towered over the sergeant, a threatening figure. Lacking the subtlety of his chief, Reiner used initiative. He kicked out hard, his foot striking the man over his testicles. The man jack-knifed forward and Reiner brought his knee with force into the gasping face. The second man went down.

Yet these were professionals. Despite their agonies, they were quickly on their feet again. But only to face Lohmann's Mauser.

'That's it!' said Lohmann. 'Finished!'

Unheeding, one of the men moved forward.

Lohmann's finger tightened on the trigger. He had no desire to fire, much as he abhorred the type in front of him. No thought and little mind. Yet killing the man would solve little. Still he had learned, early in his police career, the very old adage, 'Never point a pistol unless you are prepared to fire it'.

'I wouldn't,' Lohmann heard himself say. 'I'm a police

officer so, if I blow your brains all over that wall, it's all in the line of duty. I like doing my duty.'

The man stopped. Motionless. Reiner now had his revolver in hand.

'You've made a mistake, policeman,' the man said.

'Not tonight, Herr What's-your-name. Not this week. Maybe later it'll be a mistake but not now.

The man backed away, looked at his companion and feeling his throat gently where Lohmann had hit him, he moved to the door. The companion followed him, walking with an awkward gait.

'One other thing,' Lohmann said. 'Please inform Doctor Goebbels it'll be safe for him to come backstage later. Much later. By then we will have everything under control.'

A glare from the man with the sore throat. 'Who the fuck are you?'

Reiner answered. 'That's Inspector Lohmann. Second most powerful man in Germany.'

Another glare and they were gone. Lohmann turned to find Leni helping Ferdy Mann from the floor. The MC's chin was covered in blood, and every movement caused him to wince.

'Are you all right, Ferdy?' Leni asked, ignoring the obvious.

'No,' said the small man. 'I'm sore. All over.' He felt his groin carefully. 'And my sex life will be impaired for some weeks. Otto will not like that.'

Leni shook his head dejectedly. 'I warned you. How often I warned you. Using such material.'

Something resembling a grin flickered over the blood-stained lips. 'Ah, but you should have seen the look on Goebbel's face. If I live to be a hundred, I'll remember that look.' He now faced Lohmann. 'I have to thank you, Inspector. You see, it was my last gesture. The thumb to the nose. And then, well, I have two tickets to Vienna on tonight's express. Otto will be waiting at the station.'

'Then be sure not to miss the train,' Lohmann replied. 'And then, go further than Vienna. These people have long arms and memories to match.'

'Yes. Thank you again, sir.' He winced. 'I think they

have broken my arm. Among other things. Herr Leni, if you would call a taxi . . .'

'You have time. Rest,' said Leni. 'I will show Herr Lohmann Fräulein Lysander's room.'

He escorted Lohmann and Reiner into the corridor. Four chorus girls and numerous members of the stage crew crowded Ferdy's doorway, curious faces peering in.

'Come now!' the club manager exhorted. 'Back to work. The sideshow is over.'

They dispered reluctantly.

'That is Fräulein Lysander's room,' Leni said, pointing to the next door. 'But, before you go in . . . oh, there's no hurry, she's still on stage . . . about Ferdy?'

'What about Ferdy?'

'Will they allow him to reach the station?'

Lohmann nodded thoughtfully. 'Stay with him. Tidy him up. After we see Fräulein Lysander, we'll make sure he gets his train.'

Leni left the two detectives alone in the singer's dressing room. In shape it was the same as Ferdy Mann's room. But the furnishings were more lavish. A couch and two deep armchairs faced the seat in front of the dressing table. The electric bulbs were unbroken and, reflected in the mirror, cast even more light into the room. The walls were decorated with photos of film stars and posters of their films. At once Reiner was drawn to these.

'I love the cinema,' he announced, staring at a portrait of Peter Lorre in *M*. His voice dropped to a low whining tone, and he hissed his next words. 'I didn't . . . didn't mean to harm ze child. I like children . . . I didn't mean to . . .'

Lohmann gave him no encouragement, his face blank.

'Peter Lorre,' Reiner explained. 'As the child-murderer in *M*.'

Lohmann still said nothing.

Reiner moved to the next photograph. This time it was of the American comedians, Laurel and Hardy. Reiner's face ballooned. His movements became a model of elephantine grace.

'Here's another fine mess you got me into, Inspector Lohmann.'

This time Lohmann gave an exaggerated sigh. 'I should be used to working with whores and comic singers,' he said.

'Into what category do I fall, Inspector?' Reiner enquired.

Lohmann smiled now. Reiner's timing, he knew, was impeccable. When relief was needed the sergeant sensed when to provide it. The tensions of the day were assuaged.

Then the door opened and Lys Lysander came in.

SIX

To Reiner, the haunter of picture palaces, the singer's entrance heralded the arrival of a necessary leading lady in the case. Certainly an aura of glamour surrounded the singer. Yet she appeared to be smaller than she had seemed on the stage, pretty certainly, but not beautiful, and young, very young. (In fact she was twenty-one.) The large eyes, in close-up, were closer to purple than blue. The face, too seemed thinner, almost prematurely pinched and waif-like. To Lohmann, the first impression was of a child with the body of a woman. And, for her age, considerable self-assurance.

She said nothing at first, but looked from one policeman to the other, an appraising look, pencil thin etched eyebrows slightly raised.

'You may shut the door behind you, Fräulein,' said Lohmann. 'We're police officers.'

She walked coolly to her dressing table. 'Herr Leni told me. He also told me you helped Ferdy. Was that wise?'

'We were keeping the peace. Herr Mann was not the disturber of that peace.'

'It may be worse for him now. You're going to help him catch his train to Vienna? If you don't, well . . . he . . . he hasn't . . . finished with Ferdy . . .'

'He?'

'Josef. Doctor Goebbels.'

'Bears grudges?'

'Enjoys bearing grudges.'

Lohmann swung around to face the sergeant. 'Reiner, you'll take Mann to the station. Take a taxi and make sure you're not followed. They may not know he's going away, so if you're not followed he should be in Vienna before they realise he's gone. Then you can go home and I'll see you in the morning.'

'Sir,' said Reiner, showing every evidence of extreme reluctance to depart. However, he went glumly, sensing Lohmann would take no arguments on the subject.

'Now, Fräulein, my name is Lohmann. Inspector Lohmann, Criminal Police. I want to talk about Karl Bruckner.'

Lohmann watched her. Beautifully controlled, he thought. A slight flicker below her right eye; a feeling, now, of tension in the room.

She said, 'I heard about it. I'm sorry.'

'Yes? That's all? One small sorry for the murdered man?'

She showed a sudden flash of nervous anger. 'What more can I say. He's dead. He can't know . . .'

'What should he know?'

She looked towards the door. With apprehension.

'There isn't time,' she said.

'I'm in no hurry.' God, he thought, I sound pompous. Or smug. Or both.

'He'll be here now.'

'Goebbels?'

She nodded. The lost girl.

'He can't wait.'

'No, he won't wait.'

'I have the authority to make him wait,' Lohmann insisted, forbearing to add that he would enjoy doing so.

'It's all right for you,' Lys Lysander said. 'But he'll take it out on me later. One way or another. Please, go now. Come and see me later. At my apartment.'

He studied her for a moment, without replying.

'The Mannheim building. Apartment 4-A,' she went on. 'Please, in about two hours. Yes, give me two hours. I have one more spot here. And then, he'll have to go home to his wife tonight.'

'Yes, all right.' He went to the door of the dressing room. As he put his hand on the door knob, he felt it turn from the outside. The door swung inwards.

He was small, very small. In a plain uniform, decorated

only by the swastika armband. Large eyes, under a bulging forehead, stared up at Lohmann. The black hair was slicked back and shining under the lights. Behind him were two aides. Not the men who had tried to beat up Ferdy Mann.

'Good evening,' said Goebbels. 'You would be Inspector Lohmann, I imagine?' The mouth twitched into a smile. But the eyes were dead.

'Doctor Goebbels, I believe,' Lohmann replied. 'You look much smaller than your photographs.'

The smile became fixed. The Doctor was obviously not amused. 'May I . . .?' he said, and moved past Lohmann into the dressing room. Turning then to stare at the Inspector. Ignoring the girl. Simply staring at the Inspector.

Lohmann was not unaccustomed to fear. He had felt the ice of it on his spine on many occasions. The other night, while Glauber had held the shard of glass at the boy's throat. Other occasions, too. Facing a heavy automatic held by a gunman who had already killed two policemen and had nothing to lose. During the war, watching the Tommies charging towards the trench he was huddled in. It wasn't the men, or even their rifles that had frightened him. It had been the bayonets on the end of the rifles, steel gleaming in the rain. And now, it was the expressionless face of the little doctor. There was, in that gaze, a power as frightening as those bayonets so many years before.

'You are investigating a series of murders, Lohmann?'

'Yes.'

'Here? In the Club Hawai?'

'Yes, here in the Club Hawai.'

Goebbels looked around, a mock searching of the room. 'I see nothing here that might aid such an investigation.'

A deep breath now. To hell with the little doctor. 'You haven't the training to see anything, Herr Doctor.'

'So you say, Lohmann. But I have something more than training. I have authority. And the power to enforce that authority. Your investigation does not permit you to bother senior Party members.'

'According to a letter I have in my pocket, it allows me to do anything I think fit. The letter is signed Adolf Hitler.'

This had an effect. A small effect. The doctor's large eyes blinked myopically. Then the reply came out like a whiplash.

'I think you may believe yourself to be more important than you actually are, Lohmann. You may have to test the extent of your own authority. And it certainly does not permit you to aid enemies of the State, such as Jews.'

Lohmann came back quickly. 'I have only stopped a German citizen being assaulted by thugs tonight, Doctor. That is a part of my professional duty.'

'I suggest you consult your superiors as to the range and extent of your duty, Inspector. You will find changes are coming in this country of ours. We are no longer concerned with the decadent weakness of Weimar law. You see, we are the lawmakers now.'

'For how long, Doctor Goebbels, for how long?'

The doctor scowled. No affectation of a smile now. The unpleasant face of the New Germany.

'Good night, Inspector Lohmann. Doubtless we'll meet again.'

The small doctor turned to face the singer. Lohmann had been dismissed. He went out into the corridor, pushing determinedly past the Reichsminister's two aides.

Leni was waiting in the club's foyer.

'Your sergeant got Ferdy away. Thank God! But I'm sure those two thugs of Goebbels were after them.'

Lohmann reassured him. 'Reiner's an expert. He'll shake them loose and get your man to the station. He'll be in Vienna by morning.'

'He told me to thank you. When the times comes, I hope you'll be able to help me get out.'

'You're not Jewish?'

'Does one have to be a Jew to see what is happening here?' said Leni. 'I make my living entertaining people, Inspector. Oh, I make money at it. Maybe I even come near to breaking the law doing it. But I don't hurt people. Unless giving them what they want hurts them. These people that are taking over Germany, they can hurt people.'

'I have noticed.'

'And not just the Jews. Soon it will be all of us.'

'You think it'll be as bad as that, Leni?'

'Worse, Inspector, worse.' Leni stared bleakly towards the door. 'And it is starting to rain again. Only a lunatic would run a club called Hawai in this climate.'

He let Lohmann out of the door into the alley. 'Come whenever you like. You will always be a welcome guest here.'

The alley was awash with rain. Another downpour. Puddles forming underfoot. He was forced to jump from one piece of raised paving to another. The Kurfüstendamm was a gleaming ribbon of shining light stretching into the infinity of darkness. A few pedestrians scurried from doorway to doorway, sheltering and then moving on, as the rain showed no sign of letting up. Lohmann felt infinitely depressed. It wasn't just the rain, which he was accustomed to; had always felt it had a cleansing effect on the city. But not now. Now it was part of a metropolis that seemed to be dying; decaying, flaking off, coming apart at its cemented seams. Despite the years of inflation and unemployment, there had been life in Berlin, a frenetic striving to endure and more, to find value in that endurance. Survival with a struggle even to attain laughter; a belief that, whatever passed, everything would be better in time. Now time had passed, and something else was rising to the surface. A disregard for the very essence of living; the imposition of a dead hand; one man's nightmare over all. And the people were accepting this as the better time to come. They had no need to concern themselves any more with the business of trying to survive. The Party would do that for them; and even if it decided that some of them were not to survive, the rest would accept this without question. Soon, no-one would dare to question. The new Germany would provide answers for all. And, in return, all the Party asked was complete dominion.

Only a few, like Leni, could see it. Only a few . . . like Lohmann? Or were his eyes tightly shut, his ears plugged to avoid the truth?

He was sitting in the driving seat of the car now, eyes fixed on the dashboard. He barely felt the first prod of the cane on his shoulder. The second prod caused him to turn, irritatedly. To face the Blind Man.

'I've been looking for you.'

'Sightless, he looks. Eyeless in Gaza, he searches.'

The Blind Man laughed. 'Everybody with eyes looks to the outside. I look to the inside. That's where I find you. In my head.'

'The places I get to . . .' said Lohmann.

'Müller wants to see you.'

'I've been wanting to see him for years. In prison.'

'But not yet Inspector. I've to take you to him.'

Lohmann opened the off-side door of the car. 'Get in.'

The white stick tapped its way around the car. The Blind Man climbed in with ease.

Lohmann said, 'I sometimes wonder about you, Blind Man.'

'Everybody does. You want proof?'

'Out of curiosity, yes.'

The Blind Man removed his black spectacles. In the light from the street lamps, Lohmann looked into his eyes. Milk white. No pupil in either eye.

'Don't say you're sorry,' the Blind Man replied. 'You're not, I'm not. But then I'm used to it. And I cannot see what you can see. Now will you please drive to the end of the Kürfüstendamm. Then turn right and straight on 'til morning.'

'That far?'

The Blind Man gave a throaty chuckle. 'A joke. Something I read in an English book. When I was a child. Barrie. The way to the Never-Never Land. I'm always looking for it. No, turn right. Down to the canal. Oberstrasse. A big warehouse.'

'I'll find it.'

Lohmann drove in silence for some minutes.

Then the Blind Man spoke again. 'We're close now. I can hear the canal.'

Pulling the car to the kerb, Lohmann said, 'We're here. Oberstrasse. The warehouse on the right?'

'That's it.'

They climbed down from the car and stood on the kerb.

'I always thought you worked for Müller,' Lohmann said.

The Blind Man shook his head. 'I don't. I work for myself. And whoever pays me. The door should be right in front of you. Go through it and to the end of the workshop. You'll find another door there.'

'You're not coming?'

'I told you. I don't work for him. I just do odd jobs. I don't want to know anything about anything. Best that way. Every time somebody knows something, they get into trouble. Anyway, it'll be dark in the warehouse. I might lose my way.'

He turned and, tapping on the cobbles, he walked away from Lohmann and the warehouse.

The door was open. Lohmann went in. Walked carefully through a dimly-lit one-time workshop of considerable size. It was now devoid of machinery although markings, barely discernible on the floor, indicated where machines had once stood. Slowly Lohmann made his way to the far end of the workshop. The door was easily seen, light coming from behind it, showing up the cracks around it. He opened it and stepped into a brilliantly illuminated anteroom. Two doors. One, straight ahead, was shut. The other, half open, led to a long corridor. The walls were papered with a thick flock, cream paper.

Lohmann opened the door in front of him and stepped into the room beyond.

It was like the study of some wealthy business tycoon. Panelled walls, bookcases in front of them. None of the Spartan simplicity of Heydrich's study. Here was ease, and luxury and comfort. Deep leather armchairs, a deep leather sofa; a desk, Louis Quinze period, ormolu on the legs. Paintings where there were no bookcases. A Cezanne, not a print, but the original; a Renoir, a plump ballerina adjusting her dancing shoes; one, of which he could not identify the painter, of a woman with a long swan-like neck and oriental eyes. Lohmann stood staring at it.

'A Modigliani,' said the solitary occupant of the room. 'I bought it when no-one had ever heard of him. He's now becoming recognised. Not in Germany, of course. All of it comes under the heading of decadent art.'

The speaker was a man in his fifties, very erect, though not particularly tall . . . about five-foot six, Lohmann estimated. Of course he had seen the man before. Once in dock, when the verdict had been not guilty. Accused of organising an armed robbery from a bank. Not that he'd been near the bank. Only the organiser. An unprovable fact. Dressed as he had been in the dock. Like a bank manager, or perhaps the director of the bank. Dark suit, striped trousers, and wing collar with black silk tie. Impeccable and expensive.

'Come in, Inspector Lohmann,' said the man, Müller. 'Do take a seat. We haven't actually met though we've seen each other several times.'

Lohmann walked to the centre of the room. He noted two other doors behind the desk.

'However,' Müller went on, 'you probably know more about me than I do. Such extensive police records. You know, I often thought, if I was ever to be arrested again, I'd hope it would be by you.'

'A kind of compliment,' Lohmann replied. 'I'll keep it in mind.'

'Oh, it'll never happen now. You see, I'm leaving Germany. Tomorrow. For Rio de Janeiro. An early retirement.'

'A lot of people will be pleased.'

'I hope so. I like pleasing people. A drink? Scotch whisky, schnapps, vodka?'

'Whisky will be fine.'

Müller poured two large whiskies, and handed one to the police officer.

'Yes, I've always regretted we never crossed swords.' The wing collar bobbed up and down over the prominent Adam's apple. 'Like Sherlock Holmes and Moriarty. I like that. Great reader of detective stories, I am. Conan Doyle, Edgar Wallace, especially Edgar Wallace. But then you were always so busy with those grotesque murder cases.'

'You're telling me you never committed murder?'

Müller had a look of mock indignation on his face. 'I abhor murder. Principally because it is rarely profitable.

Of course, if someone was being awkward, standing in the way of the progress of my little organisation, then I had to arrange for him to be removed. Nothing personal about it. Nor was I involved. But there was never any need for you people to worry. As an American, I think an associate of Mr Capone, said – we only kill each other.'

He took a sip of whisky before going on. 'Of course you have to admit, my organisation was good.'

'It was good,' Lohmann said. He didn't grudge the admission. It was a matter of simple fact.

'Mind you I was greatly assisted by a number of dishonest policemen and judges. Avaricious people. Of course, I never really considered myself as big as Mr Capone.'

'You tried.'

'Yes, I did, didn't I?'

'I was looking forward to putting you away, Müller.'

Müller laughed, a high pitched cackling sound. 'Come now, what harm did I do? A few bank robberies, a little intimidation. What was it Brecht said in *The Threepenny Opera*? What is the difference between the robber of banks and the founder of banks? Both are great robbers of the people.'

'Why give it all up now?'

Müller hesitated before replying. He took another sip of whisky, paced to his desk and, with an almost loving caress, ran his hand over its gilded side.

'With the rule of law, one had a sporting chance. And, if one was arrested, there could be no regrets. I would have accepted arrest. Not with pleasure, but I would have accepted it. I did once, you wouldn't know that, when I was younger. In another place under another name. But now . . .' He shrugged.

'Now?' Lohmann prompted him.

'Another set of villains has taken over. A bigger gang. They would not tolerate my survival. And soon, there will be no more rule of law. They won't bother trying to prove my guilt. They'll simply execute me. I have no desire to experience the executioner's axe.'

'And this is why you want to see me? A farewell drink?'

Müller gave a sweeping gesture with his right arm. 'I'm

a great romantic, Lohmann. I wanted to say goodbye to one honourable adversary at least.'

Lohmann said, 'Goodbye, Müller.'

'Ah, you try hard to be a cold man, Lohmann,' Müller replied. 'But, I hear otherwise. From Madame Kitty.'

Lohmann frowned. Of course he knew Kitty, but he didn't like the thought that Müller knew of the acquaintance. Madame Kitty, other names unknown, ran the most expensive and elegant brothel in Berlin. And as such, the place was a useful source of information for the Criminal Police.

'Was it a year after your wife died, Lohmann? Certainly the decent interval. One of her girls, isn't it? Lucy or Lucette? That's the name.

'You hide under beds, too?' Lohmann said quietly. Nevertheless he was now uneasy. It was true; over a year after his wife died, on a routine investigation he had called at Madame Kitty's. And there had met Lucy. Came to like the girl. Despite a knowledge of what she was . . . and she had made no pretences to Lohmann . . . he had liked her. Perhaps more. A strong fondness for her honesty. Maybe it was the old cliché, the whore with the heart of gold. It hadn't mattered at the time. It didn't matter now. Except that Müller knew about it. It would seem too, that Kitty had betrayed a confidence.

As if reading his mind, Müller said, 'Oh, it wasn't actually from Kitty I learned about it. I have contacts in the Gestapo. They know about it. Useful to them, if you misbehave in other ways. I suppose they could take your job away from you.'

It was the kind of information the Gestapo stored, Lohmann knew. Would use when it suited them. At least he was warned.

'Comes under Kaltenbrunner,' Müller went on. 'You know, Kaltenbrunner has installed listening apparatus in most of Kitty's rooms. He doesn't need to hide under the bed. And it is a source of information for the Gestapo. Kitty had no choice. Either agree or be closed up and arrested. What could she do? Kitty could never survive a place like Dachau.'

He added, as an afterthought, 'is anybody meant to?'

Lohmann frowned. Something new? 'I agree Kitty wouldn't survive prison. But is Dachau anything else but another prison?'

Müller peered at him from under heavy eyebrows. 'Ask anyone who has managed to get out of that place. They are very few, and should be cherished. They are so fortunate.'

Lohmann made a mental note. Ask about Dachau. What was so different from ordinary penal practice? Müller came over and topped up his tumbler with whisky.

'No more,' said Lohmann. 'I'm driving myself tonight.'

'Of course. Leave what you cannot finish. I myself will be leaving so much behind. But all this talk, it is not what you came here for. You came to ask if I had heard anything on the grapevine about these murders you're investigating, didn't you? That's what you asked the Blind Man.'

'You know about most things that happen in Berlin.'

'It's true.' Müller gave a deep sigh. 'Alas, no more after tonight.'

'About these murders . . .?'

'Ah, yes. You know of course there's no future for you in this investigation. None at all. You find the truth, you're a dead man. You don't, the Führer will no longer love you. Which is the same thing. In Germany, from now on, if the Führer doesn't love you, you're as good as dead.'

'You know more than that, Müller.'

Müller gave a shrug. The bank manager refusing an overdraft. 'I'm no pigeon, Lohmann. Even against . . . the likes of them.'

'Them?'

'The Party. For or against I will not get involved. I open my mouth on this one, I won't even be safe in Rio.'

Now was the time to take the hard line. Lohmann stared evenly at Müller. 'You don't open your mouth, you won't even get to the boat, far less to Rio.'

Müller smiled again, wearily. 'We will have to see about that. You arrest me now, you'd never get me out of the building. You see, Lohmann, once I make up my mind, I am not put off. By anything. I shall enjoy Rio. I shall enjoy my retirement. Nothing will stop that. I intend, in time, to travel the world. I have always wanted to climb Kangchenjunga. Not Everest. Everyone wants to climb Everest. No, for me, Kangchenjunga.'

'You'll never get there.'

'If you'd said, I'll never climb it, I won't argue. Perhaps I'm too old. But I will stand on the slopes of that mountain. And I will go on. I will see the snow on Mount Fuji. Row into the lagoons of Tahiti and Samoa.' Suddenly Müller's face flushed with anger. 'Why do you think I've done what I've done? Lived as a criminal. Killed, yes, killed and robbed. Not because I liked it. But because, as a boy, a child in a Potsdam slum, I dreamt of seeing them. An impossibility? It seemed so. But now I can do it. I can go to these places and leave this . . . this festering dung heap of a city. Leave it behind to crumble into the ruins of that maniac's dream. That screeching lunatic in the Wilhelmstrasse.'

Lohmann saw it then, very clearly. 'Is it that you're jealous, Müller?'

The rage was still on the lined features under the heavy eyebrows. 'Jealous? Jealous? No. Not jealous. Happy to go. But go, knowing I could have done it so much better. With the resources he had, the banks that didn't have to be robbed because they opened their vaults to him, oh, yes I could have done it better. One thing Hitler knows, and I too know. Once they open the vaults to him, he will never allow them to be closed again. You see, I know the technique.' He took a deep breath. 'Because of all this, you will never stop me getting away.'

Taking a final sip of whisky, Lohmann laid his tumbler aside.

'You will be in my office at eight o'clock tomorrow morning. Otherwise I will see you never leave Germany.'

Müller flushed, his neck bulging. 'If I am there, I will never leave Germany alive . . .'

'I will guarantee your safety . . .'

'You can guarantee nothing! Oh, put up your road blocks. Search every ship sailing from Hamburg or any other port, you'll never stop me. You see, Lohmann, I have this in common with Hitler. I have the will to do what I say. And I have no need to talk now or tomorrow morning. You have only to look out for yourself now. I'm already beyond your authority. So, no heroics. Just go, now!'

'And if I arrest you now . . .?'

'It would be painful for you even to try.'

He pressed a button on the desk. One of the doors behind him opened and two large men came into the room. The marks of their life were written large on their faces. Things they had done, and things that had been done to them, were there to be viewed and thought upon.

Lohmann acknowledged their presence and the threat of that presence, with a shrug. He said again, 'Eight o'clock tomorrow morning, Müller. Be in my office.'

'I'm sorry I will have to disappoint you,' Müller replied. 'But I'll give you one tip. Being a sporting man, as they say. Look for the common factor, Lohmann, look for that.'

'The common factor?'

'Goodbye, Inspector.'

Lohmann went out. Through the hallway, across the warehouse floor and into Oberstrasse. It was still raining heavily. Lohmann climbed into the police car and drove off. He drove through a haze of moisture, back into the centre of the city. A sheen, a shining patina of smooth dampness, covered everything. Swastikas hung limply from balconies and flagstaffs. Lights, yellow in the seemingly unceasing downpour, winked over the night city. In the streets, life had become extinct.

Except for Lohmann.

INTERREGNUM

What occurred after Lohmann left the warehouse is of course a matter of speculation. Lohmann could, a day later, only surmise. And Müller's two men, although they both survived that night, would say nothing beyond the fact that, after the police inspector's departure, they too left. (For a time these statements were suspect. Later, events indicated they were true.) One thing is and was certain. Müller was left alone in his office in the rear of the warehouse in Oberstrasse.

One large cabin trunk, packed with clothes and personal items, had already been picked up by a carrier and was on its way, not to Hamburg as Müller had said, but to Bremen. (A small subterfuge by which he hoped only to delay police action.) Another suitcase, small enough for Müller to carry personally, was being packed, shortly after the two men had gone. The suitcase was to contain, not marks, but every other currency; dollars, pounds, Swiss and French francs; indeed did contain these to the value of nearly a million dollars. All were recovered by the police, scattered around the elevator and the elevator shaft at the rear of the warehouse.

As far as the police could ascertain, Müller, having packed this case, donned his overcoat, switched out the lights in the room, and made his way along the corridor Lohmann had seen on his arrival. At the end of this corridor was an elevator which sank down to a landing stage on the canal. Here, a small powerboat was waiting to take Müller across the canal to where his car was waiting, petrol tank full, pointed in the general direction of Bremen. Müller never reached the landing stage.

The elevator was of that design which consisted of iron lattice work. Müller, carrying his case, had stepped into it and closed the metal gate behind him. As far as can be determined, as he did this a length of rope, some three or four feet, was thrown around his neck. The rope was attached to a thick, strong section of wood which was on the outside of the elevator's metal work. At the same time as the rope was looped around his neck, the button was depressed and the elevator started to descend. As it reached the level of the floor, the wood caught outside. And effectively, indeed with mechanical efficiency, Müller was garrotted.

In his short death throes, he dropped the suitcase. Filled, indeed overfilled, it burst open on the floor of the elevator. This floor was at once covered in notes of large denomination in various currencies. Many of these somehow flew out of the lattice work and were later found at the bottom of the shaft. Certainly the motive for Müller's killing was not robbery.

The body was not discovered until late the next morning. And then, of course, it becomes again part of the story of Lohmann's investigation.

Müller's death was mourned by few. Known to be the force behind many of Berlin's major bank robberies, it was also learned that he was involved in extortion, smuggling, prostitution and illicit drug smuggling and distribution. He was, in short, the brain behind most of Berlin's current rackets, as we Americans would say. His death did not, of course, bring these rackets to an end. His successor, a former aide, flourished only for a short time, was eventually arrested, sent to Dachau where he became a trusty, and, much later was transferred to a then new camp at Auschwitz. There he disappeared into that horrific miasma the French called 'Night and Fog'.

It is one of the strange side issues of National Socialism and Fascism that the state is more successful in combating organised crime than the democracies. I once attempted to write an article for my newspaper, the New York *Post-Enquirer*, on this very subject. My editor roundly rejected the article which he believed erroneously to be pro-Fascist. It is still true, the dictator countries eradicated crime. Probably because the clever criminals were only too willing to become members of such governments and their parties. Müller's mistake, if it can be said to be a mistake, was in not aligning his people with the Party. In his favour, perhaps he had more honour, was saner, than those who had become the masters of Germany.

Of course his murder had little to do with this. As you will know, it was related to the investigation of the three murders of minor Nazi officials. To Lohmann's investigation. As you will know . . .

SEVEN

The Mannheim apartment building was comparatively modern, having been built in the early twenties to accommodate a number of wealthy Berliners, many of whom had made money in the earlier part of the war and quickly transferred it to Switzerland and other currencies more secure than the mark. Thus had they weathered the slump and massive inflation. The building also accommodated the scions of wealthy families from Prussia. Their wealth had been so vast as to be able to survive all major economic cataclysms. Known to the rest of the tenants as the 'vons', they were aloof and intent on stressing their inherited superiority. Others of the tenancy included some rising bachelor Party officials; and also the female friends of prominent, but married, officials who generously arranged and paid for such accommodation. These females, in their turn, became known as the 'Frau-Fräuleins'.

Lohmann arrived at Apartment 4A of the Mannheim building some two hours and ten minutes after leaving Lys Lysander's dressing room. True to her word, she was alone as she ushered him into a luxurious if rather garishly furnished lounge. The lighting was subdued, shadowing what were known at that time as modern, art-deco furnishings. All were heavily influenced by American design, the decor of the Jazz age. Lohmann found it smart, ugly, and oppressive; and he was thankful for the subdued lighting.

'You will please pour yourself a drink, Inspector,' Lys Lysander said, face averted from him, indicating a gold-rimmed trolley containing a variety of bottles and glasses. 'And a cognac for me.'

Lohmann poured the drinks, confining himself to a small whisky.

'You were able to get rid of your . . . your friend all right?' he asked as he handed her the brandy glass.

Her head still turned away from him, she said, 'Yes, I got rid of him. For the time being.'

'You know why I'm here?'

She nodded. 'Bruckner's death.'

'Bruckner's murder. And two others. Bruckner was a friend of yours?'

She nodded.

'Did you know a man called Rudig. Or Preuss?'

'No.'

'But Bruckner was a good friend.'

She made to turn towards him, seemed to think better of it, and turned back. 'If you mean, did I sleep with him . . . yes. For a time. Then I . . . I broke with him.'

'On account of your meeting Doctor Goebbels?'

Her body visibly stiffened. A tense quality had appeared.'Yes, if you like. I may not be a very moral person, but I don't happen to believe in sleeping with two people at the same time.'

'And of course, Doctor Goebbels would be a more valuable contact for a young girl starting out on her career?'

Now she was angry. But she still had her back towards him. 'I've no doubt you are right. The Doctor would certainly have more influence. Indeed he has. But that is not the reason why I . . . I became friendly with the Doctor. I genuinely preferred his company.'

Lohmann was deliberately trying to stir up her anger. In rage, control was lost. Things were said that might not otherwise be said. It was a way of gleaning information.

'You would of course have to tell yourself that!'

'It's true! And Doctor Goebbels has nothing to do with Bruckner's death!'

'He told you to say that?'

'No! Why should he? He barely knew Karl.'

Pressing forward now. 'Oh, he did know him then?'

Flung over her shoulder. 'They met once. Once! That's all. Before I really knew the Doctor.'

'But he knew of your liaison with Bruckner?'

'I . . . I suppose so. It was no secret!'

'And when you left Bruckner, he may have wanted to make sure you didn't go back. Or even that you weren't . . . despite your principles . . . sleeping with two men at the same time.'

She turned now quickly to face him, unable to control her anger.

'Goebbels had nothing to do with Karl Bruckner's death! I've told you. Anyway, you say there were other deaths. He would hardly kill complete strangers . . .'

'Unless he was cleaning up a number of enemies and included Bruckner with a couple of others.'

'That's ridiculous!' she said, realised she was facing him, and turned away again. But not before he could see, even in the dim light, the marks of bruising on her cheek and around her right eye.

'The Doctor is known to have enemies. Most prominent Party people have. It seems endemic among them.'

'I know nothing about that.' Trying to bring herself under control. 'Is this necessary? If I assure you I know nothing about Karl's death . . . I was shocked and . . . and sorry . . . really, I was . . . can't you leave me alone?'

'I'm conducting a murder investigation, Fräulein Lysander. That's not your real name, is it? Anyway I have to explore every avenue. Shall we go on?'

'I'm tired.'

'Makes two of us. Did the little doctor do that to your face?'

Her hand flew to her face. 'I had an accident . . .'

'One of Goebbels's propaganda messages?'

'I suppose I should think myself lucky, eh?' she said, viciously. 'After all, according to you, he had Karl strangled. Or did he do it personally?'

Lohmann gave a sad smile. 'I haven't said the Doctor killed Bruckner. Or had him killed. I'm merely exploring the possibility.'

'Then why don't you explore it with the Doctor himself?'

There was a degree of truth there, Lohmann told himself. He should be questioning the Doctor. But he doubted, after the incident with Ferdy Mann, if he would be given the opportunity. Even with the Hitler letter,

Goebbels could practise evasion with considerable ability. And, even if he was involved in the three killings, he would have ensured they were carried out by others. He decided to change tack.

'When you were with Bruckner, did he have any other enemies?'

She relaxed. Sitting down she sipped her cognac. A sense of relief, moving away from the subject of Doctor Goebbels.

'None that I knew of. He was a minor Party official. Too minor to have real enemies. He used to say, only at the top does one collect enemies. And he was far from the top.'

'He knew Hitler.'

'My father knew the Kaiser. He was a gardener at the Palace.'

'Other women?'

She shrugged, giving a small smile. 'Not while I was with him. Unlike the Doctor, Karl was a one-woman-at-a-time character. Oh, there had been others, but I never knew them. And I wasn't interested. Karl was . . . was . . .' She hesitated, took another sip of brandy, and became silent.

'Anything about Bruckner you can tell me will be of use.'

'He was . . . a kind man. A considerate man.'

'A sterling character. Without fault?'

'Oh, he had his faults. A very careful man with money.'

'Usually comes of not having very much.'

She agreed. 'I don't think he ever had. We had that in common. And another thing.'

'That was . . .?'

'Ambition. He . . . he wanted to rise in the Party. Believed he would.'

'By diligence and hard work?' Lohmann smiled now himself. 'It doesn't often happen that way. In the Party, it seems to be who you know, and how much that "who" will do for you.'

'Why do you think I left him for Goebbels?' The reply had an element of bitterness in it. 'You know, he understood. That was his fault. He too was ambitious.'

'And he had no Doctor Goebbels to help him.'

Her head jerked up. 'But he thought he had.'

He felt at once a sense of excitement. Something new might be added.

'Who?'

'I don't know.'

'Go on, please.'

'He would never tell me. He just said . . . there was someone . . . that he had great hopes . . . it was only a matter of time . . .'

The excitement died. 'Perhaps he meant Hitler? He was hoping to use that connection.'

'Perhaps. But I think there was someone else.'

'Or perhaps he was simply trying to stop you going to Goebbels?'

She contemplated her foot for a moment, then, standing, went over and poured herself another cognac. Lohmann realised that she had been drinking before his arrival and was close to inebriation. Swallowing the brandy, she laughed harshly.

'Bruckner couldn't stop me going to Goebbels,' she said. 'And he knew that.'

'Why?'

'Because only at the end, before I left him, did he begin to understand.'

Lohmann stared at her with unabashed curiosity. There was something he too did not understand.

She walked across the room towards him, brandy glass in her hand, swaying slightly.

'You see this,' she said, pointing to the bruises on her face. 'And not just here. Not just on the face. Other places.'

'Goebbels did that?'

'But not just because he likes doing things like this to women. I'm not even sure he does.' She stood facing Lohmann now. Still swaying. Brandy slopped over from the glass onto her hand. She brought hand and glass to her mouth and licked the back of the hand.

'No, I'm not even sure he likes doing it,' she giggled. 'You see, Lohmann, I'm the one who likes it. Likes having it done to me. You understand now?'

He should be able to understand. He'd seen it before. At times. The beaten wife who enjoyed the beatings. The baffled husband, who eventually began to enjoy beating her. Not commonplace, but there were enough of them.

'I'm sorry,' he said, not knowing what else to say.

'Why are you sorry?' she replied. 'There is nothing to be sorry about. I am . . . what I am. I like being what I am. So you see, Inspector, if you ever find you have some excess energy to work off, come and see Lys. She can always help . . . she enjoys helping . . .'

She sat down. Unsteadily. Smiling. And weeping at the same time. Tears carving deltas through face powder, running over bruises, the lividity of which did not concern her. The next day powder and make up would cover everything. And if it did not, she was beyond caring.

She looked up at him. 'You can stay with me if you want to. Until morning. Goebbels would not need to know.'

'I'm sorry,' he replied. 'But I have to go.'

'Your wife expects you? Of course.'

'My wife died two years ago.'

'Oh. I didn't know. Stay, then. I . . . I don't like to be on my own. It gets so cold in the early morning. Lohmann . . .?'

'I'm still sorry,' he said, and meant it. There was a temptation here. One he had to resist. Perhaps, within him, there was a strain of Lutheranism, an old-fashioned, pompous morality. It was a thought hard to accept. Inspector Lohmann of the Criminal Police, who, on his nights off, was a customer at an elegant brothel; why should he refuse this attractive gift, self-offered, from an attractive woman? Yet, a woman who took pleasure in the physical abuse of her own body by anyone to hand. There was something here he could not take. As if such abuse was against life itself. Christ, he was aware, at once, of his own pomposity.

'Lohmann,' the girl said. 'Lohmann? You have a first name? Everyone has a first name.'

'I'm just called Lohmann. Or Inspector Lohmann. Or Herr Lohmann.'

'You must have a first name?'

'I've forgotten it. Now I have to go, Fräulein.'

'Stay. Have another drink. Please.' Desperation now. She started to shiver. 'You like me, don't you? Then stay. I don't like to be alone.'

'I'd like to,' he lied, with kindness. 'But I have work to do. I must go now.'

He moved towards the door.

She threw the brandy glass at him. It shattered against the door. Fragments of glass landed on the sleeve of his coat.

'You fucking bastard!' she said evenly.

The throwing and smashing of the glass had somehow lightened Lohmann's mood.

'I may be a bastard,' he said. 'But for the rest, that's been only too infrequent. I will have to do something about that soon.'

He went out of the apartment. It wasn't worth taking the elevator to descend one floor. He walked down the stairs.

Into a dark foyer. No lights on. Only street lights shining faintly through glass doors. Street lights at a distance. Very little illumination.

So little that he did not see them until they were upon him. The first blow took him low in the stomach. The second, a kick, aimed at his testicles, was averted by his doubling up and took him on the thigh. He tried to look up, identify his assailants, but now the blows came thick and fast, from fists and from booted feet. He tried to strike out in retaliation, landing one good blow on a heavy face. But, for the rest, he was outnumbered and knew it. There were three of them, bulky figures, shapes pressing upon him. There was a fleeting recognition of one of them, one of the two men in Ferdy Mann's dressing room. Then he was forced to curl up to protect himself. Still blows rained on his back, head and legs. Pain, like a series of massive electric shocks, jerked through his body. He was unaware of his crying out, although cry out he did, and at least once, screamed. He did become aware, with some certainty, that the men attacking him would not care if they actually killed him. With this thought in his mind, he tried to accept death. Here. Now. But, in place of acceptance, there came a great rage. It wasn't time, he wasn't prepared. His daughter would not manage without him; not in the way he wished her to manage. He determined not to die.

Then the lights went on. Someone had heard the noise. Lohmann was barely aware of noise or indeed of the lights. He was still conscious but dazed. The pain, which had been considerable, did not increase but to his surprise seemed to disappear. As if he had become so inured to it as to no longer feel it. He was then aware of a distant whistle being blown, a familiar sound. The blows ceased to rain upon his body, and there was the sound of running feet.

After some moments, hands helped him to his feet and sat him on a bench-type seat in the corridor. He was aware of a policeman standing over him. Behind the policeman, other faces, curious, peering down at him. With some difficulty he reached into his inside jacket pocket and produced his warrant card. He showed this to the policeman who, officious though he had been, suddenly became solicitous. Lohmann was assisted into the caretaker's apartment where he was allowed to bathe his face. He also managed to dissuade the policeman from calling an ambulance.

'I'm all right. Thanks to a thick coat. In a moment, I want you to help me to my car.'

He was anxious to avoid going to a hospital where he might be forcibly detained. And where he would be a target, if his attackers decided to finish the job they had started. He was unsure as to whether he had merely been beaten or whether homicide was to be the end product. At the same time, while he washed his face, bathing the bruises and cuts, he knew he should not go home in this state. He had no wish to alarm his daughter or their housekeeper. Yet he needed to rest for a few hours. Only when the policeman helped him into his car did he decide where he would go.

He was surprised again by his ability to drive. He had a pounding headache, and every movement caused him pain. But behind the wheel of the car, the pain, to his relief, became minimal.

Ten minutes later he brought the car to a halt beside a

short flight of stairs leading to the door of a large house. The windows were heavily curtained yet, despite the lateness of the hour, light spilled from the edges of these curtains. He staggered up the stairs and, still swaying, rang the doorbell.

The door was opened by a negro. The man wore black striped trousers; a scarlet waistcoat over a white shirt; and a black bow tie. He recognised Lohmann at once.

'Mister Lohmann, what has happened to you!' He spoke German with a distinct American accent.

'Hello, Georg,' Lohmann said. 'I'm afraid I have a small but distinct amount of pain.' He stepped into the large hall of the house. 'Could you call Madame Kitty?'

But Madame Kitty, in a stylish black evening gown, was already descending the wide staircase that led into the hall. Red hair, elegantly styled, swept upwards from her white neck, forming an array of smooth curls on the top of her head, swept over to a fringe on her forehead. A startlingly attractive woman, she was in her early forties. She instantly recognised the new arrival.

'Lohmann?' she exclaimed. 'What has happened?'

'An encounter with disgusted clientele.' He swayed gently now, in the centre of the hallway. He presented a ruffled figure, flecks of blood on his shirt collar, livid bruises on his face.

Kitty now faced him, hands on her hips, a look of mock indignation on her face.

'You should be in hospital,' she insisted.

'Too many forms, too many questions. And the treatment here is better.'

'I'm not running a nursing home.'

'There are those who would disagree with that. One night, Kitty?'

Her face softened. 'I shall get annoyed if you think you have to ask. She turned to the negro. 'Georg, help him to the end bedroom.'

Gently, George took Lohmann's arm.

'Is that one of the rooms wired for sound, Kitty?' Lohmann asked.

'You heard about that? I suppose you would. Although I did think it was solely Gestapo business.'

'It is. I heard about it indirectly.'

Kitty shrugged. 'What could I do? They're bastards, but I can't fight them. Still, your bedroom isn't wired.'

'Good!'

'It's one of the rooms I use when the girls are sick.' Then, to Georg, 'Oh, and when he's up there, call our doctor.'

Lohmann grinned and the effort caused him two stabs of pain up each cheek. 'If he doesn't do much for the bruises, he'll tell me whether or not I've got a social disease.'

'I don't find that amusing,' Kitty replied. 'Get that ungrateful bastard upstairs. Before he puts the customers off by bleeding all over the carpet.'

An hour later, Lohmann lay between crisp white sheets. The doctor, a plump little man called Weil, had finished examining him.

'Nothing broken. For which you can thank God and that leather coat of yours. Fairly extensive bruising. And from head to toe. Very efficient beating you've taken.'

'They were probably medical students,' Lohmann said from between clenched teeth. The examination had increased his aches and pains.

'You'll have the bruises for a couple of weeks,' the doctor went on. 'But you should be all right after four or five days in bed . . .'

'No! Tomorrow, I have to be up.'

'I sometimes wonder why people like you bother calling me . . .'

'I didn't. Kitty did.'

'Doesn't matter. You get up tomorrow, I should certify you insane. Still, apart from being agonising, it probably won't do you too much harm. Unless you have a cerebral haemorrhage, and then you'll be dead.'

The bedroom door opened and Kitty came in.

'How is he?' she enquired.

'Unlike my usual patients in here, he is at least not pregnant.' Weil picked up his medical bag. 'No other calamities for me?'

'No, doctor.'

Weil went to the door, half turned, and looked back at

Kitty, his eyes twinkling. 'You know, If I wasn't a married man, I'd move in here as physician in residence. Only trouble is, I'd over-indulge in your merchandise, Kitty, and die young.'

He went out, leaving the policeman alone with the Madame.

'Did you . . .' Lohmann began.

'I telephoned your sergeant,' she cut in. 'He'll be here in the morning. Also he is telephoning your housekeeper to inform her and your daughter you will be working all night. Anything else?'

'Thanks, Kitty. You've been good.'

'I've few real friends. When I have one who is also in the police, I must keep him happy. Would you like some champagne? Medicinally I recommend it.'

Lohmann smiled. 'One small glass.'

'It's on its way. Anything else. Food?'

'No food.'

Kitty smiled now. 'A little orgy with three or four of my girls? Or have you had enough sado-masochism for one night?'

'Quite enough. Although, if she isn't busy . . .'

'I already anticipated that request. She's waiting outside. And I've given her the rest of the night off.'

'Kitty, you are superb. A beautiful, understanding woman . . .'

'As the ageing madame of a whorehouse – oh, a superior whorehouse, but still just that – I thank you.' She went to the door, opened it and called. 'Lucy!'

Lucy came in. Kitty went out and left them alone.

She was in her middle twenties, dressed in a flowing white evening gown, a pearl choker at her throat. Her hair was raven-black and hung to her shoulders. Her skin in contrast was very white and unblemished. She came quickly to the side of the bed, her face expressing genuine concern.

'You're hurt, Lohmann!'

'Bruised, but unbowed. I daren't bow. It would be sore. Have you a cigarette?'

She produced one from a small reticule in her hand, lit

it and handed it to him. Gently, she sat on the edge of the bed.

'Eventually someone will kill you, Lohmann.'

'Occupational hazard,' he replied. 'I have mine, you have yours.' The moment he said it he regretted it. Long ago he had agreed to accept her occupation and not cast it up at her. On this occasion, she ignored the remark.

'Did they intend to kill you?' she asked.

'I don't know. It may have been simply a warning: stay off their grass.'

'You'll do so?'

'Depends.'

'Doesn't it always? It's a terrible job you have.'

'Swimming in sewers. I know. But I'm a good swimmer. And it is all I know.' Suddenly he started to shiver uncontrollably.

'You're cold?'

'Reaction, I suppose.'

She stood up, without hesitation. Quickly she undressed until she stood before him naked. Her waist was slim, her breasts full, a large aureola around each nipple.

'Move over,' she said and raising the sheets climbed in beside him.

'I don't think I'll be much good to you tonight,' he said quietly, feeling a rare embarrassment.

'You are not meant to be good to me tonight. I am simply going to keep you warm.' So saying, she embraced him gently, with an infinite tenderness. Her touch seemed to ease the pains, her warmth taking the chill from his body.

After a time, they slept.

EIGHT

In the morning when Lohmann woke, Lucy had gone. The identation in the mattress was warm, and the aroma of her perfume was everywhere. He tried to move and at once stabbing pains brought back the memory of the beating he had taken. He shuddered. He was then angry at having been beaten by three of Goebbels's hirelings; but it was more than anger. There was a raw humiliation too, even stronger than anger. As if their blows had in some way defiled him, threatened his individuality, reduced him from the impartial law-enforcer down to one of the victims. He'd seen too many victims, felt pity for them. God forbid that anyone should feel pity for him. Inspector Lohmann, Criminal Police, was above that. He felt angry too at himself, allowing the girl Lucy to lie beside him, when he was in such a condition. As if he had been touched when he did not care to be touched.

Ever since his wife had died, he had built a wall around himself, yes, he could acknowledge that now. He did not wish to be placed in such a position again; where he loved and relied on another human being. Apart from Anna, there was no-one to whom he wished to give anything other than the most superficial affection. Not to Kitty, not to Lucy . . . there was no-one, he repeated that to himself. Anything other than that would confuse him, impede him from carrying out his job. No hatred either, he must have no hatred. Another unnecessary emotion. Magda, his wife, there had been enough pain there. Even remembering was still painful.

Remembering. Looking back . . . to that time. Her

friends, their friends, they had all been Magda's. Lohmann had only had acquaintances. Still only acquaintances or subordinates. Only one person, he could claim knew him; and not well. That was Reiner. Well, when you worked closely with someone, it was necessary to know and trust him. As he should know and trust you. But there was no emotion there, no need for it. A simple understanding was enough.

And then there was Lucy. The perfume all around him. Not cheap, Kitty would never permit cheap perfume, but pungent. Clinging. Six months after Magda died, he'd met Lucy. Here, during an enquiry. A matter of routine. Of course he had known Kitty, but then everyone knew Kitty. She would help, if she could, if it was a capital crime. Otherwise, no business of hers. That, he had always respected. Petty crime, what the hell . . . in the days when there'd been starvation in the streets . . . not important. Kitty had introduced him to Lucy. Six months after Magda. A decent interval. That's what they called it, a decent interval. Comprising of desolation, loneliness, night thoughts of suicide, wishing to be negated, dead, anything to rid himself of sorrow and pity and self-pity. All this, the decent interval.

The next night, he'd returned to Madame Kitty's and gone to bed with Lucy. An anodyne. They'd made love gently at first, but that had only stirred old memories. He had then turned to something else; a savage caressing, a rough entrance into her body as if accumulated pain had suddenly found release. Surprisingly she had responded, not in her customary professional simulation, but as if she too was undergoing a catharsis, she, too, ridding herself of the hypocrisy, the affectations of her profession. He had sensed this and later she had confirmed it. The relationship had begun.

Of course, it was ideal. The whore who loved me, he told himself. No, not loved, had an affection, but nothing more. No possibility of further grief.

He lay, staring at the white ceiling, Smooth, white, not even the slightest crack in the plaster, nothing to trouble the eye, nothing to disturb his contemplation. A watery sun shining through the open curtains. The temptation to go back to sleep.

He must not do that! There was work to be done. The investigation must continue. He forced himself to a sitting position, ignoring the stabs of pain through his body.

The bedroom door opened and Lucy came in carrying a tray.

'Breakfast,' she said. 'And how are you feeling?'

'Hungry.' It was true, he was very hungry.

The tray contained coffee, fruit juice, hot rolls and smoked sausage.

'And you have visitors,' she went on, turning to beckon Reiner into the room. Behind him, grey-uniformed, was Zoller.

Reiner said, 'Christ, they worked you over.'

'They enjoy their work.'

'Do we go after them?'

'Only if we find Goebbels is involved in the killings. Which I doubt.'

'I shall report this to Colonel Heydrich,' Zoller said. 'He will be interested. And angry.'

Lohmann said nothing but swallowed his fruit juice.

'We have news.' said Reiner. 'Müller.'

'He was to come in this morning.'

Reiner looked at his watch. 'You've overslept. It's one o'clock in the afternoon.

'Damn! Lucy . . .'

She was half way through the door now. 'I let you sleep. You needed it. Eat your breakfast and talk. It's not my business.' She went out, shutting the door behind her.

Reiner went on. 'Müller didn't come in. But then he couldn't. A caretaker in a warehouse by the canal found him. In the elevator. Garrotted. Surrounded by American dollar bills and Swiss francs. Not that they did him any good.'

Lohmann swore, very deliberately. Then he proceeded to eat a sausage.

'Müller's no loss,' said Zoller. 'A cheap gangster.'

Reiner threw him a cold look.

'Anything else?' Lohmann asked.

'I had a talk with Bruckner's housekeeper again. Funny

thing. Thought he'd got interested in the occult, she did. He was looking for some crackpot astrologer. A Doctor Gisevius.'

'I know about that. For once, Holtz has beaten you to it.' Lohmann was aware that he sounded unnecessarily smug.

'Who's Gisevius?' Zoller asked.

'Bruckner doesn't sound the type to be going in for astrology,' Reiner said.

'Stupid superstitions,' the SD man added.

Reiner stared bleakly at him. 'I should be careful, Captain Zoller. They say the Führer has quite an interest in matters of the occult. As does Himmler.'

He was pleased to see Zoller, for once, nonplussed.

'Holtz is out looking for this Gisevius character,' said Lohmann. 'You might check the SD and Gestapo files, Zoller. See if they have anything on him. Holtz was checking our police records.'

'We'll find him,' Reiner said with assurance. 'Maybe Bruckner did get tied in with some crackpots and they killed him.'

'And Preuss and Rudig too? And now Müller?' Lohmann threw the bedsheets to one side. He was naked. 'You two had better wait downstairs while I get dressed.'

They left. Lohmann, investigating the wash basin in a corner of the room, was pleased to discover shaving soap and an open razor. Donning only his underpants and trousers, he was shaving when he heard voices raised excitedly, and footsteps in the corridor.

The bedroom door opened yet again, and this time an excited Madame Kitty came in.

'You have another visitor, Inspector Lohmann,' she said with unaccustomed formality. Turning she stood aside. In SS uniform, Heydrich came into the bedroom.

'Thank you, madame,' he said, with a small nod of the head which served as a bow. 'If you would be good enough to leave us . . .'

Kitty gave a small bob, as if she had just been presented to at least the Kaiser, and went out. Heydrich waited until he heard the door shut behind her, before speaking.

'I was informed about your assault last night,' he said solicitously. 'I hope you are not badly injured.'

'I survived. If I can shave, I'm well enough.'

Heydrich surveyed the room, turning on the heels of his shining boots. 'You choose an interesting hospital, Inspector. I believe the nurses render every service.'

'And a few that aren't in the nursing manuals, Colonel.'

Heydrich smiled, and for the first time it was a genuine smile.

'I can imagine, Lohmann. You see, I'm quite human, despite your obvious reservations . . .'

'I wasn't aware I'd made any,' Lohmann replied, continuing to shave.

'Ah, but I know how you non-party people look on the SS and the Gestapo. As if we are not quite . . . ordinary. We too have our needs and emotions. As a matter of fact, it was on account of a woman that I left the navy.'

Lohmann nodded. 'It was in our police files for a time. Until that particular file disappeared.'

'A small precaution on my part,' Heydrich admitted. 'But, it happened. And is now forgotten. You know, I was pleased when I heard you were here. And come often, I believe.'

'From a time after my wife died. It's no secret. Why does it please you? To have something on me, Colonel? Senior police officer consorts with whores?'

Again the laugh. This time, more calculated. 'No, no. You're not important enough for us to condemn you for that, my dear fellow. It merely illustrates your own basic humanity. I was, I must admit, slightly in awe of your Olympian detachment. Afraid I suppose that your ability as a detective came from such a strong detachment from the world of ordinary mortals. A little, if I am not being blasphemous, Hitlerian. Yes, not unlike the Führer. Even to your omission in not joining the Party. Of course Hitler is the Party, but you choose to stand to one side. There are actions of ours you don't approve of?'

'Does it matter?'

Heydrich looked thoughtful. 'Yes. Just now, for me, it matters.'

Lohmann was washing traces of shaving soap from his

face. 'You people seem so anxious to justify your actions. As if you had a conscience about them.'

'Yes, perhaps.' It was a surprising admission, especially from a man like Heydrich. 'You must understand, Lohmann, everything we do is for the future of our country.'

'Even the burning of the books of which you disapprove?'

Heydrich's gesture was dismissive. 'A symbolic gesture. A turning-away from a dead past.'

'Very glib. Facile. And how do you explain the Party's anti-Semitism?'

'Of course I have nothing against the Jews myself . . .'

'Strange. Göring said exactly the same thing.'

The Colonel flushed. 'I do not echo Göring! I mean what I say. Nothing against them. Nothing, you understand? I have to carry out certain duties which are not pleasant to me.'

Lohmann turned from the shaving mirror and the basin to find Heydrich mopping his brow with a large handkerchief. The man was sweating profusely. Seemed almost depressed. Making an effort. But what kind of an effort? And why?

'It is necessary that you understand my position,' Heydrich went on. 'I have to be hard. It is expected. They have said it. Necessary to be hard. So that everything can be done. There is no room for emotion, for sentimentality.'

'Is that an official decree?' Lohmann asked not without irony.

'Yes. Yes, it is expected. You don't think I like it. You don't think I enjoy my job?'

'As a matter of fact, yes, I thought you enjoyed your job.' Lohmann struggled into his undervest.

'You can't think that. I . . . I have to steel myself daily to carry out many actions I abhor. That's bad enough. But to know that, as we gain strength, there will be many more such actions, that is infinitely worse. But necessary. We are rebuilding German society. To rebuild, one must first demolish. From inside. As I say, without sentiment or emotion.'

'You would even demolish that which is worth keeping?'

Heydrich's head moved up and down. 'Yes, yes, yes. Necessary. To start afresh. To build from new foundations. To rid ourselves of the dry rot of Weimar. To eradicate the curse of Jewish international finance bleeding the nation . . .'

'You people keep coming back to this fantasy of Jewish international finance. Even if it exists, what has it to do with the Jewish university professor, the small Jewish shopkeeper, the Jewish ex-soldier who won an Iron Cross fighting on the Western Front? They have nothing to do with international finance.'

Again the Colonel nodded violently. 'I know, I know. But we have to be seen to be fighting them . . . even the small man. We have to be seen to be doing this. That is why you have to understand my position. I am forced to be hard. But, inside, you have to see I hate it all.'

'Then . . . resign, Colonel, resign.'

Heydrich stiffened. 'It is my vocation. To be a part of the building of the new Germany.' A long pause. 'Please. I . . . I wish you to understand.'

Lohmann had now donned his shirt and was taking his time buttoning it. Time to think. To absorb his surprise at Heydrich's need to explain.

'Why me, Colonel?' he finally asked.

'Because I feel it is necessary for you to understand.'

'Perhaps it's just too ambivalent for me.'

Heydrich suddenly drew himself to his full height. He seemed to tower over Lohmann, a blond giant, the ideal representative of the new Germany.

'I was concerned with your welfare, Inspector Lohmann,' he said formally. 'I am pleased you are on your feet. And will be able to carry on your investigation.'

'I am able to do that.'

'Very good! As you will know, the Party rally starts at Nuremberg tomorrow. I am expected to be present. Your reports will be forwarded to me, and I will of course pass these to the Führer. I look forward to a successful outcome quickly. This matter is . . . an irritation.' He clicked his heels and turned away from the inspector.

And then he said, face averted, 'Remember what I have said. I do not like what I have to do. But it is necessary, and I have to live with it.'

He went out of the room. There were whispers and scurrying feet in the corridor. Lohmann finished dressing, small aches all over his body. As he was carefully pulling on his jacket, Reiner came back into the room.

'The hospital visitor, what did he want?'

'Solicitous about my health. And I think he wanted me to feel sorry for him.'

'What?'

'Yes, I think he wanted that.' A pause. Lohmann adjusted his tie. 'Come. I want to go home and change into a clean shirt. And suit, I think.'

They went downstairs. Lucy was waiting alone in the hallway.

'Wait in the car with Zoller,' Lohmann said to Reiner. When the sergeant had gone he turned to the girl.

'Thank you.'

'You don't have to thank me,' the girl replied.

'I do.'

'Come back tonight.'

'I'd like to. But I'm not sure.'

'Please.'

'Maybe.' He held her by the shoulders. 'You should get out of this place.'

'Why? I like Kitty. She's decent to us. I make money.'

'There are other ways of making money.'

Lucy laughed. 'Oh, not from you, Lohmann. Not that kind of thing from you. You'll ask me next how I got into the game. They all ask that, all the kind gentlemen.'

'I never have.'

'Thank God for that. Otherwise you get the answer you want. That's the way to handle such questions. The answer the customer wants. The poor country girl seduced by the cruel Prussian landlord. Or the little shopgirl who lost her job in the depression and would have starved to death. Or, how about, I'm just naturally a nymphomaniac? You'd be surprised how many men like that one.'

'Maybe I'm not saying you should get out of here. Maybe I'm saying you should get out of Berlin.'

'Why? I'm a Berliner.'

'It won't be the same. The rats are taking over from the people.'

'You would take me out of Berlin, Lohmann?'

A pause. Lohmann staring over her shoulder into the middle distance.

He broke the silence. 'Perhaps. In time.'

'You would take me? And your daughter?'

Lohmann, staring at her now, 'Yes.'

'You're a bloody fool, Lohmann,' she said evenly.

'Maybe.'

'I'm a whore! Oh, it's fine, you visit me now and then. That's what I'm for. We get on well, we fuck well, you're kind and generous. Not like some of the others. And remember, Lohmann, there are others. Always.'

'Not important,' he said and believed it.

'Go away, Lohmann, and don't paint pretty pictures. The whore with the heart of gold, she doesn't exist. So go on, get on with your work, and I'll get on with mine.'

He kissed her gently on the lips and went out. She stared after him. No sign of emotion. Just staring.

Lohmann climbed into the rear of the car beside Reiner. Zoller was at the wheel.

'You don't have an easy life, Inspector,' Reiner said, grinning.

'Don't be envious, Sergeant. When you're my age, it may all fall upon you. Until then, all life is but a training.' He leant forward. 'Good of you to drive, Captain Zoller. We will go to headquarters first. I want to hear from Holtz. Then I think, a trip home to change my clothes.'

Despite his bruises, Lohmann felt good. For once. And not, he was sure, for long. As the car moved off, a beggar, tattered coat be-medalled was singing, almost to himself, *The Watch on the Rhine*.

Later that afternoon. Lohmann's office.

Lohmann, speaking to Reiner. 'Holtz? Where is Holtz? I sent him to find this Gisevius character.'

'He hasn't reported in.'

'Nothing? Not even a telephone call?'

'Nothing.'

'Very well. Two jobs for you, Reiner. Find Gisevius. And find Holtz. He should have found Gisevius by this time.'

'One more thing, Inspector.'

'Yes?'

'Nothing in SD or Gestapo records.'

'I don't believe that. They know every charlatan in the game. I told Holtz not to report to the SD before he came to me . . .'

Reiner coughed loudly, deliberately.

Lohmann looked up. 'All right, what is it?'

'I don't like Holtz but you can't expect him to obey an order like that. If he is SD . . . and he is . . . he has no choice.'

'All right, Sergeant, see if you can find him. And this . . . Gisevius. Incidentally, we haven't even looked in our own records. You might check there on Gisevius.'

'Should have been done first thing,' Reiner mumbled.

'Do it now. First thing. I'm going home to change.' He rose and his ribs creaked. More pain. Damn Doctor Goebbels! At the door, he stopped, looked back at Reiner.

'You know, if the Gestapo say they have no file on Gisevius, if Holtz goes to look for him, Gisevius just may be important.'

'That's if Holtz didn't make him up to keep you looking the wrong way.'

'Impossible. I look both ways at once, Sergeant.'

Lohmann drove himself to his apartment. Aching still, his body demanded a shower and clean clothes.

His housekeeper, Frau Anselm, faced him in the kitchen.

'Ach, what has happened to you, Herr Lohmann?' She was plump, in her sixties, and expansive in her facial expressions. Also, hands were wrung in distress.

'A small accident,' he replied. 'No need to concern yourself.'

'No need,' Frau Anselm wailed. 'No need, he says. Comes home looking as if he's been beaten to death and he says, no need.'

'I would like a coffee.'

'Iodine, you should have, all over. But, I'll make coffee.'

After his shower, wrapped in a large towelling bathrobe, Lohmann sat at the kitchen table drinking coffee. Leaning on the cooker, Frau Anselm stared down at him. He became self-conscious, and decided to change the subject.

'The house is no trouble for you?' he asked.

'The house? No, the house is no trouble.'

Something in her voice caused him to half turn in his chair.

'Something else? Anna?'

Frau Anselm's shoulders rose and fell briefly.

'Tell me,' Lohmann persisted.

'She is . . . a nice girl. But now, is difficult.'

'In what way?'

'It was all right when she was smaller. But now . . .' Then, at once, the housekeeper showed her irritation. 'What can you expect? Her mother is dead. Her father . . . is rarely here. Oh, I know you have to be at your work. But it is now . . . Anna is subjected to . . . to these influences . . . these new ideas.'

She broke off and Lohmann was aware of a sudden flash of fear on her face.

'Oh, I don't say they are wrong . . . after all, they are taught them at school. Anyway I know nothing of politics . . .'

'But you know they are wrong,' Lohmann said quietly.

Hands twisted around a dish towel. 'My husband, Herr Lohmann, my late husband, he was an engineer on the factory floor. A working man. An artisan. That was his work. Maybe he was a Communist . . . certainly he was a Socialist. . . .'

'You've never talked of him before.'

Frau Anselm straightened up defiantly. 'These people . . . these Nazis. They killed him. On the street, one evening. They beat him, and he died. I don't talk about it. I was told, if I want to go on living, I must be quiet. You understand?'

'I understand.'

'I have to keep quiet. Especially in front of your daughter.'

Lohmann sipped his coffee in silence for a moment. Thinking. That a fourteen-year old girl should engender fear in a middle-aged widow. Not right. Humiliating for the housekeeper. For him, too. For his home.

'I'll speak to her,' he said.

Ten minutes later, he was dressed, when he heard Anna come in from school. Banging upstairs and into her own room. When he had finished tying his tie, he went into her room.

She was lying on her narrow bed, a book open. As he entered, she twisted around to stare at him.

'What happened to you?' she said.

His hands went to his face. He had almost forgotten his bruises.

'Some of your friends,' he replied, looking around the room. His eyes settled on the Hitler Youth uniform laid out on a chair.

'Not my friends!' she insisted. 'Father, you don't think that?'

'I know it. You wear this?' He indicated the uniform.

'We're all in the Hitler Youth. We have to be. If only I'd joined sooner I might have been at Nuremberg this week. At the rally.'

'They really sew it all up,' Lohmann said.

'It . . . it shows we're all one country . . . one Party.'

'And if you don't want to join the Party?'

She scowled. 'Only Jews and gypsies . . .

'And what's wrong with Jews and gypsies? They served in the front line in the last war! Now what happens to them? They take people like that away at six o'clock in the morning. The Gestapo believes that is the best time. Resistance is low, people are less likely to resist. With most of them, they're not heard of again. They disappear into the cellars at Albrechstrasse. Gestapo headquarters. Sometime, I'll tell you what goes on in there.'

Anna flared up indignantly. 'Lies! Spread by the Jews . . .'

'Not so! I'm not a Jew. I'm a policeman. I know. I've even been there. I've seen the results.'

She looked around, baffled. 'No . . . not so. Enemies. Enemies of the State!'

'Merely people who disagree with the Party. They don't

allow disagreement, Anna. Don't you think there's something wrong there?'

Silence. A long moment. Then, 'But you still work for them.'

'I work for the police. To maintain the law. Eventually, they'll take over the police completely. That's when I shall resign.'

He thought, he'd never put that into words before. Never made a definite decision. Now he had.

'Anyway, at this minute, I'm still working for the police. And I have to go on duty. I've told you my thoughts. I want you to think now. And look around you. You're an intelligent girl. You'll see. But, until you do, I don't want you wearing that uniform in the house. And I don't want you worrying Frau Anselm. I would hate to think of my daughter as a professional informer. For the State. Especially this State . . .'

'I . . . I wouldn't really have informed on her. Not really. I think I was just joking . . .'

'Then don't! Especially about her husband. He was beaten to death by Nazi Stormtroopers. That's the truth. Because he just didn't happen to believe in the philosophy of Adolf Hitler. I don't think that's such a crime. Anyway, think about it.'

He went out of the room. Out of the house. It was time he was back at police headquarters.

There were fewer uniforms on the streets. A small relief. They were out of the city, moving on Nuremberg and the big rally. What was it Goebbels had been quoted in the newspapers as calling this year's rally? 'The Triumph of the Will.' All roads leading to Nuremberg. The Führer would speak. The masses would 'heil'. And a Star of David was scrawled on the window of a shop near police headquarters. People still begged in the streets. And the Führer will ask only for time. One thousand years. The thousand-year Reich.

Reiner was waiting in his office.

'You look human again,' said the sergeant. 'And I found out why Holtz didn't report back here. He went straight to the SD. They say they've borrowed him and sent him to Nuremberg. Part of the police detail.'

'Nuremberg! The bastards. They wanted him out of the way.'

Reiner looked puzzled. 'I don't understand. Why should they . . .?'

Lohmann sat behind his desk and studied his finger tips. 'I don't know. Let's get Heydrich on the phone.'

Two minutes later they were connected to Heydrich's office. A cool female voice answered. 'I'm sorry but the Colonel has left for Nuremberg.'

'Of course,' Lohmann replied. 'He told me he was going. All right, put me through to whoever's in charge of personnel.'

He waited. Reiner lit a cigarette and Lohmann beckoned to him to give him one. He was lighting the cigarette when he was connected.

'SD and SS personnel.' A thin, slightly hesitant voice.

'To whom am I speaking?' Lohmann asked.

'Lieutenant Eichmann.'

Good, I outrank him, Lohmann thought. 'This is Inspector Lohmann of the Criminal Police.'

Unctuous now, as well as hesitant. 'What can I do for you, Inspector?'

'One of my men, Detective Holtz, I believe he also works for the SD.'

The hesitancy became more apparent. 'I'm sorry, I have no information on that. Occasionally we are assisted by your people. For which we are very grateful. I believe you are assisting Colonel Heydrich yourself . . .'

'You're wrong. Colonel Heydrich is assisting me! I've been informed that Holtz has been seconded to Nuremberg . . .'

'That's quite possible, Herr Inspector. Because of the rally we have drafted a number of men into the city. There were rumours the Communists might try and disrupt the various parades.'

'Holtz was engaged in an investigation of mine. Your people had no right to . . .'

The voice cut in, less hesitant now. 'There has been some misunderstanding here, Herr Inspector. We requested from Chief Inspector Murnau a number of men. They duly reported. Your Holtz must have been one of them. Of course all he had to do was inform us he was on a case and . . .'

'Yes, yes, Lieutenant. I've heard the story before. Thank you and goodbye.' Lohmann hung up.

'Not helpful?' Reiner asked.

'A good and efficient liar. All right, we look for this Gisevius character ourselves.'

Reiner smiled. 'I've already started. He may not have had a record with the SS or the SD but he has got one with us. It's on the desk in front of you.'

Lohmann glared at him. 'Sergeant, you too are a bastard.'

'But I'm one of the good ones.'

The file was lying on the top of his in-tray. One arrest, one conviction. Hamburg, 1927. Lohmann read on.

'Gisevius, Hans Albrecht. Born Saxony, 1893. (No further details.) Former engineer, Imperial Navy. Dishonourable discharge, 1925, after court-martial for desertion. Worked in Carlos' Circus as fortune teller. Then set up in Hamburg as a consultant in the Occult. Used this to blackmail Avrom Hersheimer, a Cologne business man. Arrested on Hersheimer's evidence. (Arresting Officers, Sergeant Haller and Detective Braun, Hamburg Criminal Police.) Sentenced to two years' imprisonment, Hamburg. Released on parole 1929, after serving eighteen months. Informed parole officer of move to Berlin. Last known address, 14 Alexanderplatz. No further convictions.'

Lohmann closed the file and looked up at Reiner.

'Oh, he's gone from the address in there. 1930, he moved,' said Reiner.

'Holtz said something about him writing a book . . .'

'There's a note attached to the file. H. A. Gisevius, Doctor of Occult Philosophy . . . I think he awarded himself the degree . . . the book was called *An Approach to the Unseen Universe*. Old Sergeant Charlus of Records has a magpie mind. He saw the book advertised. I think he knows every name in our files. Anyway, he recognised the name, clipped out the advert and attached it to the file. Just in case.'

Lohmann turned over the charge sheet. Clipped to the

file was a two line book advert. '*Approach to the Unseen Universe*, occult experience by Dr H. A. Gisevius. Pub. by Kreisler GmbH, Morgengasse.'

'I've always thought Charlus should have been promoted to inspector years ago,' Lohmann said. 'You telephoned this place?'

'Phone's been disconnected. For non-payment of bill.'

'Anything known about this Kreisler?'

'One-man firm. Vanity publishing. You pay the costs, he gets your book printed and published. Strictly esoteric stuff.'

Lohmann nodded. 'In other words, crackpot stuff on the occult, covering up a nice little trade in pornography.'

'That's about it. The Vice Squad know him. But he's never been charged.'

'Right. That gives us a lever. Let's visit Herr Kreisler.'

Morgengasse 11 was a small shop in a narrow alley. Window panes were thick with dust, completely obscuring the titles of the few volumes behind them. Inside, a low ceiling weighed down on a small counter surrounded by half-empty bookshelves. A row of magazines ran along the counter, all of them in plain brown paper covers, titles inked on the paper. These ranged from *Servant of the White Slavers* to *School Girl Chastisement*. There was no-one behind the counter when they entered. Lohmann picked a hard-back volume from the nearest bookcase and glanced at the title: *The Roman Empire Under the Whip and the Lash*.

'Highly specialised tastes,' he murmured to Reiner.

'Oh, I don't know,' replied the sergeant thumbing through one of the brown-paper covered magazines. This seemed to specialise in close-up photographs of pudenda. 'Something for everybody here.'

From a door behind the counter came a diminutive figure, a bald-headed little man, wing collar and tie protruding from under a greasy pullover. The head shone under the solitary electric light bulb illuminating the shop.

'I can do something for you, gentlemen?' The voice was high pitched and reedy.

'Herr Kreisler?' Reiner asked.

'I am he.'

'We believe you published a book by a certain H. A. Gisevius?'

Small eyes became smaller. 'I published a book by a Doctor Gisevius. It is out of print, but I could probably find you a second-hand copy.'

'We're not so much interested in the book as the present address of the author.'

A pause. The eyes seemed to become hooded like those of a snake.

'I'm afraid I'm not at liberty to furnish such information.'

Lohmann stepped in front of Reiner. 'I'm afraid you'll have to be. We're from Criminal Police. You will give us Gisevius's address.'

The bald head flushed. 'I . . . I'm not sure if . . .'

Now Lohmann leaned forward. He could smell Kreisler's breath, a rancid odour with a distinct trace of onions.

'You will be sure. Otherwise, within one half-hour the Vice Squad will be here, and five minutes after they arrive, you will be under arrest for disseminating pornographic material.'

Kreisler nodded. He kept nodding as he called out, 'Otto, Otto, bring my ledger . . .'

Otto turned out to be an acne-scarred youth in his teens, dressed only in a discoloured vest and crumpled woollen trousers. He appeared a moment later from the back-shop carrying a large ledger which he placed on the counter in front of the nodding Kreisler.

'My . . . my nephew,' Kreisler nodded towards the youth who at once scurried back through the doorway into darkness. The bookseller thumbed through the ledger.

'It's here . . . it's here . . . just let me find it. Ah, yes, Gisevius, here we are. Rosenthaler Platz. Number 32. That is an apartment. Gisevius's apartment.'

Reiner had written the address in his notebook. 'Thank you, Herr Kreisler.'

'My privilege, gentlemen.' The sigh of relief was audible.

'One thing more, Kreisler,' said Lohmann. 'Someone else was asking about this address? Another police officer?'

The bald head nodded again. 'That is so, sir. A Detective Holtz.'

'You gave him the address?'
'I did. Was it wrong to . . ?'
'No. But you haven't been in touch with Gisevius? You haven't warned him that the police are looking for him?'
'No, no, not at all. Why should I? Gisevius is nothing to me. A writer. Not a good writer. . .'
'You published his book.'
'Ah, but he paid for it to be published. Occasionally one gets such people. Had he not done so, I would not have published the book. No merit there, I'm afraid.'
'Not a great deal anywhere,' Lohmann replied, with a final glance at the dusty shelves. 'Good day, Herr Kreisler.'
It was starting to rain again as they climbed into the police car.
'Holtz was there,' Reiner said.
'Yes,' Lohmann replied. 'And despite my request that he report to me, he had to go to the SD first. I think Holtz will have to make up his mind who he is working for.'
'Why send him to Nuremberg?'
'To get him out of the way. To . . . delay the investigation.'
'But why?'
Lohmann settled into the passenger seat. 'You have to understand the Party mentality. Nobody really wants anybody else to be successful. Only themselves. The SD doesn't want the Criminal Police to solve these murders. For the simple reason that they want to solve them themselves.'
'So Heydrich will put every obstacle in our way?'
'I doubt if Heydrich cares too much. He's rather well-established with the Party. No, someone lower down.'
Reiner grinned. 'Zoller?'
'Possibly. Perhaps the SD as a whole. Conditioned reflex. Don't encourage the Criminal Police to achieve success. The *Sicherheitsdienst* must not only be perfect but it must be seen to be perfect. Now, for God's sake, drive and stop asking questions!'
Reiner started the car as the rain began to beat down on its hood.

NINE

There was always a time during any investigation when Lohmann felt a growing sense of anticipation. As if he was approaching the final solution, the lead that would result in his completion of the case. It was too often a deceptive feeling. Any prolonged murder case brought out such a feeling more than once before the affair was finished. There was too a conflicting emotion. If a murder case was not solved within forty-eight hours, then the chances that it would be solved at all were greatly reduced. Most murders took place within families, and guilt was so often obvious. But this was different. Three seemingly unconnected individuals had been killed over a period of weeks. And Lohmann himself had been working now for around the forty-eight hour period. Yet he could not say that he had any idea who had committed these murders, nor had he the slightest idea of why they had been committed. He was inclined to dismiss the trail that had led to Reichsminister Goebbels. Had Bruckner been the only victim, there might have been enough motive certainly. But there was no motive on Goebbels's part for the slaying of Preuss or Rudig. Now, there was a tenuous lead to Gisevius. Tenuous was the word. Who was Gisevius? How was he involved? No reason to presume on the man's guilt, no reason to be sure of even his involvement. And yet there was that strange sense of anticipation.

Lohmann put it from his mind. Senseless to live in hope. That would indicate his own frustration; the feeling that he was running in circles, getting nowhere.

They parked on Rosenthaler Platz. The rain had settled

into a dismal drizzle. Lohmann sat in the car while Reiner went into the square to find Number 32. Prerogative of rank, Lohmann thought. The sergeant gets wet while his superior keeps dry. Until necessary.

Reiner returned to the car three minutes later.

'Down the alley. Number 32. Not exactly the most salubrious dwelling place.'

Buttoning his coat up to the neck, Lohmann descended from the car. They moved past scurrying pedestrians into the alley. As they turned the corner they were greeted by a familiar figure. Hand clutching innumerable strings attached to innumerable coloured balloons, the Blind Man, oblivious of weather, was approaching them.

As he came closer, the Blind Man hesitated, his nose seemed to twitch, he took a deep breath, and said. 'Buy a balloon, Inspector Lohmann. It is Inspector Lohmann, isn't it?'

Lohmann stopped in front of the figure, glanced up at the balloons. 'I thought you could always tell.'

The Blind Man wiped the rain from his dark glasses. 'At night, I can. Not so easy in the daylight.' He paused, coughed, and then said. 'The man you're looking for? He killed Müller too, didn't he?'

'It's probable.'

'He's been here. Looking for Gisevius. Like you are.'

Lohmann stared at his own reflection in the dark glasses. His astonishment was obvious to Reiner.

'How the hell . . .' Lohmann started to say, and stopped.

'Herr Holtz was looking for Gisevius,' said the Blind Man. 'So I presumed you were too. Of course I know Gisevius. Not that I would have shopped him to Holtz. I don't like Holtz. And Gisevius, what's he trying to do? Grub up a living like the rest of us.'

Reiner couldn't contain himself. 'You said you saw the killer here?'

The Blind Man's mouth turned down at the edges. 'Not saw, Herr Reiner. I can't see. I'm blind. No, after Holtz was here, sometime after, another man came. I heard him. And I knew. You see, Müller was decent to me. And that man killed Müller. I could smell it. The smell of death. If

I'd had my eyes, he'd be dead. Under the grass in the Tiergarten, sleeping with the maggots.'

'He got to Gisevius?' Lohmann asked.

'No. Gisevius was out. Doctor Gisevius, not at home. Doctor, eh? The clever one, Gisevius. But with the other one looking for him, he's in trouble.'

'We can get to him first, then?'

'The place is at the end of the alley. Number 32. Up the stairs.'

'Thanks,' said Lohmann and meant it.

'The other one's still around. Still the smell there. Like blood.'

The blind Man shuffled on, stick tapping, balloons in the air. Lohmann and Reiner moved, quickly now, down the alley and into the doorway of Number 32.

What happened to the Blind Man next can only be surmised. It is a fact that he never got out of the alley. At the time Lohmann and Reiner were climbing the narrow stairway of Number 32, the Blind Man certainly came to a halt. He must have sensed the other man. And would have stopped. There was no place to which he could have run. He could only stand, whatever senses he had alive and alert. Words may have passed. The Blind Man would inevitably have excused his presence, as he did to strangers.

'I'm blind. I see nothing. May I pass?'

Yet if he could truly smell blood, he would have been smelling it just then. And the other man may well have spoken; almost certainly so, a small justification, and a rare opportunity to give one.

'For a blind man, you say too much. And you see too much.'

Somewhere on Rosenthaler Platz, a car may have sounded its horn. Certainly there must have been some noise. The Blind Man's throat would have attempted a protest as the cord curled around it. The expert, because he was an expert, would have timed his move to the first available sound. And, as the cord tightened, of course the sound was cut off, becoming a subdued, unpleasant, choking gargle. Fingers released the strings of uncounted coloured balloons which, against the falling rain, floated gently upwards. The white stick fell from the other hand. And as the assailant twisted the segment of wood, the Blind Man would fall, first to his knees on the cobbles, then face down, smashing the dark glasses . . . they were so discovered . . . fragments cutting into his eyebrow. But, by then, he would not have felt the glass slivers. Or even the soaking dampness of the cobbles. He would have been beyond sensation of any kind.

Number 32 was on the second landing. The door had a piece of paper tacked to it. 'Doctor Gisevius' was the legend, carefully printed in large letters and black ink.

Reiner knocked on the door. Heavily and sharply. They waited. After a moment, the door opened some two inches. A large eye stared out at them.

'No consultations at this time!' said the voice behind the eye.

'Open up, Gisevius. Criminal Police,' Reiner spoke the accustomed words in heavy tones.

The door did not move.

'I've done nothing. Leave me alone.'

'Did anyone say you had?' Lohmann said.

'You are the Gestapo!'

'We told you. We're Kripos.'

'Investigating the murder of Karl Bruckner . . .' Reiner added.

The door moved. The voice was trying to shut it. Reiner put his booted toe in, hard. The door stayed open.

Lohmann said, 'You knew Bruckner!'

Another voice, a woman's, came from behind the door. 'What's happening here?'

'Police. Not the Gestapo. The Police.'

'You can't keep them out. Let them in.'

A moment. Silence. No movement. And then, the sound of a chain being unlatched. And the door opened.

Gisevius stood back as they entered. He was of medium height, balding, with large, protruding eyes. Some kind of thyroid deficiency there, Lohmann thought. A shirt, minus collar, an old woollen jumper, threadbare at the sleeves, and heavy corduroy trousers. This was Gisevius, nervous, eyes never still.

Behind him, the woman. Small, in her thirties, dressed in a black shirt and a blouse once white. The face was marred by a large purple birthmark across the right cheek and lower jaw. And the woman walked with a limp. A club foot. Again, Lohmann thought, someone with a large share of misfortune.

'I am Gisevius,' the man said, straightening up.

'Come in here,' the woman said, ushering them from the tiny hall into the nearest room. A living room. A lived-in room. A sofa and two old armchairs, stuffing coming out of all of them at awkward corners. There were a lot of awkward corners. A table stood in the centre of the room. On this was a bottle of milk, half full, two cups containing the dregs of coffee, and a plate with several segments of black bread, and a wedge of unhealthy looking cheese.

'Leave us, Paula,' said Gisevius.

'No. The Fräulein will stay,' Lohmann responded. There was something about the woman, a sense of concern about Gisevius, that might be useful.

'I am Inspector Lohmann. This is Sergeant Reiner. You are Hans Albrecht Gisevius. And the Fräulein . . .?'

She replied before he could. 'Paula Korman.'

'Fräulein Korman is a . . . a friend,' Gisevius added.

Lohmann acknowledged the relationship with a curt nod. Reiner took his cue to start the interrogation.

'Hans Gisevius. Two years' imprisonment, Hamburg, 1927. Blackmailing one Avrom Hersheimer.'

Gisevius looked at the woman, as if to see her reaction. There was none.

'A mistake. A misunderstanding,' said Gisevius.

'The mistake was yours, 'Reiner replied. 'You were known as a confidence man.'

'Only that one conviction, 'Gisevius insisted. Another look at Paula Korman. 'It was a difficult time. You understand, Paula?'

'You don't have to explain to me, Hans.' Spoken again without expression. But with sincerity.

'She is good for me,' Gisevius explained to Lohmann.

'Paula. Very good. Everyone needs some . . . some affection.'

'We're only interested in the murder of Bruckner. And two others. Rudig and Preuss.'

If he had heard of them, Gisevius gave no indication.

'Come on, Gisevius. You must have known Bruckner. He knew you. He was looking for you before he was killed.'

Yet another look at the woman. And back to them after a barely perceptible nod from her.

'I knew him. He came to me for a reading. His fortune. I told him he was going to die.'

'How did you know that?' Reiner went on.

'I cast his horoscope. It was there.'

There was something too glib about the answer. Also a touch of the actor, Lohmann could see. As if he enjoyed the interrogation now.

'The sergeant asked you how you knew. Now tell us,' Lohmann persisted.

'I told you . . .'

Lohmann suddenly, but with deliberation, kicked out at the leg of the table. The table shuddered.

'Don't waste my time, Gisevius! I'm not a client, a mug, a customer to be conned or spooked. I want the truth about Bruckner. Now! Why Bruckner looked for you. What he wanted from you. He wasn't a believer in your hocus-pocus. He was a hard-nosed Party man. And, I, Herr Gisevius, am a steel-nosed policeman. So, tell me!'

Gisevius was staring at the worn carpet underfoot. His eyes seemed to protrude even more. The woman stepped forward.

'Leave him alone. He's not well . . .'

'He's afraid,' said Lohmann. 'And he will have more to be afraid of, if he doesn't give me an honest answer.'

Gisevius gestured with his right hand as if to quieten them down. 'It's . . . it's all right. I'm all right. You see, Bruckner was an old comrade. We knew each other before.'

'In the navy?' Reiner asked.

'Yes. In the navy.'

'He merely came to you as an old comrade . . .?'

'That was it!'

'You think we're stupid, Gisevius. Now, try the truth.'

The man's face was chalk white. His hands started to tremble. He started to swallow hard, Adam's apple moving up and down in the thin neck.

'No! No more. Please!'

'The truth. The whole story.'

The woman stepped forward. 'Can't you see he's terrified?'

Reiner stepped in front of her. 'Please, Fräulein, do not interrupt.'

Gisevius turned his back on Lohmann. His shoulders were sagging, his head down.

'I will say nothing. It doesn't matter. I'm already a dead man.'

'So you're a dead man. Then it makes no difference if you talk. So talk to me now.' Lohmann insisted.

Gisevius paced. Five paces forward, five paces back towards Lohmann. Hands rubbing against each other. Brow beaded.

'Bruckner knew I'd been in prison,' he gasped hoarsely. 'He was using that knowledge to make me help him.'

'Help him do what?'

Gisevius ran his hand through thinning hair. Lohmann thought, a man despairing, a man close to the end of a rope, twisting and turning to be free. Something here, larger than one man seeking a way out; something common to the entire city, to the whole uncommitted populace. God knows why, but Lohmann could feel a sympathy for these people. The Berliners. These plump figures, dressed in heavy coats, ugly, ill-cut suits, the bowler hatted bourgeois of Weimar; the thinner, cloth-capped artisans and workers, split between the National Socialists and the Communists, turning one way and then the other. Behind all this, something simpler; a search for bread, for food, for thousand-mark notes which overnight became worth pfennigs. Gisevius was only one of so many. Less moral than some, perhaps more moral than others. 'I will talk, I will dupe, I will steal. But I will not kill'. A small ugly, petty philosophy.

'Help him to do what?' Lohmann repeated.

'He . . . he had a plan. Bruckner. With the other two. You see, we were all Saxons together. Came from the small town. Five of us . . .'

'Five?'

'Four . . . five . . . we were all in the navy together. So! So, they knew me! And they had this plan. They . . . they had information which they wanted me to confirm.'

'What information?'

Gisevius stopped. Still. Now unmoving. 'No! If I am to live, I . . . only I . . . must hold that information. If you find it . . . all right. But I must not tell you. Otherwise, I'm speaking into the muzzle of a gun. Or is it with the garrotte around my neck?'

Lohmann stared at the immobile figure. 'We will guarantee you protection!'

Gisevius laughed. A hollow sound. 'You must know, you can guarantee nothing.'

Reiner said, 'You can be arrested as an accessory to three murders.'

'Yes, yes, do that! Arrest me! Arrest me. In hours I will be transferred to Prinz Albrechtstrasse. And never heard of again. So arrest me. But there is only one man who can save me.'

'And that is . . .?' Lohmann asked quietly.

'The Führer.'

Again a moment of silence. Broken by only the heavy breathing of Gisevius. Lohmann tried another tack.

'Can you tell me why Bruckner came to you?'

'He wanted . . . no, I cannot tell you. Leave me alone!'

'Would it be wise to leave you alone, if you are so afraid?'

Gisevius shot him a puzzled, almost alarmed look. A possibility had arisen he had not considered.

'Do what you have to,' he said. 'I . . . I am tired. In the bone, I am tired.' He went to the door and out into the hall.

Lohmann nodded to Reiner to follow. Reiner went out. 'He will only go to the bedroom,' the woman, Paula, said. 'He will try to sleep. As an escape from fear.'

Lohmann faced her. The purple mark stood out in the dim light. Even without the mark, she would not have been an attractive woman. Not to Lohmann's eyes. But he had learned that other eyes saw other visions.

'Do you know why Bruckner came here?' he asked the woman.

She shook her head. 'He didn't want me to know. He sent me from the room when Bruckner came.'

'Nothing was said in your presence?'

'Bruckner knew of Hans's conviction. He said it might be useful. Such experience. And that Hans would benefit from the knowledge they had.'

'But you didn't know what that was?'

'No. If I did I would tell you. To . . . to help him.'

Lohmann believed her.

'There was one other thing. Bruckner seemed to need confirmation of something. Something important. Hans said he should go to a synagogue. The Beth-Din synagogue at Wannsee. I was asked to tell Bruckner how to reach the synagogue.

'You? Why you?'

The woman took a deep breath. 'My temple. I am a Jew.'

She had a great deal against her in Germany today, Lohmann thought. The ugly birthmark, the choice of partner, the fear engendered by that partner. And she was a Jewess. Lohmann felt sorry for her. And wondered why, in this twentieth century, he should have to do so. The sorrow irritated him.

'I am not the Gestapo, Fräulein,' he said. 'I'm also not a Party member.'

The woman's sigh was audible.

Lohmann went on. 'You say, the synagogue at Wannsee Why there?'

'I don't know. Something in the records. Bruckner was to ask the Rabbi if he could see the records for a certain period.'

'The period?'

'Again I don't know. But tell me, what are you going to do to Hans? He has committed no crime. If there was to be a crime, it would have been Bruckner's. Whatever it was. Yet Hans is in fear. Whatever he is afraid of, you must protect him. You are the police. It is your duty.'

The woman was right. Gisevius could not be left here. If the Blind Man was right, Gisevius was a hunted man. The killer could be close. Of course they could wait, prepare a reception for the killer. But would the killer risk such a trap? And, if he arrested Gisevius, it was true the SS or the Gestapo might well claim him. No, Gisevius must be protected until Lohmann completed his investigation. The identity and the motive for the killings had to be made available to Hitler. Yet even if Gisevius knew, it would take time to make him talk. The man was bound to silence by his own fear. The longer he remained silent, the greater the opportunity for him to be killed.

Lohmann paced the room now. The woman stood, watching.

It was possible the solution lay in the Wannsee synagogue. Bruckner had gone there, seeking information. He, Lohmann, must follow in Bruckner's steps. But meantime Gisevius had to be held in safety.

'Reiner!' he called out sharply.

'Chief?' Reiner came back into the room.

'Where is he?'

'Lying on his bed. I think he's trying to sleep.'

'Wake him, in a few minutes. After I'm gone. Out the back way. There is a back way out of the building?'

The woman nodded.

'Good,' Lohmann went on. 'Take Gisevius and Fräulein Paula to Kitty's. And wait there for me. Let no-one get to Gisevius. No-one, you understand?'

'I understand. But you, Inspector . . .?'

'I shall be paying a visit to the synagogue.'

Reiner grinned. 'Well . . . mazel tov!'

'Very amusing. If our garrotter is around, he may just follow me. But, in case he doesn't, keep the Mauser handy. And tell Kitty, the room I was in. It's not wired . . .'

'You sure it wouldn't be better to put him in a cell . . .?'

'No, I don't. Now, wait fifteen minutes. The Fräulein will show you how to get out. I'll be back at Kitty's within a couple of hours. I take the car. You take a taxi.'

He went out. Down the stairs and into the alley. Still,

it rained. Puddles forming between the cobbles; drains filling in torrents.

A crowd had formed a circle at the mouth of the alley. Lohmann approached slowly, and pushed his way through. He could see, in the middle of the crowd, the square hat of a policeman.

'One side, please,' said Lohmann.

The policeman looked up. 'Wait a minute. Who do you think you are?'

'Lohmann. Inspector. Kripos.'

The policeman came to attention with a smart clicking of heels. 'Sorry, sir. Didn't recognise you.'

'What's happened?' Lohmann asked. The question was unnecessary. He followed the police officer's eyes to the ground.

'The Blind Man, sir.'

A small, neat man in an expensive raincoat was crouched by the body.

'Who's he?'

'I'm a doctor, sir. I happened to be passing. This man's been strangled.'

'No, doctor, he's been garrotted. Would you please go and phone for the Criminal Police? Ask for the Murder Squad. The officer will have to remain here.'

'Yes, of course, at once,' said the doctor, rising.

Lohmann turned to the police officer. 'None of these people to get out of the alley without being questioned.'

An indignant groan from the crowd.

'If necessary, use your revolver to keep them here,' Lohmann added.

He turned full circle. Slowly. Surveying the crowd. Curiously flat features. Always the same with the morbid spectator. Like cardboard cut-outs of people. Two-dimensional. The curious Berliner. Lohmann looking for something familiar, a recognisable feature; someone, something that might relate to the death of the Blind Man. To any of the deaths he was investigating. He saw nothing.

Yet somewhere near was the man who had used the garrotte.

'You'll be waiting, Inspector?' said the policeman.

'No. I'm on another matter. If the investigating officer wants me, I'll be available at headquarters.'

He went out of the alley and straight to the car. He sat behind the wheel for some moments thinking of the Blind Man. Another killing. For what? Bruckner, Preuss, Rudig and Müller. And now the Blind Man. Someone was following in his footsteps, dogging his every move, and wiping out every lead. Only Gisevius was left. For how long? For the next few hours, that was Reiner's problem. If they were lucky, the murderer would follow him rather than Reiner; the man would be curious as to what lead Lohmann was following. Later, Gisevius could be attended to. If Lohmann was right, that's how the killer should think. How Lohmann hoped he would think.

And the death of the Blind Man? Unnecessary. A stupid, futile act. An act of deliberate cruelty. Or, something else? No place in the New Germany for the disabled. He'd heard that philosophy too. Eradicate the weak, eliminate the sickly strain. Himmler's philosophy. The puny, watery-eyed master of the SS, the self-appointed guardian of the future nation of blue-eyed, blond supermen.

Angry, he started the car.

The synagogue was a tall, three-storeyed building, stucco peeling from the walls. A large stained glass window, a number of panels shattered and jagged-edged, black against the remaining coloured glass. To the side of the double doors, a few feet from the ground, scrawled crudely in white paint, was one word, 'Juden'. Above the double doors, an inscription in Hebrew had been chipped and scarred by the throwing of stones.

Parking the car at the foot of the short flight of steps that led up to the doors, Lohmann climbed out and ran through the still-falling rain up the steps. The doors were locked. He knocked. Knocked a second time, heavily with his clenched fist. The sound echoed deep inside the building. There was no response. He waited, then knocked again. There was still no reply.

He came back down the steps, the rain running damp on his collar and trickling under it. He looked around. There had to be another entrance. Between the left hand wall of the synagogue and the building next to it was the entrance to a narrow lane. He ran towards it and, treading carefully to avoid puddles, moved along the lane. Some twenty yards along, Lohmann came to a door set into the synagogue wall. It was unlocked. He stepped inside.

Five steps led up to another door. Beyond this second door, Lohmann found himself at the side of the main hall, the Temple itself. He moved into the centre of the hall and stared around. A full three hundred and sixty degree turn showed him everything. He stared on rows of smashed wooden pews stretching back under a high balcony. The wood of the pews was white and splintered. Between them and scattered over the aisles, mixed with unpleasant damp puddles and small mounds of human faeces, were what appeared to be pieces of torn altar cloth and ripped parchment. A wooden rail in front of the raised dais was cracked and broken, sagging towards the floor. And, at the rear of the dais, the Ark which should have contained the scrolls of the sacred Torah had been broken open, the inner door to the cabinet ripped off. The scrolls had gone. Lohmann knew now what the parchment fragments scattered over the Temple floor were. The desecrators had done their work with efficiency.

A sound from behind a pillar to his left caused him to spin around. It was a harsh scraping noise. He walked, carefully avoiding the debris, to the pillar. On her knees, frozen in the act of scrubbing a section of the floor, a grey haired, elderly woman looked up at him.

'What you want?' she demanded in a thick accent that owed more to the Polish language than to the German she was attempting.

'I'm a police officer.'

The face, skin seamed by time, almost cracked into a joyless grin. 'Took your time, wasn't you? Where was you when we needed?'

'I'm sorry. I knew nothing of this.'

'Three days since. When they break in and do this. Brownshorts, they call themselves. Gonifs, I call them. And three days it takes to send around a knocker like you.'

'I'd like to speak to the Rabbi.'

'Du! Du, the Rabbi, he wants. For a rabbi, you have to have a synagogue. You see a synagogue around here?'

'This is the Beth-Din . . .?'

'For a synagogue, you have to have the Torah. You see the Torah here?'

She looked towards the smashed Ark.

'They tear up the Torah, may God forgive them, which I hope he won't. And now you come. What for? You want to arrest the Rabbi for attacking twenty Brownshirts?'

Lohmann shook his head. 'This is something else. I'm investigating a murder case . . .'

'So investigate somewhere else and let me continue to clean what is dirty.'

'Now, that is enough, Sarah.' The voice came from a doorway somewhere in the dim light beyond the pillar. 'This man has nothing to do with what happened.'

The speaker stepped into the light. He was a tall thin man in black clothes, heavily bearded, wearing a black hat.

'Is another of them,' the woman on her knees protested. 'Calling himself a policeman. I know what I call him.'

'Please to be quiet, Sarah. I will attend to the gentleman.' Turning now to Lohmann. 'I can help you, sir?'

'My name is Lohmann. Inspector, Criminal Police. I'm investigating a murder case and I believe you may be able to help me.'

The man stood aside. 'I am Rabbi Cohn. Or was. After this . . .' He made a gesture with his hands, ' . . . I don't know what I am. You will please to come into my study.'

The room was small and filled with books. There were books in bookcases, books on chairs, books on the top of a roll-top desk. Heavy volumes, bound by leather and dust. The Rabbi cleared a chair and beckoned Lohmann to sit. He himself then sat on a high leather chair beside the desk. Outside Sarah, whose name was Frau Leibovitz, recommenced her scrubbing. After a moment, she stopped again, staring up at the balcony, an area of darkness. She listened. An imagined sound had come to her. Then she called out.

'Somebody is there?' A silence. 'You come to finish the

job? To set fire to us all? Ach, but not now. We got a policeman here. He might just set fire to you!'

The Rabbi had left the door open. He rose and closed it quietly on the woman's last words.

'You have to excuse Frau Leibovitz. She is . . . excitable.' He returned to his seat. 'You will doubtless know we had a visit from some Brownshirts.'

'I didn't. And I'm sorry.'

The Rabbi raised his eyebrows. 'Why should you be sorry? You are an official of the government.'

'And I was an official of the Weimar government. And I am a member of no political party. So I am genuinely sorry. What has been done is a criminal act of vandalism . . .'

'More, Inspector. Sacrilege. Unfortunately our local police official *is* a member of a political party. He is a National Socialist. And sees no crime here.'

Lohmann nodded. It was all he could do. A brief nod. Indicating understanding. Of something of which there was no understanding.

'You would like a glass, tea?' The Rabbi asked with old-world courtesy.

'For now, no thank you.'

'Then tell me in what way I can help you?'

'I believe a man called Bruckner came to see you some weeks ago?'

Rabbi Cohn nodded. 'That is so. He was a Party official. But not . . . not quite like these others. He was polite. I was surprised. Which is why I remember him.'

'What exactly did he want?'

The Rabbi drummed his fingers on the top of the desk. 'Let me see. These recent events, they have been a disturbance, you understand? What did he want? Ah, yes. He wanted to study the records of the synagogue. I was surprised. Who should, outside my people, want such a thing?'

'Did he say why?'

'I remember, I asked him. He said he was trying to trace a Jewish family from the district. Yes, now was the little trouble. You see, I thought, why should he do this? Unless to create more trouble for this family. I was inclined to refuse him. But then he said, yes, he said it was his own family. I didn't believe him.'

'Why not?'

'Inspector, I am not an old man. I am sixty-two. Not old, not young. I do not have expectations of becoming an old man. Not in Berlin today. But I have experience of human nature. You have to take my word this man was lying. I am able to tell.'

'You let him see the records, though?'

'In the end I decided a man that could lie with such sincerity should have what he wanted. Also I didn't wish to create trouble for the synagogue. I didn't know it would happen anyway.' A thought struck the Rabbi. 'You think his visit is connected with the vandalism?'

'Were your records tampered with? Or destroyed?'

'No.'

'Then I don't think there was any connection. I would like to see the records myself . . .'

The Rabbi raised his eyes to the ceiling. 'There are volumes upon volumes.'

'I would like . . . if you can remember . . . to see only the volumes Bruckner saw.'

'Of course. I am very meticulous. I write in my register what he wished to see.' He hesitated. 'You say this is a murder investigation? How does all this concern Bruckner? He is a suspect?'

'He was murdered three days ago.'

A sharp intake of breath. The Rabbi shook his head. 'So he is the victim. Sad.'

The man's compassion was real. Yet, to Lohmann, the fact of it was unreal. Bruckner had been a Nazi, a supporter of Nazi policy, an anti-Semite; yet the Rabbi showed his genuine sorrow.

'There have been others too,' Lohmann added.

'Terrible. But I find it difficult. The records Herr Bruckner wished to see, they are old. They go far back. Before my time, before my predecessor.'

'How far back?'

'I think . . . the beginning of the century. Perhaps a little earlier. I will look first in my register.'

Turning, he rolled up the top of the desk and proceeded

to rummage among a small mountain of papers. These rose from the surface of the desk, bulged from a row of pigeon holes at its rear, each of them overflowing with documents.

'In time, I will need to tidy this desk,' the Rabbi murmured. 'Yes, in time. Perhaps now.'

He glanced around at Lohmann. 'Yes, this would be the time. You see, for now, this not a temple any more. Not after the desecration. Of course, in time perhaps . . . when we restore the Torah . . . and always presuming the authorities will permit. You think they will permit?'

'I wish I could answer that to your satisfaction, Rabbi.'

'Indeed, I too, Herr Lohmann,' said the Rabbi, turning back to the desk's clutter.

After a moment, he gave a small, satisfied exclamation and withdrew from the desk clutching a long ledger book.

'Here we are. The ledger. It will be the last entry. And there are not so many. Only eight pages in fifty-four years.'

He opened the book and turned over the first few pages.

'Yes. This is it. He wished to see volume four. Now all we do is find volume four.' He replaced the ledger under the mountain of paper and rolled down the desk top. Rising, he twisted past Lohmann's chair and over to a shelf of thick, leather-bound volumes. He selected one of these and turning back, placed it in Lohmann's hands.

'Here! Records of families of this Temple. Births, marriages, bar-mitzvahs, deaths. Also something of the families themselves. For the Rabbi's own information. We cannot keep it all in memory.'

'You'd have no idea where he . . .?'

The Rabbi anticipated his question. 'Under the letter S, I believe. But I will leave you with the book for a few moments. I go make a glass tea. You . . . read, read, please.'

Then Lohmann was alone. Aware only of the book. He found what he was looking for quickly. Under the name 'Suess'. The details were there. All he needed. The family 'Suess'. Date of the wedding, births of children. And two additional notes.

The Rabbi returned carrying two glasses of lemon tea.

'Thought you might have changed your mind,' the Rabbi said, handing him one glass.

'Thank you.'

'Frau Leibovitz enjoys a glass, this time day. You find what you are looking for?'

'Yes. There aren't too many families under the initial S. But there are some symbols here I don't understand.'

The Rabbi adjusted a pair of wire-rimmed spectacles and peered over his glass of tea at the book.

'Ah, yes. Old Rabbi Mosevitz used his own shorthand. A marvellously inventive old man, so they used to say. I never knew him. This sign here . . .' he pointed with a long finger ' . . . that means the bride was a *shiksa*. A Gentile, marrying a Jew of this temple.'

'You allow such a marriage in the synagogue?'

'Also the sign indicates she was a convert. She took instruction before marrying this man Suess. This means she becomes a Jew and her children are therefore Jewish. You see the religion, as you might say, is through the mother. In Judaism, always.'

'I see. And here . . .?'

'The children of the marriage.'

'This one . . . the daughter, what does that sign mean?'

'A sadness.' The Rabbi shook his head mournfully as if reacting to the sadness. 'This daughter, she reverses the process. She marries a Gentile. A civil marriage. To this man . . .'

The Rabbi hesitated over the name, frowning. Well he might, Lohmann told himself. In the name was the answer.

'So she's no longer a Jew?' Lohmann asked.

'Ah, Herr Lohmann, to us a Jew is always a Jew. Even in the outer darkness of the gentile world, if you will excuse the expression. And her children will be Jews because she is. Even if she ceases to practise.'

'And this note here?'

'The daughter and her husband moved from Berlin with their children. Also, they move to another town, a small town, probably without a synagogue. So even if she wished to continue to worship, it might not be possible. Also, as you may know, in these small towns the Jew might well be an unwanted curiosity. One would suspect, the daughter might take the easy course and quietly forget she was a Jewess. Sad but so likely.'

'She was still half Jewish and her children would be quarter Jewish?'

The Rabbi smiled but still sadly. This time, perhaps for Lohmann.

'We do not recognise these halves and quarterings, Herr Lohmann. That is something the Nazi has thought up. However, I suppose, technically, you are correct.'

Lohmann indicated a final entry. 'And this . . .?'

'The town they went to. Halle en der Saale. It is, I believe, in Saxony.'

Lohmann closed the book. 'Thank you. I have what I want.'

The Rabbi was frowning. 'The name of the man the daughter married . . . I have heard . . .'

'Forget it! Lohmann cut in abruptly. 'Put it out of your mind. Recognition, I assure you, sir, would be unhealthy. Leave it to me.'

'Yes. Yes, perhaps that would be wise.'

Lohmann rose wearily. He should feel excitement. He had what he wanted. He held the solution to the murders. Yet he felt exhausted, drained of energy. Not a good sign, not when he would need all his energy and care to conclude the case. If that were possible. He was aware of a great and growing danger.

'Thank you for your help, Rabbi Cohn,' he said, gently placing the half empty glass of tea on a small table between two stacks of books. He rose and went to the door of the study.

'You will be back, Herr Lohmann? the Rabbi asked.

'If everything goes well. Please look after volume four. We may have to ask for it in evidence.'

'You will not take it with you?'

Lohmann considered this. 'I would rather take it from you legally. As a possible court exhibit. If this ever gets to court. Also, it might be safer here than with me. If there has so far been no attempt to steal it, then it is possible that they . . . he . . . our murderer does not know of it.'

'I will lock it away,' the Rabbi said.

'And, Rabbi, I hope I haven't brought you more trouble with this business.'

An expressive smile. 'What more trouble? To me, death is a lesser trouble than what has already happened.'

He ushered Lohmann out of his study and into the derelict temple. Frau Leibovitz was still on her knees scrubbing. An empty glass was by her side. She looked up.

'I was thinking they was back. I was thinking someone is up on the balcony.'

The two men looked up into darkness. At the rear of the balcony, the broken stained glass window was shrouded by a thick tarpaulin.

The old woman went on. 'But then, I think nobody is there. Nobody is running about making a noise.'

Lohmann stepped forward, eyes trying to pierce the upper darkness. He was fortunate. As he did so the first shot rang out, reverberating around the temple walls. And a fragment of wood on the floor behind him flew up into the air.

It was a sound Lohmann was accustomed to, and he reacted quickly.

'Under the balcony,' he shouted to the old woman and the Rabbi. 'Move! Now!'

They moved, Frau Leibovitz with amazing alacrity. As they did so, a second shot ploughed a furrow in the wood flooring, this time in front of Lohmann. Then he too was sheltered by the balcony.

'How do I get up there?' he demanded of Rabbi Cohn.

'Staircase. At the back!' The Rabbi replied with surprising calmness.

Lohmann ran, an erratic course through broken pews to the rear of the hall. Dimly he made out the staircase and was running towards it, Mauser drawn from under his shoulder and now in hand. At the foot of the stairs he slowed almost to a halt, and then, gun in hand, mounted the stairs, peering upwards. He was an ideal target climbing the stairway if the would-be assassin appeared at the top.

He was still fortunate. He came onto the balcony before the next shot echoed across the area, plunging through the tarpaulin behind him and, with a tinkle of glass, breaking another part of the window. At the same time, the force of the bullet pulled the tarpaulin aside for a second, casting a flashing ray of fading light across the balcony. Lohmann was able to make out a dark figure at the far end of the balcony, outlined against a door. He tried his own first shot but the figure threw open the door and disappeared, after one more shot which threw a puff of dust from the wall behind the policeman.

Lohmann now ran towards the door, kicked it open and fired another shot up the narrow stairway beyond. This shot clanged against a metal door at the top of this stairway. Slowing down, he climbed the stairs, Mauser in front of him. Again he used his foot to open this door. A rush of cold, damp air and rain blew into his face. The man had gone onto the roof.

Carefully Lohmann edged out onto a small flat section of roof. He was on some kind of buttress at the side of the synagogue. Behind him, the third storey of the building rose upwards. Ahead of him was a drop to the pavement, but at the side of the flat area was a rusting metal ladder leading upwards to the main section of the synagogue roof. The man must have climbed the ladder. There was no other way.

With even more care, he mounted the ladder. The rungs were damp, treacherous and rusty. His foot slipped twice on the way up but he held on, regaining his foothold. He continued to climb.

As his head came over the parapet at the top, another shot rang out, and chips of stone flew at his face. He felt a nick on his forehead. With a sudden, fast leap he threw himself over the parapet, and lay gasping, face downwards on a piece of concrete between slating and a gutter pipe. Slowly he raised his head. The sky was darkening above as the day went, but he could still make out a shadowy figure, arm wrapped around a chimney stack. Another shot smashed into slating inches from his head.

Then the figure disappeared behind the chimney.

'Six shots,' Lohmann muttered to himself. 'The bastard's fired six shots. His revolver should be empty.'

He stood up and, edging his way onto the slated roof,

moved towards the chimney stack. The Mauser was in his hand and he had fired only two shots from it. He reached the chimney, a thick, solid edifice, and flattened himself against the damp stone. Slowly he moved around it. The man had gone. He was slithering down the roof, a leather coat shimmering in the rain and the dying light. Lohmann braced himself against the chimney and essayed another shot, aiming not at the body but at the flailing right arm of the man. The arm seemed to jerk as if it had been hit but then the man seemed to straighten up at the edge of the roof. In front of him was a yawning gap, some five or six feet. Steadying himself, he jumped. And landed on the opposite roof, swaying slightly before stumbling forward behind a parapet.

Lohmann looked down. Below the sloping roof was a drop of three storeys to the ground, some sixty to seventy feet. He took a deep breath, feeling the nausea of vertigo in his stomach. He abhorred heights. Training as a young policeman, he had been forced to steel himself against such a feeling. Yet, it still recurred on occasion. And this was, such an occasion. He studied the slope in front of him, and the roof of the next building. It was an ornate roof, with stone buttresses, cupolas, ancient and twisted chimneys that seemed to be leaning against the wind. The dim light and the driving rain seemed to distort everything. Shapes altered, distances seemed greater than they should be.

Another deep breath, and then he was sliding down towards the edge of the roof. As he did so, he saw a movement from the other roof, the assailant flitting from behind the parapet further onwards, behind the ornamentation.

Lohmann knew he would have to jump and jump quickly. Any hesitation would give the man time to reload . . . if he hadn't already done so . . . and conceal himself where he could easily pick him off. Below, the street seemed deep and distant, a scar between the two buildings.

He jumped.

And landed, heels over the gap, throwing himself forward and into a narrow parapet, a drainpipe filled with running water under his legs. Crawling forward some feet, he half stood, crouching on uneven slating. Again he was aware of distorted vision, narrow passages around chimneys; roofs, level at one point, sloping at another. A grotesque quality diffused his forward view. Like the rooftop scenes in Lang's *Caligari*, nothing seemed as it should be. A statue, to his right, became a chimney; a cupola, a dome rose up on his left. He glanced downwards briefly. Strange buttresses protruded from below. The whole was like some nightmare of Gothic fantasy. Or was it the death of light and the distortion by the falling rain?

Around the cupola wound a narrow passage and it was to this that Lohmann now moved. With care, but as fast as he could against the rain which was beating into his eyes and face, he came around the side of the cupola.

He came face to face with his assailant. And with a revolver pointed at his chest. He heard the click of the trigger. The firing-pin fell on a used shell. The man hadn't managed to reload!

The face was in shadow under the shining brim of the uniformed cap. Above the brim, also shining in the rain was the Death's Head badge. The man gave a muttered curse and threw his revolver at Lohmann's head. Ducking, Lohmann fired at the man's legs and was gratified by a sudden scream as the figure dropped to the damp stone. Yet, despite his obvious agony the man threw himself forward onto Lohmann, grappling with him. It was a last act of desperation. The policeman lashed out with his gun hand and the cap flew off as the gun barrel connected under the man's chin. The figure, on one knee now, spun backwards, battered against the edge of the cupola and then slid sideways down a sloping area of the roof. Hands went out, grasping at slates, but, with the surfaces running with rain water, somehow the fingers failed to grip. Another scream rang out, this time prolonged as the figure slid off the roof. For one small fraction of a second, Lohmann saw the face, eyes wild with final terror, hair wet across the forehead. Then Captain Zoller disappeared over the edge of the roof. A second later the scream was abruptly terminated with a thud.

Zoller!

Lohmann shook his head in an effort to clear both vision and thought. The SS Captain had tried to kill him. The observer of the hunt had turned into the quarry. Lohmann moved over the slated slope, first assuring his hand grips were firm, before peering over the edge of the roof.

Some fifteen feet below him, an ornamental buttress seemed to grow from the stone of the building. From the buttress, as a form of decoration, there protruded a steel lightning conductor. Impaled through his chest on this was the body of Captain Zoller. Head back, eyes staring upwards, he hung like a broken toy soldier.

TEN

When the police arrived fifteen minutes later, Lohmann was in the Rabbi's study, drying off in front of a small, single-bar electric fire. Detective Werner, in charge of the squad, found his way to Lohmann's side.

'That's Captain Zoller up there, isn't it? 'Werner asked, a naive puzzlement on his face.

'Is he still up there?'

'Well, yes, sir, but . . . it's going to be difficult to get him down.'

Lohmann sighed. 'Has it occurred to you to telephone the Fire Department.'

'Yes, yes, of course, sir.' He disappeared only to return a few minutes later.

'They're on their way, sir.'

'You too will take a glass of tea?' Rabbi Cohn asked, entering with a steaming mug for Lohmann.

'Oh, well, eh . . .' Werner looked uncertainly at the behatted, bewhiskered figure of the Rabbi; and then decided that if Jewish tea was good enough for his inspector, then he could, without prejudice, accept tea from a rabbi. '. . . thank you, I will.'

The Rabbi disappeared with an appreciative smile. There was hope for Germany yet, if the police would take tea in the synagogue.

'You'll be reporting the circumstances of the Captain's death?' Werner asked nervously.

'No, you'll be,' Lohmann replied, nursing the mug of tea with both hands. 'I am still involved in an investigation.'

'But . . . how . . . how do I report it? Captain Zoller fell while aiding you in pursuit of an assailant?'

Lohmann stared bleakly at Werner for a moment. The thought, he admitted to himself, had not occurred to him. If Werner reported it, then he could, if necessary, correct the report later. If it would ever be necessary now that he knew; now that he'd studied the records on the wall facing him. Yet it would still buy him time.

'That's right. You report it that way.'

Werner nodded eagerly as the Rabbi entered with another mug of tea.

'I'll be going now,' Lohmann said, picking up his coat. 'You're in charge here. Clean everything up . . .'

'Where's Sergeant Reiner?'

'He'll be with me. You're in charge here. Get the body down and then report in. As you said.' Lohmann struggled into his still-wet coat. 'Oh, and see the Rabbi isn't bothered. Zoller's body was found on the building next door. It has nothing to do with the synagogue. Understand?'

'Yes, sir.'

Werner was a stolid, unimaginative type. But he would do what he was told. And he would do it efficiently.

Outside in the street, it was night now, and still raining. Despite the rain, a small crowd had gathered, plump, solid citizens, filled only with a morbid curiosity. They were peering and pointing upwards to where Zoller's body still hung. In the distance he could hear the approaching clanging of a bell. The fire brigade was on its way. Lohmann climbed into his car and drove, slowly at first, down the street. Some distance from the synagogue, he accelerated, heading back into the centre of the city.

He drove to Kitty's, parking on the opposite side of the street some fifty yards from the front door. He walked back to the door, noting the few passers-by. Very few, and none to be viewed with suspicion. Georg admitted him into the brightly lit hallway.

'Upstairs, Inspector. The room you were in.'

Reiner was pacing the room when Lohmann entered. The woman Paula was sitting hunched up on the bed. There was no one else in the room.

'Where's Gisevius?'

Reiner spun around on his heels. 'Oh, it's you, sir . . .'

'I asked, where's Gisevius?'

Reiner gulped, opened his mouth and said nothing.

The woman said, 'He's gone.'

Lohmann ignored her. 'I told you to keep him here,' he said to Reiner.

'I tried, sir. The minute he got here he wanted to leave. But I stopped him. And . . . and then he seemed to settle. After a time, he went to the . . . the lavatory. Well I mean, what could I do? Follow him there?'

'Yes, if you thought he was going to run. You would have done it at the police station.'

Reiner literally hung his head. 'I know . . .' he murmured in a whisper.

'Anyway where the hell did he think he was going?'

The woman answered. 'To Nuremberg.'

'What?'

'He told me. He said, if he could get to Nuremberg, he would be all right.'

'The bloody fool! Doesn't he know he's walking towards them.'

The woman shook her head. 'No, no! He said, he thought he could get to Hitler. With what he knew. Once he talked to Hitler, he'd be all right.'

'He won't get near Hitler! Do you think anybody would let him?'

She shook her head, eyes becoming vague. 'I don't know. He said, years ago they were all comrades. Bruckner, Preuss and . . . and a man called Rudig. And . . . and they knew Hitler. In the early days. After he came out of Landsberg, they met him . . . the four of them.'

'Four, Paula?' said Lohmann.

'Yes. Four of them!' she suddenly sounded afraid. 'He told me, only four of them.'

'Five, Paula. Five. All of them in the navy. Isn't that so?'

She shook her head again, this time violently. 'No! Only four. He only mentioned four.'

Lohmann sighed. 'All right. You can go.'

The woman sat, unmoving.

'I said, you could go.'

'But . . . what about Hans . . .?'

'If you want to stay alive, go. And forget him. He's already a dead man.'

She started to tremble spasmodically. It was not pleasant. As if she was suffering from a sudden ague. Slowly she rose and went to Lohmann.

'You can save him.'

'Perhaps, if he had remained here. But not now.'

'You have to try. You have to . . .'

'Yes, 'Lohmann replied and then turned away from her. 'I have to. But there's little chance . . .'

'Please . . .'

'Go! Out of here. Now!'

Her face contorted, tears streaking her cheeks, she went, still shaking and shuddering.

Rainer said, 'What's happened? What happened at the synagogue?'

'Zoller's dead. I'm pretty sure he did the garrotting.'

'Zoller's the killer? Then the case is over.'

Lohmann shook his head. 'No. Reiner, you've no family, have you?'

'Just the wife. And a brother in America.'

'You want to stay alive?'

'I'd prefer it. What are you on about?'

'You've a choice. Tomorrow morning, either you denounce me to the Gestapo, or you and your wife take a train and get out of Germany.'

Reiner, baffled, ran a nervous hand through his hair. 'What are you talking about? Denounce you? Why should I denounce you? What have you done?'

'You have to say that, in this investigation, you have reason to believe I'm working against the Party interest. That I'm using the investigation to blacken the reputation of members of the Party. And I already killed an SS Captain, Zoller.'

'For God's sake, chief, why should I do that?'

'To save your own life. Early on in this investigation, someone, I think it was Müller, said I couldn't win in this business. If I didn't find the truth, I'd have failed Hitler . . . something not done. And if I did discover the truth,

I'd be a dead man. He was right. And the same applies to my assistant. Unless you change sides. Or get out.'

'I'd rather get out.'

'Then do it. Tomorrow morning.'

'You're serious?'

'I'm grim.'

'What about you?'

Lohmann hesitated. Considering. Then after a moment, he spoke.

'I'm getting my daughter out. Then I'm going to Nuremberg. To finish it. I might just be able to save that fool Gisevius. And, with luck, I may just get out myself. But you, you must do what I say. Or go to the Gestapo.'

Reiner was silent only for seconds. 'I've always wanted to see America,' he said.

'Good. Go to the bank first thing in the morning. Draw out everything. You have enough to get to America?'

'Just.'

'I'll write you an authorisation to take money out of the country. You will be on a special investigation which requires you to go to Paris. From there, you're on your own. You should have enough time before this blows up.'

Lohmann wrote the authorisation, in official jargon, sitting at the dressing table in the room in Madame Kitty's salon.

'That and your badge should get you through.' He handed the note to the sergeant. Reiner looked at it uncertainly.

'You really believe all this is necessary?'

'I've told you . . .'

'Yes. All right.'

'There's a hotel in Paris. Left Bank, near the Cafe Flore. Stay there for a few days. If . . . when I get through, I'll contact you.'

'Yes, sir,' Reiner still hesitated. In two minutes, his world had disappeared under him. It took a little getting used to the fact.

'Go on then, Reiner. And good luck.'

'Thanks, Chief. And to you.' The sergeant backed out, closing the door behind him.

Lohmann was alone now. For a few moments. A little

time to think. He was aware of what he had to do, but like Reiner he was trying to anticipate the feeling of giving up the world he had been born into, the existence he had known for all of his working life. It had certainly changed before for him, the day his wife had died. At least then he had buried himself in work. But now even that would go. Another place, another country, another life; that had to be the future. Yet the alternative was not to be contemplated.

A few minutes later, he went down to the hall.

Georg was alone behind the desk. He was sitting back, reading a porno magazine. It seemed to Lohmann somehow superfluous in these surroundings. The black face looked up at him and grinned.

'Heil Hitler!' he said, teeth gleaming. 'How 'bout me for the Master Race, Inspector?'

'Good enough for me, Georg. But you'll need a lot of whitewash to keep the Gestapo happy.'

The smile vanished. 'I think I head back to Paris. They appreciate me back there.'

'Do it,' Lohmann replied. 'But before you do, I'd like to see Madame. And afterwards, Lucy. If she's . . . free.'

He was surprised as he said the last three words. There was pain there. 'If she was free'. The acceptance of an unacceptable profession. Until now he had not only accepted Lucy for what she was, he had been aware that in no way was he committed emotionally. Now he was not so sure.

Behind him, Kitty appeared.

'Lohmann?'

'Kitty, I have to thank you. I may be going away for some time.'

'You don't have to thank me. You've been a friend.'

'With house privileges,' Lohmann said ironically.

'You were always welcome.'

'Thanks for that.' He paused. 'Kitty, I'm going to ask Lucy if she wants to go with me.'

Kitty stared at him evenly. 'She's not a prisoner here. If she wants to, that's all right.'

'Thanks again.'

'But, Lohmann, she may not want to.'

The idea had never occurred to him. That she should want to stay on here, in a house like this; that anyone should want to stay, other than for reasons of necessity.

Kitty seemed to read his thoughts. 'Oh, the naivety of so-called worldly males. Girls don't always work here because they have to. In fact very few of them do. Oh, don't ask me for reasons. There are so many. But ask her, Lohmann, ask her.'

He nodded. 'I will.'

'Georg'll bring her to you.'

Lucy came down the stairs moments later. She was wearing a white satin evening gown, cut low at the front.

'Hello, Lohmann. Excuse the working clothes.'

'I want to talk to you,' he said, and told her what he wanted to do.

She looked down at her shoes when he had finished. 'You want to take me with you?'

'Yes, if you want to go.'

She looked up. 'Why should I want to go?'

The question took him by surprise. 'Look,' he said after a moment's pause. 'Berlin is going to become a very unpleasant city.'

'It's never been anything else for me,' she replied. Not until I came here. And even then . . .' She shrugged.

'Will you come with me?'

'As what?'

Again he paused, searching for the right words. 'Anything you like. As . . . as my wife?'

'It would be easier to get me out that way, wouldn't it?'

'Anything you like. As a friend . . . mistress, whatever.'

'Thank you for the offer, Lohmann, but no.'

For once he was at a loss. 'I . . . I think you should get out of Germany . . .'

She cut in on him. 'Lohmann, I'm a whore. We both know it. Other people know it. I'm not ashamed of it. I'm a whore from choice. If I don't die a whore, then I'll get out my own way, when the time comes. I'll have saved up enough to buy a cafe or a small *Bierkeller*. I'll end up in black bombazine, an eye always on the till. Maybe I'll marry a labourer or a farmer, somebody who doesn't know or care. . . .'

Lohmann said, 'I know and it doesn't matter . . .'

For the first time since he'd known her, her voice had a cutting edge to it. 'How nice of you, Lohmann. How broadminded! And will you tell your daughter of my previous profession? And your friends? Or will you just worry whether or not they'll find out.'

'I don't give a damn!'

'You would, Lohmann, you would. Anyway I like it here. Kitty runs a good house. I can make a lot of money. For my cafe. And . . . and I like the clients. Oh, I liked you, Lohmann, I liked you a lot. But, in between, there were others. Remember that. The others. I liked a lot of them too. You see, I . . . I need more than one man.'

Lohmann stared around the hall. The chandelier cast small diamonds on the walls.

'Come out with me. No strings, Kitty could . . . could fix you up in a house in Paris. If that's what you want. Germany's going to be a different place, Lucy. A very different place.'

'It doesn't change for whores. Goodbye, Lohmann.' She turned away but he noticed she was trembling.

He said, 'Goodbye, Lucy.'

She went to the foot of the staircase, and then turned quickly.

'Lohmann, I never did know your first name.'

A long moment. But then it had been a long time since he heard anyone use his first name.

'Ernst,' he said.

'Ernst.' She echoed him. 'Yes, I should have known.'

She went up the staircase then, without looking back. Lohmann waited until she had disappeared. Somewhere, a lingering thought that she might change her mind. Yet, when she disappeared into the upper regions of the house, there was also a sense of relief. Which he did not like. He walked slowly to the front door. Kitty appeared behind him again.

'Goodbye, Lohmann.'

He half turned. 'Kitty. Look after her.'

'As far as I can.'

He climbed into his car and drove home.

Lohmann had anticipated chaos when he arrived home. Not that it came from Anna. When he suggested to her that she and Frau Anselm should leave for Paris the next morning, she was at once excited and enthusiastic. She had never been out of Germany and the thought of seeing Paris presaged an enormous adventure to the fourteen-year old. A small frown crossed her face.

'What do I take with me?' she asked. 'Clothes, I mean.'

He wanted to tell her, 'As much as you can. We'll not be coming back for a very long time.' But he did not wish to risk this. At this time all she had to know was that they were going to Paris. She and Frau Anselm would leave in the morning. He would follow on within a day or so.

The chaos erupted from the housekeeper.

'No time, no time,' she repeated, over and over again. 'How will I get everything ready? What will we need? And you, Herr Lohmann, what will I pack for you?'

'I'll be doing my own packing now. Take what you need, Frau Anselm. But not too much. You must not give the appearance of leaving Germany for good.'

The woman stared at him, blinking. 'It will be for good?'

He nodded. 'Anna doesn't know. Nor must she until I tell her, in Paris.'

'I understand. But . . .' Her lower lip trembled.

'You have, of course, a choice, Frau Anselm. You can come back. We will have to stay.'

The woman gazed now at the suitcase she had just brought from a cupboard. 'Germany is my country. I have never been out of Germany. Except when I was first married. We went then to Vienna.' She swallowed hard, thrust her jaw forward and looked at Lohmann. 'But my Germany no longer exists. I will go with Anna. And I will stay.'

'I'm very grateful. I shall go to the station and get you both tickets. And one other thing.'

'Sir?'

'I shall give you a sum of money with a letter authorising you to take this money out of the country. It will be as official a letter as I can contrive. That should allow you to get through to Paris despite any currency restrictions. If I do not join you within a week, you will be free to use this as you see fit to settle with Anna somewhere. It could last you about two years. At the end of that time,' he shrugged reluctantly, 'I'm afraid you would both be thrown on your own resources.'

'There is a possibility you would not be able to join us?'

The question hung on the air, something not to be dwelt upon.

'A possibility. However I do not contemplate it happening,' he lied without compunction. The necessary lie. 'After you leave in the morning, I shall be driving to Nuremberg. And, after completing the present case, I shall drive to the French border. Now you have passports . . .'

They had passports. A contemplated holiday in Switzerland which had never transpired, had necessitated obtaining these.

Lohmann spent the night lying on top of his bed chain-smoking. Sleep did not come easily. The image of Lucy climbing Kitty's wide staircase was with him. But it was not her refusal to come with him that worried Lohmann. It was his own sense of relief at her refusal. Somewhere there, was a weakness in which he took no pride.

ELEVEN

He was on the road to Nuremberg.

It was a drive of over two hundred miles. Two hundred miles through the heart of Germany. By midday he was driving under the shadow of Leipzig's ancient church of St Thomas, the centre of the second largest city in the Reich. He had seen his daughter and Frau Anselm onto the train to Paris and now his mind was riveted on the City of Nuremberg. Tomorrow Hitler was to speak, and probably sometime tomorrow Gisevius would try the reach the Reichschancellor. If he had not already made the attempt. Such an attempt, Lohmann was sure, would only lead to Gisevius's death. And should Lohmann himself reach Gisevius, he too knew he was in danger of losing his life. That danger was inherent in his going to Nuremberg anyway. At least, unlike Gisevius, he had the letter from Hitler as a kind of protection.

Late in the afternoon, as he came nearer to the city of Nuremberg, the traffic on the road increased. The pilgrimage to pay homage to the Party was on.

Some miles outside the city, with darkness falling, Lohmann drove into the yard in front of a small *Gasthaus*. He was fortunate in getting a small room, the last available in the establishment.

'You go into Nuremberg tonight, sir,' the landlord informed him, 'you would have to sleep in the streets. All the hotels are full. They say even private homes have been taken over by the National Socialists to house all the delegates.'

His voice dropped suddenly. 'All to hear Him tomorrow.'

'You don't approve?' Lohmann said.

The landlord became suddenly nervous. His hands trembled visibly, and he looked from side to side. They were in the tiny foyer of the small, three storeyed square building, and the foyer was empty.

'Who am I to approve or disapprove,' the landlord went on cautiously. 'I've lived under the Kaiser, under Weimar, and under Hindenberg. Now it's Hitler. It makes no difference now. During the war, it made a difference. I had to join the army. Next time, with luck, I'll be too old. I just don't understand why all these people have to come to Nuremberg to hear one man.'

He shuffled off towards a narrow stairway, beckoning Lohmann to follow him. The room was on the top storey, under a sloping wooden roof. It was small but clean, white sheets almost gleaming on the narrow bed. A china basin and jug stood on a small side table.

'I bring you hot water now and in the morning. We eat in an hour.' So saying he took the jug and disappeared.

Later, lying in bed, Lohmann tried to determine his course of action for the next day. The rally was being held at the Zeppelin grounds outside the city. With the Hitler letter as a passport, and his credentials as an inspector in the Criminal Police, he could reach Hitler. With luck, he could make his report personally. It was the possible reaction to that report that would be dangerous. If he could be sure a written report would reach the Reichschancellor, then he might be able to extricate himself from the inevitable danger. If he could find Gisevius before anyone else, then his report would have greater validity.

He stared up at the beamed roof. The thought came that he was indulging in an act of simple and wilful insanity. He should be with his daughter on the train to Paris. He had solved the mystery of the murders of Rudig, Preuss and Bruckner to his own satisfaction. Therefore, why was he here? A stubborn determination to prove to the man who had assigned him the case that he had solved it? The conscientious policeman showing how clever he was? All that with the knowledge that Herr Hitler would not be pleased with the truth. Oh, yes, Müller had been right. A situation in which he could not win. Whatever happened it would be his last investigation in Germany. The truth would be told, but justice would, he was sure, not be done. There had been crime, but there would be no punishment. Not here, in Nuremberg.

Perhaps he could delude himself into believing he had come to try and save Gisevius's life. A lie. He had no care or liking for Hans Gisevius. A crook, a confidence man, perhaps more, perhaps an informer. Yes, it was possible that, when approached by Bruckner, he had played the informer and, by doing so, caused the three murders. Perhaps he was not running to Hitler at all, but to the imagined safety of the one for whom he had played informer.

And possibly he, Lohmann, was indulging his ego, determined to show that he had indeed solved the mystery of the three killings. Yes, there was the truth he wanted to avoid; his own vanity, vanity that could kill him.

After a time, he slept.

He dreamt. Of darkness, broken, at first only by pinpoints of light. Each pinpoint grew larger and larger. Death's Heads. SS insignia, shining, threatening. Then the darkness dissolved to a bleak grey cloud. Stumbling into the cloud were Bruckner, Preuss and Rudig. Faces in photographs. Followed by Müller and the Blind Man, and others; at first amorphous shapes coming closer, resolving themselves into men and women, and filing past into the cloud, becoming enveloped in an oppressive fog. Finally disappearing. With Lohmann as a silent observer. Watching them pass. Saying and doing nothing. Afraid to shout aloud, fearful of warning dead men that they were already dead. Then Lucy came past, moving into the cloud; and others. The Rabbi from Wannsee, Holtz and Werner, Gisevius and the woman, Paula; and so many others. Faces recognisable and unrecognisable. The entire population of Germany, stretching from darkness into darkness.

Without turning, he could see behind him. Observers, standing there, motionless, uniformed figures, like waxworks. Heydrich, immaculate, elegant, watching;

behind him, the small figure of Goebbels, and by his side the large figure of Göring. Behind them, standing higher up, Himmler, spectacles gleaming in the light when there was no light, mouth a thin line; as if the man had no lips but a slit across the lower part of his face. Above him, Hitler. The Reichschancellor, the Führer, standing above them all, not looking at the long, long line of shuffling figures stretching to infinity but looking above them, into the distance, far over their heads towards some greater unimaginable nightmare. Lohmann himself could not see that nightmare, but he could sense some greater horror.

He awoke, sweating. His watch by the side of the bed showed him it was only five-thirty in the morning. He lay back against the cool pillow, aware that he could not go back to sleep for fear the dream would return. He knew it would return. The kind of dream that would always return.

Outside, greyish light was brightening into day. An hour later Lohmann rose, washed and shaved, and went down to breakfast. He drank three cups of black coffee, forced himself to eat a ring of liverwurst and three rolls. He would need food in his stomach, God knows, he had no idea when he might eat again. He left the *Gasthaus* at eight-thirty and drove towards Nuremberg.

The road filled up with traffic. Lohmann drove slowly.

An open lorry went by carrying Hitler Jugend, fresh faced youths laughing, smiling, pointing from the sides of the vehicle.

An old gentleman in knickerbockers, a row of medal ribbons pinned to his heavy jacket, saluted shortsightedly, only aware that the occupants of the lorry were uniformed.

In Bavarian peasant costume, a group of young girls, blonde hair braided, carrying flowers, came along the pavement. Their laughter was a light musicial sound. Eyes flashed and cheeks reddened as they stared at a troop of soldiers, almost as young as themselves, marching past.

As Lohmann neared the city centre, the sun came through a bank of low cloud casting a watery yellow light on the grey stones of the old cathedral. Cars, buses, lorries, charabancs crowded the narrow streets, moving sluggishly outwards towards the suburbs and the Zeppelin field. The more expensive of the cars held uniformed men, thin, elegant, high ranking army observers in their greenish-grey uniforms, or fatter men less at ease in Party uniforms newly created to cover a variety of official positions. These ran from gauleiters to youth leaders, from major to minor civil servants. Party armbands were prominent. For, at last, after over a year in power, this was their day, the Party day, the consolidation of their power. The rally today would show their victory over Conservatives, Democrats, Socialists, Communists, the army, the industrialists, the bankers, the churches, Catholic, Lutheran and all; and their victory over the Jewish-Bolshevik international conspiracy.

The cars continued to move slowly from the centre of the city. Time to watch the crowded pavements, pedestrians too heading towards the Zeppelin field; stopped momentarily by sellers of *Der Sturmer* or official Party programmes of the Rally. Fat burghers with their wives dutifully buying and showing they were buying. Their girth obscured the thinner, gaunter faces of artisans, workers and the unemployed victims of the depression. Among these too were the odd scowling faces, some ostensibly moving against the crowd, away from the Rally. Question: who were these ill-concealed dissidents? Enemies of the Reich? Jews, gypsies, Jehovah's Witnesses, Trade Unionists, members of other religious groups? Perhaps merely Nurembergers irritated at the gigantic side show on the outskirts of their city.

But in the main the Party was blind to this silent minority. All was perfection; and in movement, a great river of the faithful flowing towards the field, now a stadium with its concrete platforms and pillars, designed at the Führer's request by the young Albert Speer.

Nuremberg was in a state of excitement, noisy, *en fete*. Indeed it was as if the old city might be so shaken that pieces of its fabric would collapse with the weight of the incomers.

After a time, Lohmann reached the stadium and was directed by traffic policemen into a vast car park. Leaving his car, he made his way through the crowd towards one of the entrances where he was stopped by a twenty-year old youth leader wearing a steward's armband above his Party armband.

'You have a ticket?'

Lohmann showed his police identification card.

'But that's a Berlin police card,' said the steward.

'Berlin Criminal Police. I'm following a suspect.'

The youth leader rubbed his chin. 'You'll have to have permission from the police authority here. I can't let you in without that authority.'

And where do I find the local police authority?'

'There's a police command post inside . . .'

'How do I get to the police command post if I am unable to get inside?'

The youth leader blinked. 'I've got my orders. No one in here without a ticket of admission issued by the local Party to which you belong.'

'I'm not a Party member. I'm a policeman on duty.'

An embarrassed shuffling of feet. 'You . . . you could go to Party Headquarters at Nuremberg. They'd issue you with a pass. But, of course, there won't be anybody there . . .' The youth's voice faded into an uncertain silence.

Lohmann thought, Nazi bureaucracy at work; and already unable to cope. With an assumed sigh of reluctance he produced the Hitler letter.

'Perhaps this might get me in?' he suggested.

Eyes widening, the youth leader read the letter, gaped at the signature, and then stood hurriedly aside.

'I'm sorry to have held you up, Inspector. If you had shown me this at once . . .'

Inside, the sight that greeted him, he had to admit with genuine reluctance, took his breath away. The old Zeppelin field had been transformed. At the far end the speaker's podium, high above the stadium, was under rising blocks of concrete, draped with enormous swastikas. The field was now a vast arena in the centre of which units of Party organisations were beginning to gather. Like Roman legions, they carried their local insignia, topped with eagle and swastika, numbered by unit, denoting SS cadres, troops of Brownshirts, Hitler Youth, the Todt Organisation and so many others. All of these created by the Party and owing allegiance not to Germany but to Adolf Hitler.

Lohmann's eyes ranged over the mass of humanity. Impossible here to find Gisevius. Needles in haystacks. Thousands of faces passing. Without Gisevius, he had no corroboration. He would have to take his chance alone with Hitler. Provided he could reach Hitler when the Reichschancellor arrived. Sometime later in the day, he was to speak. And before that would doubtless make a triumphant entry; like a Roman Emperor but without the little man behind him to whisper a reminder that he was only human.

Until Hitler's arrival, Lohmann could roam the arena, searching for Gisevius. But the chances of finding him were minute.

Unless . . .

It was high above him, a platform on a scaffolding, one of several towering over the stadium. This one was the largest. High above, he could see the cameras at the ready, their operators behind them. Film cameras in place to record the Rally. He remembered reading of it in the newspapers.

> 'At the request of Doctor Goebbels, Fräulein Leni Riefenstahl, star of *The White Hell of Pitz Palu*, and director of *The Blue Light* and SOS *Iceberg* will direct a film of the 1934 Nuremberg Rally.'

The foot of the scaffolding was boxed off, a door in the wooden wall bearing the legend UFA FILM – NO ADMITTANCE. Lohmann pushed the door open to be confronted by a young man in a cloth cap, woollen sweater and moleskin trousers. He was carrying cans of film.

A petulant voice. 'Can't you read? No admittance. Bugger off!'

'Lohmann! Inspector, Criminal Police!'

'Oh! 'The young man placed the cans of film at the foot of the ladder and looked up at him. 'Sorry. Thought you were one of the cattle straying. Can I help?'

'Frau Riefenstahl?'

'Leni's up top,' he indicated a ladder leading upwards.

Also he emphasised the first name with the false bonhomie of show business. 'Go on up.'

Lohmann looked dubiously at the ladder.

'It's safe enough,' the young man assured him. 'Leads to the first of three platforms. They're all at the top.'

Lohmann climbed.

At the top of the first ladder was a platform and a second ladder. Then another platform and another ladder. Finally he was on the highest platform. Two operators were checking their cameras. A youth was stacking raw film stock in cans. An older youth was studying the arena below through binoculars. In the centre of the platform, using an upturned wooden box as a desk, was an attractive woman in her early thirties, hair held back by a carelessly tied ribbon. Behind her a wooden wall cut off the strong breeze. The woman was pointing out certain items on a shooting schedule to a middle-aged man in a short, heavy coat.

Lohmann at once recognised the woman. He had seen *The White Hell of Pitz Palu*.

'I shall be over on the wall with Number Three camera,' she was saying. 'But you have to get these shots in one take. Especially His arrival. We cannot ask Him to go back and do it again.'

The man assured her they would secure the required shots.

'Both cameras going,' she went on. 'And to hell with the amount of film you use. I want to get so much that I'll have no editing problems. Expense doesn't matter. The Ministry is paying.'

She looked up at the sky. The sun had once again disappeared behind low-level cloud.

'Damn the bloody sun!' Fräulein Riefenstahl muttered. 'We have to shoot, no matter what. And it had better be good. Especially when He speaks. Forget about sound, though. We're recording the speech right there.'

Lohmann smiled to himself. They referred to 'He' and 'Him' as if Christ had risen and would be speaking. The elevation of Adolf Hitler was never so apparent as now.

Leni Riefenstahl finally stared at Lohmann. 'Who the

hell are you? I told them I only wanted my crew. No men from the Ministry . . .'

'My name's Lohmann, Criminal Police, Berlin. I'm looking for a fugitive. Down there.' He indicated the arena below.

'Then I should think you'd be better off looking for him down there,' she replied tartly.

'It's a little busy. I want to use your binoculars or any kind of telescopic lens . . . you have adjustable lenses, don't you?'

She thought for a moment, then nodded. 'I see what you mean.' She turned away. 'Fritzie, let Herr . . . Herr . . .?'

'Lohmann.'

'Let Herr Lohmann have a look through your binoculars. And, if he needs it, put the zoom lens on Number Two camera and let him look through that.'

Fritzie, the younger of the two camera operators, nodded and prised the binoculars from the youth who had been studying the arena with them. Lohmann took them gratefully.

'Thank you, Fräulein,' he said to the woman director.

'Fine. But from now, you'll have to search on your own. I am, as you might appreciate, making a film. Stay up here as long as you like but, for God's sake don't get in the way of the cameras.' To underline her point, she looked over at her middle-aged associate who had been listening. 'Take care of him, Paul.'

She was already descending the ladder as Lohmann positioned himself at the edge of the platform and started to scan the crowds below through the binoculars. He used an old, familiar technique. Place an imaginary grid over the arena and then search every square as closely as he could. Searching for faces, shapes, anything familiar or recognisable. Perhaps an article of clothing, the shape of a head. He went through the first square of the grid, the far corner of the arena, close under the elevated stages and the podium. Gisevius, if he was still free, would have arrived early and stationed himself where he might get close to the Führer, or to the behind-the-scenes entrances. He moved to the second square, almost directly under the podium. Still it was like the needle and the haystack.

Nothing. And aware as he was that he could miss his quarry. The third square. Faces, more faces, turning, laughing, a group of young athletes limbering up on the edge of the field. The fourth square . . . no, there was movement at the edge of the third square. People were being shouldered aside by two black uniforms, moving as if they were trying to reach someone.

He lowered the binoculars and turned to the young camera operator.

'Over there, just under the podium, have you anything would give me a closer view?'

'Try the viewfinder on the camera. There's a zoom lens on it.' The youth indicated the eye piece. 'Look through there.'

Lohmann did as he was told only to find himself peering at white concrete. He was about to open his mouth when the youth interrupted him.

'I'll do the focus-pulling. Just tell me, up or down, left or right.'

'Down . . . that's enough. Now to the right. More, just a little more.'

He was fortunate that as yet the crowd was thin under the podium.

'A little more to the right . . .' he called to the camera operator. Now he saw the two black-uniformed SS men pushing their way through the group of athletes, and clearly they were searching for someone.

'Up, please,' he said and the lens moved from the SS men.

And there he was. Gisevius. Hunched up on a bench, the wall of the dais behind him. Lohmann could see the features of the man quite clearly. The eyes seemed to be half shut, as if he was dozing, arms around himself, to keep warm.

Lohmann stepped away from the camera.

'You've found him?' the camera operator asked.

The policeman nodded. 'Far end of the arena. How the hell do I get there quickly?'

'Not so difficult,' said the youth. 'Leni's got it all arranged. There's a corridor to the right under that bank of seats. To be kept clear for us cinematographers. They'll show you when you get to the ground.'

Lohmann went down the ladders at a speed which surprised even himself. He was in too much of a hurry to be worried by vertigo. On the ground the youth, more cans of film in his arms, pointed to a near-by arched entrance. The stadium was now filled with music, fed in through giant speakers. The *Horst Wessel Song* blared out above him, mercifully dulled as he entered the corridor. Long and narrow, with white concrete walls and an earth floor, it was indeed deserted.

Lohmann ran.

There were a number of side exits but he ran the length of the corridor. Breathless, he came out into the light under the dais. The crowd was thin here and he pushed his way through them towards the spot he reckoned he had seen Gisevius.

The bench under the podium was empty. The group of athletes was limbering up nearby. The nearest, his vest emblazoned with a swastika, was flexing his biceps, at the same time running on the spot, a slow but rhythmic pace.

'There was a man here . . .' Lohmann gasped.

The young man nodded without breaking his pace. 'In trouble,' he said. 'Took him away a moment ago. Through there. Bloody Communist, if you ask me.' Then, with a suspicious leer. 'Who are you?'

'Police!' Lohmann flashed his identity card. Saved time and trouble. 'Where did they take him?'

'Told you. Through there,' with a nod towards a door set in the side of the dais. Close-fitted and painted white, almost invisible.

Lohmann pushed his way towards the door. Through a group of plump men in green uniforms. And muttered protests. Another tune was blaring out above his head. *Watch on the Rhine*. Guaranteed to make middle-aged men sentimental about the war. Lohmann pushed against the door. It would not open. There was no handle or bell or knocker. He rapped with his knuckles but the sound was minimal. Clenching his fist, he battered on the door. This time it opened inwards.

'No civilians permitted,' said the tall, black-uniformed SS man standing inside.

Lohmann fumbled for the Hitler letter and thrust it at the man. Icicle blue eyes scanned the document, looked up at him, without enthusiasm.

'This is yours?'

Lohmann looked at the man. A lieutenant with the arrogance of a general. He had dealt with the type before.

'You've read the letter. You know who I am,' he said sharply.

'I know who it says you are . . .'

'I am an inspector in the Criminal Police. And as such outrank a lieutenant. Even an SS lieutenant. You will stand to attention at once. And you will note the signature on that letter. Do you question that signature?'

The lieutenant came to attention. 'No, sir.' The tone had changed instantly. The lieutenant stared over Lohmann's head, lips trembling slightly.

'You will now let me enter?'

'Yes, sir. Of course, sir.'

He stood back and Lohmann stepped through the door into an antechamber. Or so it would appear. But an antechamber to what? Apart from a door at the other side of the room, the place was entirely empty. No furnishings, nothing but bare concrete walls, whitewashed into a bare existence.

'Two of your men brought in a prisoner some minutes ago.'

'Yes, sir.'

'Where did they take him?'

'SS guardroom. Through that door, turn to the right and last door at the end of the corridor.'

'Thank you. You may stand easy, Lieutenant.'

The SS guardroom was, unlike the antechamber, furnished. A desk faced the door. Behind the desk, an SS captain, lounging elegantly, cigarette in a long silver holder. A bench, empty, ran along one wall. Against the other, sitting in hard chairs, were two SS private soldiers. They sat to attention, ready seemingly for any emergencies. Behind them were two doors.

As Lohmann entered, the captain looked up, one eyebrow raised. 'What the hell do you want?'

The same exercise as before was called for.

'Take your feet off the desk when you speak to me!' Delivered sharply and with due authority. 'I am an inspector in the Berlin Criminal Police, and I am on official business.'

Red faced, the captain swung his feet from the desk. 'This isn't Berlin. You have no jurisdiction here . . .'

Again Lohmann presented the Hitler letter. 'That is my jurisdiction. I think you will find it takes in the whole of Germany.'

As he studied the letter the red face became purple. Control was maintained with some effort.

'Yes, yes, of course, Inspector Lohmann. In what way can we help you?'

'I wish to interview the man brought in here a few minutes ago. Hans Gisevius.'

A smile appeared on the captain's face. 'I'm afraid that will not be possible. The man has been taken to be questioned by Colonel Heydrich personally.'

So Heydrich was already in the stadium. Lohmann shivered but succeeded in concealing it from the captain.

'What is your name, Captain?' he demanded.

'Milch, Herr Inspector.'

'You are a captain in the SS, Milch. Therefore I presume you are able to read?'

'Yes, sir.'

'My letter from the Reichschancellor does not exclude Colonel Heydrich. Or for that matter Reichsführer Himmler.'

'No, sir.'

'You will therefore personally escort me to Colonel Heydrich's office, Captain Milch.'

Milch hesitated, torn between two loyalties. But the signature on Lohmann's letter won out. With some reluctance he rose to his feet.

'At once, Milch!' Lohmann barked. 'And you will extinguish that cigarette. The Führer objects to such weaknesses and I hope you would not wish him to arrive here with the odour of tobacco in the air.'

Again red faced, Milch stubbed out the cigarette, donned his cap and clicked his heels, beckoning Lohmann to the first of the two doors. As they passed, the two SS men leaped to their feet and stood firmly at attention.

'Your men would appear to be better trained in the niceties than you, Milch,' Lohmann took pleasure in announcing. Milch said nothing but ushered the Inspector through the door into yet another office, desk in place, but with a blonde female secretary behind it. Beyond the desk was yet another door, of unpainted white wood. Speer's interior decorators had obviously lacked time for completion of executive offices. Lohmann walked straight towards the door, Milch at his heels.

'You are not permitted to go in there!' the secretary exclaimed belatedly. Lohmann was already through the door.

The inner office also had white walls. But here, at least, there was some attempt at decoration. Behind the large antique desk was a portrait of Hitler in an ornate gilt frame. Around the walls were SS standards, the eagles angled so that they appeared to be staring sternly down into the room. Heydrich was sitting in a high-backed chair behind the desk. In front of the desk, crouched in an ordinary wooden chair, was Hans Gisevius. On each side of him stood an SS man.

Heydrich looked up at the new arrivals.

'Of course I was expecting you, Inspector. I can hardly say, come in, since you seem to be in.' He glanced over Lohmann's shoulder. 'That will be all, Fräulein Eberhardt. And you, Captain Milch. I should of course have told you the Inspector was on his way. It doesn't matter. You may go.'

Fräulein Eberhardt went. Milch hesitated.

'You too, Milch. And take these two men with you.' Heydrich indicated the men on each side of Gisevius. 'They have my personal commendation for apprehending Herr Gisevius. I believe he was intent on getting close to the Führer. God knows what reasons he may have had.'

The SS men withdrew, Milch carefully shutting the door behind him. While they did so, Gisevius remained sitting, head down, barely moving but for an uncontrolled spasm that caused his body to tremor. Heydrich seemed not to notice this.

'Well, here we are, just the three of us,' he said, the customary thin smile on his lips.

Lohmann said, 'The survivors.'

'Exactly. I heard that you killed Captain Zoller.'

'I think the report will read he died while assisting me. In the line of duty,' Lohmann replied.

'That's exactly how it will read, Lohmann. I wouldn't want it said that one of my men was going around garrotting Party members. You know Zoller served with the Spanish Foreign Legion? He became the regimental executioner. That's how he became an expert with the garrotte.'

'I imagined it was something like that.'

'Of course I could let you name Zoller. I could do that.'

'A rotten apple in the SS barrel?'

Heydrich chuckled. To Lohmann the sound was almost obscene. 'But why bring the SS into it at all? When we have Gisevius here. The ideal perpetrator. A jealous former acquaintance of the three victims . . . we can forget Müller . . . Gisevius even has a police record. And he was a running man.'

Gisevius spoke now, for the first time. He spoke but he did not look up. 'I helped you, Heydrich,' he said. 'I told you what Bruckner and Preuss and . . . and Rudig were planning. I came to you . . . you can't blame it on me.'

'Oh yes, you came to me,' Heydrich replied. 'When you thought their plans might not work. But you played along with them too. You played both sides of the fence. And then you came running here to try and get to the Führer. You thought, if you repeated the lie Bruckner claimed to have discovered, you would save yourself. Is that not so?'

Gisevius shook his head violently. 'No, no, I came here to see you. This . . . this policeman . . .' he nodded in Lohmann's direction. ' . . . he was after me. He was trying to make me tell him what Bruckner knew.'

Heydrich gently corrected him. 'What Bruckner *thought* he knew. But then, my dear Hans, how did Inspector Lohmann find his way to the synagogue in Wannsee?'

'I didn't tell him. . . . I did not tell him!' Again Gisevius shook his head. 'It must have been that woman . . .'

'What woman?' Heydrich demanded sharply. At the same time he drew a note pad from one side of his desk, and took a gold pencil from the breast pocket of his uniform. 'Her name. Tell me her name!'

'Paula . . . Paula Korman. Just a woman I . . . I picked up.'

Heydrich carefully made a note. 'How much did this bitch know?'

Lohmann answered. 'Nothing. She only knew that Gisevius had sent Bruckner to the synagogue. She didn't know why. So you can take her name off your executioner's list.'

The Colonel now turned his attention again to Lohmann. 'And of course you visited this synagogue, Inspector.'

'It was my job to do so. Remember I was investigating the three murders. And I found out why they had been committed and that Zoller had committed them. Under orders. Your orders, Colonel Heydrich.'

There was no visible reaction. Heydrich leaned back in his seat, smile still in place, and gestured with his right hand.

'Please go on, Inspector Lohmann. I find this fascinating.'

'Five men from the same town in Saxony, Heydrich. You, Bruckner, Preuss, Rudig and Gisevius. All around the same age. All of them went off to the navy. Comrades, you could say.'

'It was rather like that,' Heydrich interjected. 'Go on.'

'Also, at various times, they joined the Party. Of course, two of them were kicked out of the navy . . . Gisevius and you, Colonel.'

Again Heydrich could not resist interrupting. 'Gisevius was court-martialled for criminal offences. I left the navy over what might be called an affair of the heart . . .'

'Conduct unbefitting an officer, were the exact words,' Lohmann pressed on. 'Engaged to one lady and another pregnant by you . . .'

'This is no secret,' Heydrich said, for the first time exhibiting an irritated impatience.

'As you say,' Lohmann continued. 'And as it happened, you prospered in the Party. Taken under Himmler's wing, and even looked upon with favour by Hitler himself. While Bruckner, Preuss and Rudig became merely minor Party officials. It hardly seemed fair to them, especially when they believed they had information about you which would terminate your career.'

'Lies, Inspector, lies. Without proof or substance.'

'Frau Preuss gave me a small clue. I thought at first she was talking about Preuss's father, but she wasn't. I think she was talking about your father. Given to rather cruel impersonations of Jews . . .'

'My father was not Jewish, if that is what you are implying.'

'No, but his wife's family had Jewish connections. Colonel Heydrich, it is in the records of the synagogue at Wannsee. Your grandmother married a Jewish citizen of Imperial Germany, a man called Suess. Your mother was half Jewish and you, Colonel, are one quarter Jewish. That was why Bruckner, Preuss and Rudig were killed. By Zoller, acting under orders from you.'

Lohmann sighed before going on. 'The stupid thing is, they didn't want to reveal this so-called heinous secret. All they wanted to do was make their way in the Party. In that, they were like any other Party member. Rise to the top, by any means to hand. And when Hitler was concerned at the killing of old comrades, insisting on a detective being put on the investigation, you made sure Zoller would be around to report on progress. If necessary take care of me, if I came too close to the truth.'

'Which you did, Inspector. And for which you are to be congratulated. The trouble of course was that I did not realise that damned synagogue kept records . . . how would you say . . . unto the third, fourth and God knows how many generations. Of course, I don't feel Jewish. But then who knows how a Jew feels? You are not an anti-Semite, Inspector Lohmann?'

'No, I'm not.'

'Perhaps I should be grateful for that. But don't you find all this pity inside you for the plight of the Jews under the Party is rather tiresome? For how long can you feel sorry for these people without becoming irritated by these perpetual feelings of sympathy?'

Lohmann stirred uneasily. He was still standing facing the SS colonel and he was weary. Heydrich seemed to sense this.

'Do sit, Lohmann. We have so much to talk about.'

Lohmann drew an upright wooden chair from against the wall and sat awkwardly.

Heydrich went on. 'You feel sorry for these Jews and in doing so you feel a liability towards them. You feel you must aid them, succour them. And then after a time, you weary of the responsibility. Why should you have it placed on your shoulders, you ask yourself. And slowly, imperceptibly, you turn against the responsibility, and the people who caused it. In no time at all you resent the Jews. Two thousand years of sympathy for persecution, that's quite long enough. In no time at all, your resentment turns to something else. In no time at all you're an anti-Semite.'

An insidious argument, Lohmann could see. The man was glib and persuasive. He was also a murderer.

Heydrich went on, the voice low and soothing in its tones. 'Much worse when you find you have a Jewish ancestry. Sympathy dissolves under the handicap. Until you begin to hate your own ancestry. You begin to hate the Jewish race for all it has done to you.'

'There are those who would be proud of two thousand years of Jewish culture,' Lohmann said quietly.

'Ah yes, what was it Göring said . . . paraphrasing some American? When I heard the word "culture" I reach for my gun. No, Lohmann, against what the Party has done, and will do, the Jews are a small sacrifice. That sacrifice gave us access to power. Blame all the ills of the State on the Jews. On an alien people. And now we are in power. Don't you see the value of that? Don't you feel like joining the Party, Inspector Lohmann? National Socialism can use your abilities. Think of what we are doing.'

'Killing people?'

'A few nonentities. And Jews. But look what is happening. We shall create a strong nation again. A nation no one can insult. We shall be able to protect all our people, wherever they are in the world. We are already conquering inflation. We will root out the Communists. Send them back to Russia. Or even more unpleasant places. We shall wipe out unemployment in time. By encouraging the industrialists by building an invincible army, backed by massive factories. The wealthy will encourage us. They will become wealthier. They will create work for the people in the factories. We will control economics instead of being controlled by that inexact science. We will build the most powerful state in the world, the ideal state by the sheer triumph of the will.'

The man was intoxicated by his own rhetoric. Although all this was delivered quietly, Heydrich's eyes were set on some imagined vision he was conjuring up in front of him. Aware of this, he at once jerked himself back into the reality of the room and his audience of two.

'Triumph of the will,' he repeated. 'I believe that is what Fräulein Reefenstahl will call the film she is making of this Rally. But that is not our concern, is it, Lohmann? We are here to decide on the final report to the Führer on these murders.'

'Yes, we are.'

'Of course all this nonsense about my having Jewish blood is a fiction. Without proof.'

'The records of the synagogue . . .?'

Heydrich reached across the desk. From under a folder he produced a newspaper. 'The latest edition of the *Völkischer Beobachter*. Column three, at the foot of the page.'

Lohmann took the paper from the colonel's desk. The story was short.

SYNAGOGUE GUTTED

> Last night, the Jewish synagogue at Wannsee was completely destroyed by fire. Detective Holtz of the Criminal Police confirmed that the Rabbi, Isadore Cohn had been arrested on a charge of arson. It is believed that the crime was intended as an insurance fraud.

'You see,' said Heydrich. 'Your evidence is gone.'

'There will be other evidence. Other records,' Lohmann replied.

'If so, they too will be destroyed. That leaves you only with Herr Gisevius here.'

Gisevius looked up. 'I know nothing,' he said.

Heydrich shrugged, epaulettes moving imperceptibly. 'So what story shall we give the Führer? This matter must be terminated satisfactorily. And now. Shall we give him Zoller as the culprit? No, I don't think so. Too close to myself. Shall we give them Gisevius?'

Gisevius looked up, eyes wild. 'You cannot do that! I helped you . . .'

'You only tried to help yourself.'

Desperate now, Gisevius rose from his seat. A bent figure, shoulders hunched, he was trembling. 'I will tell the Führer all I know. Even if it cannot be proved, it will be said. If I cannot reach the Führer, I will say it in court.'

Looking amused, yet slightly perturbed, Heydrich waved him down. 'You will do exactly as we require you to do. So please sit down, Gisevius. You were always an excitable youth back in Saxony. You haven't changed.'

Gisevius subsided back into his chair, still trembling. Heydrich opened a drawer in his desk, looked down at it, frowned, unable to find what he was looking for, opened a second drawer. He withdrew the object of his search and rose to his feet.

His right arm shot out towards Gisevius. In his hand was a heavy automatic pistol.

The sound of the single shot, in the confined space of the room, was ear-splitting. It reverberated from concrete wall to concrete wall, leaving Lohmann with his ears ringing. Not that this concerned him. He was too fascinated and horrified by the scene in front of him. A red spot appeared in the centre of Gisevius's forehead. At the same time the force of the shot threw Gisevius backwards, and the back of his head seemed to explode in a haze of scarlet and grey. It seemed to Lohmann as if it was happening in slow motion. Gisevius's chair tipped over and he settled on the floor, arms spread out, head twisted to show the back missing. On his face was an expression of complete astonishment. And then, slowly, a pool of blood, streaked with greyish matter, flowed into a small puddle behind the head.

Mouth dry, Lohmann turned to stare at Heydrich who was slowly lowering his pistol.

Then Heydrich said something. Or at least his lips moved. But Lohmann could hear nothing. The ringing sound was still in his ears. Carefully Heydrich placed the pistol on his desk, nodded knowingly at Lohmann, and sat back in his chair. The office door was thrown open and Milch appeared.

'Target practice,' said Heydrich. 'Out! If I need you, I call.'

Milch withdrew, closing the door behind him.

'Can you hear me now, Lohmann?' Heydrich went on. Lohmann nodded. He could, just.

'Gisevius attacked you. So I shot him,' Heydrich explained. 'That is what happened.'

'I didn't notice,' Lohmann said, suddenly nauseous. Phlegm rose to the back of his throat, and he could barely stop himself from choking.

'He was your murderer. That will be reported to the Führer,' the SS colonel said, nodding to himself.

'I see only one murderer in this room,' Lohmann replied, aware now that he was starting to tremble. 'Do you shoot me next?'

A hoarse laugh. 'Ach, no. Why should I shoot you? You are going to sign a report I've had typed. And tomorrow morning you will hand it to the Führer. He will be pleased. He will congratulate you. Perhaps there will even be promotion. Incidentally, today I will be promoted. To staff rank. General Heydrich. I like the sound of it.'

'I'm supposed to congratulate you?'

'It would be most civil.'

Lohmann looked away from him. At the body of Gisevius. The pool of blood was spreading slowly. Against the planking of the wooden floor it was a deep ruby red.

'And what if I tell the Reichschancellor the truth?' he said thoughtfullly.

'You won't do that. You will sign the report I have prepared. And tomorrow you will take it to the Führer. I want you to read it carefully tonight. In case questions are asked by the Führer. You will then reply in context. Gisevius, jealous of his old comrade's success in the Party, brooded until he went insane. He then garrotted them, one by one. You tracked him down, followed him here, where he obviously planned to assassinate Hitler. He attacked you but I was fortunate enough to arrive in time to shoot him. That is the gist of this report.' He held up several pages of neatly typed manuscript.

'So you are supposed to have saved my life?'

'Let's say, yes, I have. It's true. You will do as I say.'

'But, if I don't . . .?'

'You have a daughter, Lohmann.' He consulted another paper on his desk. 'Yes, Anna. I see she's a member of the Hitler Youth. Very good. You wouldn't want anything to happen to her?'

'No, I wouldn't.' By now Anna should be in Paris. Please God!

'Good. I have booked you a room at a small hotel. The Augsberghof. Unfortunately the Führer's hotel is completely full. However, he will see you at his hotel at ten o'clock tomorrow morning. An SS car will pick you up at nine-thirty. You will deliver this to the Führer by hand.' He indicated the typed manuscript. 'You may as well sign it now.'

'I can do that in my hotel . . .'

'Now, Lohmann!'

Heydrich spread out that manuscript on his desk, and Lohmann signed it.

Heydrich nodded, with evident satisfaction. 'Good. Very good. When Hitler sees this with your signature on it, the case will be closed. Gisevius will be merely another item in the history of crime. You know, Lohmann, we will eradicate crime from the streets of Germany. Law and order will prevail.'

Lohmann found himself staring at Gisevius's body. Somewhere outside of the room, a bell rang. Heydrich stood, picking up his cap.

'The bell means the Führer has arrived in the stadium,' he said, donning the cap and adjusting it on his head. The Death's Head again seemed to gleam in the light. 'I have to take my place on the platform. He makes his speech soon. The big speech. In it, he will proscribe the Jews. They will officially be deprived of citizenship.'

Lohmann looked away from the body. 'Why?' he asked. 'He's in power. He no longer needs a scapegoat.'

'You preach something for a long time, you begin to believe it,' Herydrich replied. 'It is a matter of policy. You see why I had to eradicate this story that I have Jewish ancestry. By the way, Captain Milch will accompany you to your hotel. Also he will pick you up in the morning.'

He strode to the door, boots creaking. Lohmann thought, ridiculous that I notice his boots.

Heydrich opened the door. 'Milch!' he called out and the captain appeared with a distinct click of heels. 'You will take Inspector Lohmann to his hotel, as arranged. And assign two of your men to clean up this mess in here.'

Moving through the crowds in the stadium, Lohmann was aware of Milch's hand on his arm. Not the usual police grip on an arrested person, but a seemingly guiding hand; yet firm, very firm. Around him Lohmann could sense the air of expectation in the crowd, an excitement mixed with tension. In the centre of the stadium row upon row of young faces were lifted upwards towards the podium. Exultation was on each face. As if they were greeting the Second Coming. Lohmann shuddered. And again felt sick. And thought of the body lying in Heydrich's office.

Minutes later they were outside the Zeppelin field. Milch steered him past the car park. 'We have a car for you. I will arrange for your own police vehicle to be ready in time for you to drive back to Berlin. Your suitcase is now in my car.'

Lohmann said nothing; did nothing but follow the SS captain. Everything had been arranged. They had even anticipated his arrival. In his pocket was the statement bearing his signature, naming Gisevius as the killer. It had already been typed before he had arrived at the Zeppelin field. Please God they had not followed him in Berlin to the railway station. Please God, Anna was in Paris.

The SS vehicle, a large Mercedes, was waiting on the main road, a driver behind the wheel. As Milch opened the rear door, a sound like not too distant thunder came from behind him. Thousands of 'Sieg Heils' in unison from thousands of throats.

'The Führer has arrived on the platform,' Milch said. There was an element of disappointment in his voice. On official duty though he was, the man would rather be among the thousands of sycophants paying homage.

It was only in the car on the road back into Nuremberg that the thought came to Lohmann. Something Heydrich had said. Something which had worried him. As if he'd perceived an unintentional warning, a phrase uttered by Heydrich leading to another thought. What was it? He shifted uncomfortably on the leather upholstery of the Mercedes.

Then it came to him. Heydrich had said, '. . . When Hitler sees this with your signature on it, the case will be closed . . .' But Hitler was to see him as well. He, Lohmann was to present the report to Hitler. Or that's what Heydrich had said. But the SS colonel . . . soon to be general . . . could never take the risk of Lohmann seeing Hitler. The one man left who knew the truth. If he could kill Bruckner, Rudig, Preuss and Gisevius without compunction then Lohmann presented yet another threat. But to kill Lohmann would only lead to further speculation. Unless he was killed in an accident. Yes, that would be the simple solution. An accident en route to give Hitler the final report. Of course the report would not be destroyed. It would survive to terminate the investigation.

Yes, Lohmann thought, it had to be that way. Put himself in Heydrich's place, it was the only thing remaining to be done. Hence the insistence on his being driven to his hotel with Captain Milch. And driven to see Hitler in the morning. So when would the accident take place? Outside, the streets were quiet now, but tomorrow morning they would be crowded with traffic. All that would be needed would be a strong blow to the head, and a mild automobile accident. Then, sadly, Lohmann would be dead in a most unfortunate accident. But, fortunately his work would have been done.

For the time being he was safe. Until sometime tomorrow morning. Would the accident occur in the car then, or would they make sure by killing him first? He would find out in the morning. If he was alive in the morning.

The room in the Augsberghof was in complete contrast to the *Gasthaus* of the previous night. A large room with art deco furnishings, it reminded Lohmann vaguely of Lys Lysander's apartment. A tubular steel chair stood beside a low, tubular steel-legged table. The bed was large, its headboard exhibiting jazzed-up lines of colour. The bed light was a porcelain figurine of a dancing woman holding a torch. The bathroom was similarly unpleasant in style.

Milch, who had shown him to the room, stood uncertainly at the door.

'Weimar decadence,' he said with contempt.

'Or simply dubious taste,' Lohmann replied, noting his suitcase had been brought from his car and now stood at the foot of the bed.

After a pause, Milch said, 'You will dine with me tonight, Inspector Lohmann?'

'You're staying here too?' Of course he would be. On sentry duty.

'The room across the corridor,' Milch replied.

'Then you'll forgive me, Captain, if I don't dine with you. I'm tired and I think I'll just have coffee and sandwiches sent up here. After all I do have a big day tomorrow. I shall be seeing the . . . the Führer.'

'As you wish. I shall have the coffee and sandwiches sent up now. That is satisfactory?'

'Fine. I'll see you in the morning then, Captain.'

'The car will be ready at nine-fifteen. Have a good sleep.' Another click of the heels and the captain was gone.

Lohmann looked at his watch. Late afternoon. Still daylight. He would have to wait until dark before he made a move. Time to rest, and to plan. Ten minutes later there was a knock on the door and a waiter entered carrying a tray on which was a pot of coffee, a cup, saucer and a plate of sandwiches. The waiter placed the tray on the small table.

'Is this an old hotel?' Lohmann enquired of the waiter with studied casualness.

'But completely refurbished, sir,' came the reply.

'I have noticed. But, you know, once I was in a fire in a hotel not unlike this. On the third floor. I had a narrow escape.' Lohmann was lying with conviction. 'I've been nervous of hotels ever since. And here, I am on the fifth floor.'

'There are fire escapes, sir. One at the end of each corridor. No need for concern.'

'So. Very reassuring. They lead to where?'

'The rear of the hotel, sir. Down there.' The waiter indicated the window. Lohmann glanced down. Into a narrow alley.

'Just so. Thank you.' Lohmann dismissed the man with a tip and a nod of acknowledgement.

The bedroom door shut, Lohmann lifted his suitcase onto the bed and opened it. How professional had the SS been when they had brought the case from his car? Had they searched it? He felt under the spare shirt. His fingers gripped the shoulder holster he had placed there. And the butt of his Mauser pistol. The SS were still amateurs. He checked the pistol was still loaded, and then strapped on holster and pistol under his arm. Any time from now on, it might be necessary to use it.

He drank the coffee and munched a liverwurst sandwich while staring down at the alley. His way of escape was clear. But how alert would Milch be? There was the possibility of the captain periodically checking the room. But how often? He, Lohmann, was after all supposed to believe he was seeing Hitler in the morning. Still, however amateur the SS might be in many ways, they were meticulous in carrying out the obvious. He must presume Milch would check his room. Almost certainly had a spare key. Let the first check be done, and then he would leave. That way he would give himself the maximum start.

But then, once out of the hotel, how to proceed? A taxi back to the car park at the Zeppelin field, and he could pick up his own car. If it was still there. Something to be thought upon.

He drank a second cup of coffee, ate another sandwich and lay on the bed under the counterpane. Apart from his jacket and shoes, he was fully dressed. Including the shoulder holster with the Mauser. He closed his eyes. He would sleep a little, but lightly. If the room door opened, he would know.

He slept. This time there were no dreams.

He awoke to the sound of the key turning in the lock of his bedroom door. Barely moving, he slid his right hand across his chest until his fingers gripped the butt of the Mauser. At the same time he breathed heavily, as a man asleep. He was aware of a figure coming to the front of his bed. If this were to be the time of the attempt on his life, he was ready. The figure moved around the bed and he let his eyes flicker briefly. Against what little light came through the window, he determined the shape was that of Milch.

After a moment the figure moved away and Lohmann heard the door opening and shutting. Gently and as silently as possible. He waited, allowing time for the man to move down the corridor, and then, sitting up, he switched on the bed light and consulted his watch. It was a few minutes before nine in the evening. Outside the window, darkness was punctuated by lights from other windows and the dim glow of a lamp in the alley below.

It was time, Lohmann told himself. Milch would be going down to dinner. There would be no further check-up for at least an hour, probably longer. Lohmann put on his shoes, donned jacket and raincoat and put his hat on his head. He deposited the suitcase, open, at the foot of the bed. He then switched on the bathroom light, and drew the bathroom door shut from the outside. The light in the bathroom could be seen at the top and bottom of the door. Anyone coming in would presume, at least for some minutes, that he was in the bathroom.

The corridor was empty. Lohmann came to the fire escape door. A few moments passed while he struggled to open it. Despite the recent refurbishment of the hotel, the fire door was rusted from lack of use. Finally it opened with a screech of protest from hinges and handle. Damp air struck Lohmann on the face. It was raining. The surface of the steel fire escape was wet and slippery; and he climbed down it slowly and carefully. It was not the time to slip and sprain an ankle or break a bone. The escape swayed in the wind.

On the ground, he found himself standing on ancient cobblestones in the narrow alley behind the hotel. A street lamp hanging at an awkward angle threw a twisted, distorted beam of light across the alley. The rain hazed his vision, had already soaked the shoulders of his coat. He strode towards the street lights at the end of the alley. Now he needed a car. He dismissed the idea of going out to the Zeppelin field to repossess his own vehicle. It would be a predictable move, and anything predictable he had to dismiss.

As he came into the street, not much wider than the alley, an old street in an old city, he contemplated taking the SS Mercedes which had brought him to the hotel. Finding it gone would certainly delay possible pursuers. But it would be quickly and easily identified. No, he would have to appropriate another car. In his mind, he deliberately used the word 'appropriate' rather than steal. He smiled to himself. The habits of a police officer die slowly. From now on, he could no longer count himself a police officer. Rather was he a fugitive. He walked smartly now, against the rain, into a wider thoroughfare, cars parked at intervals along the kerbside. Looking, searching for an unostentatious vehicle, yet one capable of speed.

Finally he chose a British-made car, a Riley, parked halfway down the street. Not inconspicuous, it had speed, and he would have to settle for that. With the expertise gained through studying a generation of car thieves, he broke open the door and sat behind the steering wheel. With the same expertise, and some fumbling under the dashboard, he started the engine and drove off.

Initially they would expect him to head for Czechoslovakia. The Czech frontier was less than a hundred miles away, through the Böhmerwald. When they discovered he was gone, frontier posts would be alerted. Meanwhile he would be on his way to France, a longer trip, well over a hundred miles. He could not delude himself they would not take that possibility into account. Either route would be risky. But his daughter was waiting for him in Paris.

Outside the city, heading for the Czech frontier, he filled the Riley's tank with petrol. And then, he took a detour around the city and headed for Stuttgart. From there he could drive south-west to the Rhine, the frontier and Strasbourg. He settled back behind the wheel, and lit a cigarette.

Beyond Stuttgart, some two-and-a-half hours later, Lohmann was driving through the Black Forest when he became aware that he was being followed. On a narrow road winding through the forest, the car behind him was coming up fast, too fast to be merely another motorist; not in the darkness and rain that was falling on them.

Accelerating, he found the road surface treacherous, a film of liquid flowed over the tarmac and, on braking, he was forced to pull the car out of a skid. The car behind was gaining. Again Lohmann speeded up and for a time lengthened the distance between himself and his pursuer. Yet it was still a dangerous, tortuous drive, negotiating sudden twists in the road, just averting going off the tarmac and into the trees.

Moments later, he was aware that again the car behind him was gaining. The driver was obviously an expert. Not to be shaken off. Coming up behind him at great speed. Lohmann slowed down to take a hairpin bend and then increased his speed again. The car following seemed to take the bend without losing speed. Lohmann's hands started to sweat on the wheel. He was now aware that not only could he not shake off his pursuer, but that inevitably the other car would catch up with him. Other action had to be taken. Steering with his left hand he drew out the Mauser from its shoulder holster and placed it on the seat beside him.

Another bend loomed up in front of him. He changed gear, taking the bend at a much slower speed. Around it, he drove some fifty yards, slewed the wheel around so that the Riley lay across the centre of the road, and stopped. On either side of him there was only a few feet of road between the car and the edge of the forest. He took up the Mauser and looked backwards towards the bend he had just negotiated.

The car, again a Mercedes, came round the bend at speed. At first Lohmann was sure the driver had not seen him, and would surely plough into the Riley. Then he heard the screech of brakes, the Mercedes seemed to buck like a horse, it slewed around in a violent skid and veered off the road, appeared to jump over the narrow grass verge. In its headlights a tree appeared, the long bonnet slammed into it with a loud screaming sound as metal buckled, the bole of the tree burying itself deeply into the car.

Lohmann jumped from the Riley pistol in hand, and peered through the rain at the wrecked Mercedes. Despite the impact, its headlights were still on, lighting up trees and undergrowth. Now too there was a silence, broken only by the sound of one wheel of the Mercedes which continued to spin slowly, a ticking noise like that of a clock. For a moment nothing beyond the wheel moved. Lohmann approached slowly.

A rear door of the Mercedes opened. A man in SS uniform came out as fast as he could, which wasn't too fast in view of the impact. He was full in the headlights of the parked Riley. Lohmann lifted the Mauser, took careful aim and shot him just below the right knee. The man gave one short, sharp scream . . . the yelp of a dog in sudden agony . . . and fell onto the grass. The other rear door was halfway open and without waiting for a target Lohmann fired at its centre, just below the window. Something, in shadow, fell heavily onto the grass.

Now Lohmann came up to the car. The man he had shot in the leg lay uttering small moaning sounds. Lohmann's bullet had smashed the bone just below the knee. The Inspector relieved the man of his revolver, emptied it and threw it into the darkness of the wood. Making his way carefully around the car, Lohmann almost tripped over the second SS man. The figure on the grass, that of a lieutenant, was twisted up in a fetal position. Lohmann's second bullet had gone through the car door and entered the man's body just above his pelvis, moving downwards, fracturing the pelvic bone. So Lohmann estimated. Again he relieved the man of his weapon, throwing it into darkness. While he was doing this, he was aware of the man's eyes, wide open, staring up at him.

'Bastard!' the man muttered through clenched teeth. 'You won't get away. They'll get you at the frontier.'

'Maybe. Maybe not. You're Heydrich's men?'
'So?'
'Give the colonel . . . no, general now . . . give General Heydrich my compliments. And tell him from me that, in twenty years of police experience I've always found that somehow or other murderers have always paid for their crimes.'
The lieutenant glared up at him bleakly and swore again, this time under his breath.
Lohmann peered into the front of the car. The driver and his companion were also in SS uniform. The driver was dead, impaled on the steering wheel. His companion was unconscious, forehead against the dashboard, and covered in blood. Again and with some reluctance, Lohmann reached in and took both their revolvers. These followed the first two into the trees. Another glance at the dead driver. Lohmann felt sick. Without any desire to kill, he had killed. He turned away and started to walk back to the Riley.
The shot hit him on the fleshy part of the upper arm. It was a small bullet, a .22, but he felt its sting and was spun around by the force of it before he even heard the explosion. Or so it seemed to Lohmann. It had been fired by the SS man with the smashed pelvis, from a small pistol he had concealed at the top of his right boot, taped to the leather. Spun around, Lohmann faced the man and his toy pistol, and fired the Mauser again. The shot was not aimed, rather a reaction of surprise at the man having another weapon. It was a fluke shot, hitting the small pistol in the lieutenant's hand. The pistol exploded taking a third of the hand with it. The lieutenant fainted.
In the Riley, Lohmann stripped off his jacket and studied his wound which was now throbbing. The .22 bullet had gone clean through the flesh, leaving two bleeding gaps. Ripping up one of two handkerchiefs he had in his pocket, Lohmann tied a tight tourniquet above the wounds, and then tied the other handkerchief around them as a crude bandage. Donning his jacket again, and trying to ignore the flashes of pain, he studied himself in the car window. Apart from a hole in the jacket, there was little sign of blood. His raincoat, previously discarded and

in the back of the car, he put on. There was now no indication that he had been shot. This would be necessary when he came to the frontier post.

Awkwardly, he restarted the Riley's engine, turned the car onto the road and drove on.

There was now only one obstacle . . . the frontier post . . . and he would be in France.

The frontier post. Customs and passport control. And a barrier across the road.

'Passport please!'

Lohmann ignored the request, reached into his pocket and produced the one item he was sure Heydrich had forgotten.

'What is this?' A scowling frontier official.

'You will please read the letter. And note the signature.'

The man took the letter but did not read it. 'We are notified to look for a man called Lohmann.'

'I am Lohmann!' There was no arguing with this. His name was on the passport and on the letter.

'Then you are under arrest!'

'Am I resisting? Read the letter.' A stab of pain from the wound in the arm. Around his elbow there was a feeling of dampness.

The frontier official opened the letter and read it.

'You will recognise the seal and the signature,' Lohmann said.

'Yes. Of course. But I have orders to detain you . . .'

'From whom?'

The man consulted another paper. 'The office of SS General Heydrich.'

Lohmann took a deep breath. The bigger the lie, he thought . . . the more likely to convince.

'There is a fugitive using my name. He has already crossed into France. I am under the Führer's orders to apprehend the man. You have my passport, my police credentials, and the letter from the Führer. You have to let me through . . .'

The official was baffled. 'Now I have contradictory orders, Herr Inspector. You must understand . . .'

'I understand I have a letter from the Führer . . . do you understand the consequences of ignoring such a letter?'

'If you will come with me, Herr Inspector, I will telephone the SS command in Nuremberg.'

Lohmann was reluctant to leave the car. He was sure blood was dripping from his arm.

'The SS have made enough blunders for one night. No, you will not phone the SS . . .'

The official's face hardened.

'You will phone the Wilhelmstrasse,' Lohmann went on. 'The Reichschancellor's office. You will confirm the authenticity of this letter . . .'

The official looked relieved. 'Yes, yes, of course. You will please come into my office.'

A small room in a wooden shack. Hitler's picture on the wall. A tidy desk. And a telephone.

The man lifted the telephone. 'I wish to speak to Berlin. The Reichschancellery.'

'Urgently,' Lohmann added.

'Urgently,' the official echoed.

Minutes passed. Lohmann was gambling, but he was sure the odds were with him. To have countermanded the Hitler letter would have meant telling Hitler why. If Heydrich even remembered the letter. And Heydrich had wanted Lohmann to be the successful investigator, killed unfortunately in a car accident. Therefore he had no reason to have the letter revoked.

'The Führer will be in Nuremberg,' Lohmann said, as an afterthought.'His secretary will know about the letter. Such assurances should satisfy you.'

'Of course, Herr Inspector. I . . . I am sure it will all be unnecessary, but you appreciate my position . . .'

Lohmann was silent. He had done enough appreciating of the man's position. And his arm was painful.

They waited.

Another few minutes. And then . . .

'I wish to speak to the secretary to the Reichschancellor . . .'

Someone at the other end of the telephone demurred. Now Lohmann had his opportunity. He took the telephone firmly from the official.

'I wish the Führer's secretary to confirm to this dim-witted, routine-bound official of the State that the letter I received from the Führer permits me every facility the State can provide.' A pause. 'This is Inspector Lohmann of the Berlin Criminal Police. You will please arouse someone to confirm what I am saying. Otherwise I will have to contact the Führer in Nuremberg.'

More minutes and then a cool female voice. 'That is Inspector Lohmann?'

'It is.'

'I can of course confirm the Führer's letter . . .'

'Then do so at once to this gentleman!'

He handed the telephone to the man who listened eagerly. 'Yes! Yes, of course I can read. Yes, I understand. There will of course be no need to mention this matter to the Führer.'

Replacing the telephone receiver, the frontier official turned to Lohmann.

'My deepest apologies, Inspector. You are of course at liberty to proceed at once.'

The next morning Lohmann was in Paris.

EPILOGUE

In April 1942 I had been working in London for the New York *Post-Enquirer* for four years, although by now I was an accredited war correspondent. That was my official designation, but unofficially I'd got myself involved in a little cloak-and-dagger work for an old Washington acquaintance Colonel William Donovan. He, along with some others in Washington, had foreseen America's entry into the war long before Pearl Harbour in December of '41, and with an eye to the future he had given me letters of introduction to one or two people in British Intelligence, asked me to make contact.

I reckoned at first I was viewed with some suspicion, considering I was officially a newspaperman. But Donovan's letters got me over that hurdle; and I was taken up by two British Intelligence people, Roger Hollis and Ian Fleming. These two soon confirmed that a number of items I was told about did not stray into print in the *Post-Enquirer*. It was a schizophrenic kind of existence . . . 'You can print *that* but for God's sake, don't print *this*!' . . . that was the order of my days.

Then, one day in April, I was visiting Fleming when this big man came into the office.

'I think I know that guy,' I said to Fleming.

Fleming looked up from his desk. 'Very possible,' he replied casually. 'You were in Berlin in the early thirties.'

I was discovering at this time that Fleming knew more about me than I did. Not surprising. Even with Bill Donovan's letters, British Intelligence had done a thorough spring-cleaning job on my past before allowing me in the back door.

'Some kind of policeman,' I said, digging into memory. 'I forget the name . . .'

The big man talking quietly to the operative at another desk.

Fleming called over. 'Mister Lomond. A moment, when you're finished . . .'

The man nodded and went on with his conversation.

'Not Lomond,' I said. 'Lohmann, that was the name. Berlin police . . .'

'He retired in 1934. Went to Paris and then came to London,' Fleming explained. 'A very useful name. Ernest Lomond became a British citizen in 1936.'

A few moments later the man came over.

'I believe you two knew each other,' Fleming said.

The man stared at me. 'Ah, yes. Mr David Conway. The American journalist.' The accent was minimal, but there nonetheless. His English was almost too precise. 'It has been a long time, Mr Conway.'

'It had indeed. And I'm pretty surprised to see you here.'

'It took a long time to get the powers that be to let him in here,' Fleming chimed in. 'But the German desk would not be what it is without him. Look, Conway is finished with me for the day, Lomond. Why don't you two go off and have a drink? Conway is dying to hear how you got here.'

Lomond . . . or Lohmann . . . smiled slightly. 'Is that not classified material?'

'Oh, we know we can trust Conway not to print the unprintable. Otherwise we'd shoot him. But, after the duration . . .' Fleming shrugged.

The upshot of this was that Lohmann . . . I shall call him that . . . and I dined together. During the meal, he told me his story. And later, over coffee, tied up a few loose ends.

'Heydrich still killed me off,' he said. 'I read, when I was in Paris, that I had been killed in a car accident en route to see the Führer. I presume Heydrich had a copy of his report. Of course I had the original signed copy but, with a little forgery, the copy would survive the accident and be presented to Hitler. With what appeared to be my signature on it.'

'And your daughter?' I asked.

'Fine. Married to a British naval officer. And my sergeant, Reiner, he is in your country. Cincinnati. In the brewery business.'

'And you are working for British Intelligence.'

'We each fight the Nazis in our own way. And, you know, Conway, I still have a belief in the rule of law. I believe murderers should be condemned for their crimes. Especially those I consider to be *my* murderers.'

'You solved your last case.'

Lohmann hesitated, staring into the brandy glass he was holding. 'It is a coincidence you and I meet at this time. If I can obtain permission, will you come on a short trip with me the day after tomorrow? I think you would be interested.'

The next morning, he telephoned me at my hotel.

'I have permission. I will pick you up in my car tomorrow morning. You will be back in London by the evening.'

I slept little that night, thanks to the attention of the Luftwaffe. I wasn't yet accustomed to air raids. However, it ensured that I was ready and waiting for Lohmann. He was driving a small Morris with, as he explained, a special petrol allocation from his employers. We drove to an airfield just outside Dorking in Surrey, parked and entered a small Nissen hut, empty but for some chairs and a desk. While we waited, he elaborated on the story he had told me over dinner, filling in a few details. As I said, he had not explained for whom we were waiting, or why. I finally asked him.

'We are waiting for two young men. They are going on a mission. I am part of their final briefing. It is a mission I myself would like to have undertaken. But they insist it is for young men. I am too old.'

We continued to wait, Lohmann chain-smoking while we did so. It was the first and only time I had ever seen him exhibit nerves. He seemed anxious and impatient. At one moment, he burst out. 'I pray this thing is right! These young men could be killed and I would bear some of the responsibility.'

He sighed and lit another cigarette. As an afterthought, he offered me one, which I accepted.

'They assure me . . . they assure me it is necessary. This mission. Nothing to do with me. But I still have my motives for encouraging it.'

Ten minutes later two young men in uniform were brought into the room by an army captain who nodded to Lohmann. I was ignored, an onlooker, a spectator. Both young men wore the flashes on their shoulders of the Free Czechoslovakian Forces.

'Mr Kubis and Mr Gabcik,' the captain introduced them to Lohmann.

'We have met, Captain,' Lohmann said, shaking hands with the two young men. 'Before they went to Scotland for their training. Please sit down.'

We all sat except Lohmann who stood behind the desk. He cleared his throat before speaking.

'You two have been specially picked and trained for this mission. You know the name and the look of the target. But it may help if I tell you I know this man personally. I tell you what I am about to tell you because assassination is, physically and morally, an ugly business. The Reichsprotector of Bohemia and Moravia is himself a murderer. Of course you know he has been called the Butcher of Moravia. He issues orders and people die. But, more than that, he is also personally a killer.'

Lohmann took a deep breath. Kubis and Gabcik stared at him intently.

Lohmann went on, 'He is personally responsible for a number of murders perpetrated in order to further his own career. Therefore in my personal view you are going out to execute a criminal . . . a multiple murderer. Of course, there are political and strategic reasons for your mission. To aid and encourage the Czech underground. To create havoc in an area where havoc is needed. But you will not forget that you are going out to execute a murderer. Right and law are with you. Good luck.'

Again there was a shaking of hands. And then the two young men were escorted out, presumably to a more specific briefing. When they had gone, Lohmann was silent for some moments. Then he looked up at me. His eyes seemed red and blurred.

'It should be me,' he said.

We drove back to London. The next day I learned he had driven back alone to Dorking, to stand and watch a lone plane take off.

On May 27th 1942, in Prague, Reinhard Heydrich's car was stopped by a young man with an automatic weapon. The weapon jammed, allowing Heydrich to climb out. However another young man threw a hand grenade which exploded inside the Reichsprotector's car. Heydrich, seemingly uninjured, fired at the man whose gun had jammed. Then he collapsed, as the young man ran away. Fragments of leather and springs from the Mercedes had penetrated Heydrich's body, piercing his stomach. The Reichsprotector died sometime later in hospital in the city.

The assassins and other members of the Czech resistance were trapped in a church by the SS, and executed.

I met Lohmann only once more, in London. He seemed tired and ill. Over a drink, he spoke briefly of the death of Heydrich.

'In time, you see, in time, there is justice. But I should have been allowed to go, in place of Kubis or Gabcik. That would have been right. And, if they'd caught me, they wouldn't have blamed the Czechs. There would have been no Lidice . . .'

He swallowed his brandy and ordered another.

'But that's not what they wanted. The powers that be. They wanted terror. To stiffen the Czech resistance. And I wanted my justice. Maybe it was right, but it leaves too many ghosts . . .'

Ernst Lohmann was killed three months later in an air raid on London. I suspect it was a kind of relief.